LT

D0909890

AUG

WITHDRAWN
Wilmette Public Library

Wilmette Public Library
1242 Wilmette Ave.
Wilmette, IL 60091
847-256-5025

THE EMERALD TIDE

Center Point
Large Print

Also by Davis Bunn and available from
Center Point Large Print:

Miramar Bay
Firefly Cove
Moondust Lake
Outbreak
Unscripted
Tranquility Falls
Burden of Proof
The Cottage on Lighthouse Lane

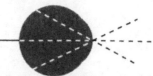

**This Large Print Book carries the
Seal of Approval of N.A.V.H.**

THE EMERALD TIDE

DAVIS BUNN

Center Point Large Print
Thorndike, Maine

WILMETTE PUBLIC LIBRARY

This book is dedicated to
ILEEN MAISEL
For the guidance, the challenge,
the friendship . . . the chance

◇◇◇◇◇◇◇◇◇◇◇◇◇◇◇◇

This Center Point Large Print edition
is published in the year 2022 by arrangement with
Kensington Publishing Corp.

Copyright © 2022 by Davis Bunn.

All rights reserved.

This book is a work of fiction. Names, characters,
businesses, organizations, places, events, and incidents
either are the product of the author's imagination
or are used fictitiously. Any resemblance to
actual persons, living or dead, events,
or locales is entirely coincidental.

The text of this Large Print edition is unabridged.
In other aspects, this book may vary
from the original edition.
Printed in the United States of America
on permanent paper sourced using
environmentally responsible foresting methods.
Set in 16-point Times New Roman type.

ISBN: 978-1-63808-400-6

The Library of Congress has cataloged this record
under Library of Congress Control Number: 2022937404

WILMETTE PUBLIC LIBRARY

Chapter 1

On the day his life changed forever, Derek Gaines rolled his road bike from the garage at half past five. He normally set off about then, a habit that his neighbors and few remaining friends assumed was Derek's way of racing into the new day. Derek saw no need to correct them.

In truth, he no longer fled the dawn light. His days were not burdened with the pain of an internal vacuum. Four years since his wife's death, he was beyond all that. To say he was restored was of course absurd. But he had healed. He had moved on. He had no choice in the matter.

Dawn rides were part of the daily routine. Routines shaped his existence. He gave the practice no more conscious thought than brushing his teeth.

Two years back, the last session he'd attended of his bereavement recovery group, the leader had asked him to describe his current state of mind. Derek had known the answer before the counselor had finished shaping the question. He replied that he had accepted the new normal with stoic grace. The new Derek got on with life. Or rather, with as much of life as he could.

Darkness still dominated the town of Miramar.

The moonlight was so strong it cast the road in a pewter glow. His going was clear as he headed east toward the first faint light of day. Mornings like this, he relished the quiet. Birds offered him sleepy chirps as he rode Miramar's empty main street. His tires whispered silklike past the town hall. His breath stayed measured and calm as the road curved along the rise marking the town's border. The few cars he met passed with an almost apologetic air. Slow, quiet, another murmur of sound and they were gone, and the predawn was his once more.

Derek's ride of choice was a Felt endurance frame with Shimano 105 mechanics and Campagnolo wheels. Many of Derek's Iron Man buddies considered his bike nothing more than a decent step in the right direction. They spent more on wheel-sets than he had on his entire bike. Though Derek had little interest in what they classed as critical upgrades, he liked how their conversations never strayed from the ride, the workout, the next competition. It was one of the reasons why he felt safe in their company.

Derek was midway through his return loop when his cellphone rang. He always carried it when cycling alone, a just-in-case emergency connection. But as he stopped and drew it from his rear pouch, he could not remember the last time it had rung.

The readout said it was Trevor Coomes, his boss. Derek answered with, "Did I forget something?"

"No. And I hope you were already awake. That's me being polite. Actually, I'm too excited to care."

A delivery truck rumbled up the ridge, heading for the supermarket on the outskirts of town. Derek pulled his bike over the verge and onto the grass. "What's up?"

"I just received a call from Gwen Freeth."

"Should I know the name?"

Trevor snorted. "You academics in your ivory towers."

"Former academics. No tower within sight. Just your employee struggling to keep his home."

"Gwen Freeth was married to Santa Barbara's number-one bad boy. Which is saying a lot, believe you me. He passed away, leaving her a huge pile of debt, a gorgeous house she may soon be losing, and an art collection that has me positively salivating."

Derek would have resented anyone else invading his morning quiet. But Trevor had been Erin's best friend and the only other person alive who had fully known the extent of her illnesses. Right after Erin's funeral, Trevor had offered Derek the position of managing his new Miramar Bay store. In the dark days when he was still busy crawling out of his own shallow grave, it had meant the world. Derek would do anything for the man. "What does that have to do with me?"

"She asked for you."

"This woman I've never heard of before."

"The only reason she's willing to meet is because of you." Trevor gave a theatrical sigh. "I suppose now is the point when you hold my feet to the financial flames. When can you get down here?"

Trevor's Treasures was located on Anacapa, one block and a world removed from the tourists and grifters who now dominated Santa Barbara's State Street. Anacapa was home to high-end restaurants and professional offices with enough clout to clear away panhandlers. Patrons were able to sit at the sidewalk tables and remain undisturbed, but only if they could afford to pay ten dollars for a cup of coffee. Most tourists found the area overly boring and overly quiet and far too expensive. Trevor's antique store catered to the people who liked quiet. And paid to keep things that way.

Derek entered the municipal lot and took a space reserved for Trevor's clients. He was supposed to park in the alley behind the shop, but the way was often blocked by delivery trucks. There was no telling what this mystery lady required. He assumed she wanted his help in valuing a painting without provenance. Since his life went through the unwanted overhaul, this work had become a major sideline. And one thing about

Trevor's Santa Barbara clientele: The rich hated waiting.

The Spanish Mission buildings lining Anacapa glowed in the morning light. Shops along Trevor's side of the street were fronted by a broad raised sidewalk. The steel shutters over Trevor's two display windows glinted bright as mirrors in the sunlight. Derek tapped on the glass-fronted door and exchanged greetings with the waiter setting up sidewalk tables at the restaurant next door.

Trevor's face appeared in the glass. He was aged somewhere north of fifty-five. Slender and extremely well-groomed, hair frosted and trimmed to hide every feather of gray, perfect smile. Derek had liked Trevor from the first time they met. The quick wit, the snippy tone, the acidic comments about clients he disliked, all of these were matched by a brilliant mind and an impeccable eye for genuine antiques.

"Well, *finally*." Trevor gave his feather-duster a frantic wave. "Grab the keys and get started!"

Trevor had a thing about clocks. Timepieces had been his passion since childhood and was why he had entered the highly competitive antiques trade. Selling one of his beloved pets—that was what Trevor called them, his pets—caused the man very real pain.

Derek had not been down to Santa Barbara in almost two weeks, so he did what Trevor both expected and wanted. He took the winding keys from the desk drawer, found a clean dustcloth, and began a slow circuit. Searching.

He found it on a French Empire side table near the front window. "This is new."

Trevor was instantly beside him. "Yes, I'm rather pleased, if I do say so myself. Art deco, date stamped on the base, 1929. And the artist who carved the crystal was none other than René Lalique himself."

The sterling silver timepiece was housed in a block of polished crystal, with two birds of prey forming the side pillars. "It's magnificent."

"I'll probably take it upstairs, once I decide which item I'm ready to give up. Which could take months. Until then, my new pet should be happy here, don't you agree?"

Trevor lived above the shop. His apartment reminded Derek of a Fabergé jewel box. "Dare I ask?"

"Oh, I couldn't possibly assign this a price." He adjusted its position a fraction of an inch. "Perhaps in a few years, to a buyer who convinces me they'll give it a good home."

"Gun to your head . . ."

"A steal at fifty thousand dollars."

"Get out of town."

Trevor's response was cut off by a shadow passing in front of the display window. "Gwen is here."

• • •

Gwendolyn Freeth wore a cashmere sweater set, a Hermès scarf, and pearls. At ten thirty in the morning. Her hair was perfectly coiffed, her cosmetics so precise as to go almost unnoticed. Derek had met any number of such clients. He neither liked nor disliked them, or their airs. The rich were different, no doubt about that. The rules that governed so much of their lives were baffling.

Gwen Freeth endured a few moments of Trevor's nervous greetings, then asked if she might have a private word with Derek. She left the shop, clearly assuming both men would see her command for what it was.

Derek followed her along the sidewalk, held her chair at the neighboring restaurant's first table, seated himself, and waited. Gwen Freeth took her time, building up to whatever had brought her out this day. She sipped her coffee, then asked for a fresh OJ and finished that too. Derek's chair was angled so he could observe Trevor stepping into the shop's sunlit window, pretending to adjust an article so he could check on their progress.

"Do you miss lecturing at UC Santa Cruz?"

Derek figured the question was mostly to show she had researched his past. "I miss the routine. Feeling like my life was set on a secure path. I liked that about university life. A lot."

"My investigator claims you were also a very good teacher."

She seemed genuinely interested, so he answered fully. "I focused on the few students who shared my passion for the history of art. The rest I tolerated because I had to."

"And you researched. And you wrote. Six books in seven years. Two by mainstream publishers, the rest academic. All to excellent reviews."

"It was good to find an outlet for my passion."

"But you've developed a new passion, haven't you. Since . . ."

He said it for her. "Since my wife died. Yes. I have."

She surprised him by changing directions. "I suppose you've heard all the terrible things they're saying."

"Only what Trevor told me this morning. You were once rich. Now you're not."

"It's so easy to claim Bernard was a late great louse. But the truth is not so simple. It was all his money to begin with. Which should make it easier to learn I'm almost penniless. But it doesn't. I positively loved being rich, you see."

"From what Trevor says about your art collection, you still are."

Gwen's head moved slowly, side to side, a sorrowful rejection. "You can't imagine the debts that man left me. I am facing utter ruin."

Derek had no idea what to say, other than, "I suppose that brings us to the point."

"My attorney is Megan Pierce, a precise and

intelligent young woman who has never failed to impress. I set her the challenge of Diogenes. I assume you know what I mean."

"Diogenes of Sinope," Derek replied. "Lived in the time of Alexander the Great. He stood at the gates of Athens, shining a lantern into the face of everyone who passed. Searching for someone honest."

"I expected Megan to come back with some drivel about how I should go with one of the major auction houses. Instead, she told me about a fresh young man who gave up his position as professor of art history at UC Santa Cruz to care for his ailing wife. For two and a half years. Since she died, he's struggled to make ends meet. Doing odd consulting jobs for the Getty and working for poor nervous Trevor."

Derek made a mental note to call and thank the attorney. "Not so fresh. Nor young. Not any-more."

"Yes, tragedy will do that to a soul." She toyed with her empty cup. And surprised him with yet another shift in direction. "Can we ever fully heal? Start over? Change one life for another?"

He had never heard it expressed like that. Changing lives. But it was how he secretly thought of his existence. It suggested a bond between them. Derek had no idea how he felt about it. Which made answering very difficult.

He was aware of how the silence weighed on

her, bringing the sorrow closer to the surface. "I never found any other way to move forward. I had to change to survive."

"It's all I think about these days. That and how my new existence could very well be shaped by debts I can't pay. Bankruptcy. Even more shame. All the so-called friends who pretend to be concerned." She slipped her sunglasses into her purse and studied him intently. "How did you manage?"

The woman's evident need pushed him to reply, "At first I did it because it's what Erin would have wanted. Her last request and all that. Later it became habit. Grief counseling follows the same course as AA. Taking it one day at a time. And then, like you say, I found a new passion. Which helped. A lot, actually. The loss doesn't just vanish. Life isn't the same. But it can still be good. Different. But good." He probably should have left it there, but the act of revealing his innermost thoughts left him with a pressing need to finish. "The world has shifted on its axis. Sooner or later it settles into a new orbit. What we want and how we feel about it doesn't change a thing. Either we find a way to make peace, or we don't. That's the only real choice we face. Move forward and heal as much as we're able, or not."

He felt like he had done a terrible job, trying to express his secrets, seeking to help this bereft woman. The longer she sat in silence, staring at the empty street, the more he wished he had not spoken at all.

Finally she breathed deep, cleared the edges of her eyes, and said, "Which brings us to the subject at hand."

Derek saw Trevor step again into the display window, this time with butterfly flutters of both hands. "We should take this inside the shop."

She stood and handed Derek her keys. "My Bentley is parked just there. Be a dear and fetch the item in the trunk."

Chapter 2

Derek escorted Gwen to where Trevor held open the shop entrance. Then he returned to the sky-blue Bentley and popped the trunk. Trevor held the door open, so eager he almost danced in place. Derek balanced the frame on the rosewood secretary Trevor used as his desk. He cut away the padding, taking his time, refusing to let Trevor's nerves hurry him.

If Gwen even noticed the proprietor's two-step, she gave no sign. Instead she sipped from a glass of water and told Derek, "I need the answer to one question today. Just one."

Trevor fluttered closer. "Actually, there's also the small matter of our commission."

Gwen ignored him. "Can I pay off my debts and keep my home and my life? Yes or no."

The quilting fell away, revealing a steel frame perhaps four and a half feet square. The backing was simply another sheet of glass. This permitted the examiner to study both sides of the artwork. This sort of casing was used by professionals—restorers, universities, and museums.

Trevor deflated with a soft, "Oh."

The double glass held an unfinished painting. A middle-aged man looked down upon a woman seated in a high-backed chair. The woman held an infant. The woman and child showed no awareness of the man who observed them. Beyond the completed portion, the canvas was yellowed by time, the color of old bones.

Trevor took a step back, crossed his arms, and sighed. "Well."

Gwen stared longingly at the unfinished artwork. "My late son Allen was an adventurous spirit from birth. He seldom stayed more than a few months in any one place, including our home. Did you know him?"

Derek felt an electric current build in his gut, spreading out to where it caused the fingers holding the frame to tremble. "We met a couple of times. I can't say I knew him well."

"At least my Allen was mostly sober, and mostly honest, and led a mostly respectable existence. All the attributes my late husband lacked."

Derek said, "Hand me your glass."

Trevor slid open the central drawer and pulled out an antique Celestron hand lens. Derek knew his boss was trying to hide a bitter disappointment. Having a wealthy woman like Gwen show up with a scarred unfinished painting set in an industrial frame suggested she did not consider Trevor's shop worthy of the major items she would soon be forced to sell. Derek would correct his boss soon enough. But not yet. "And Allen died . . ."

"Ten months ago. According to the US embassy in Rome and the Italian police report they sent us, Allen was swimming off the coast of Sicily, near a smaller island called Lipari. His loss marked the beginning of my husband's final decline." Gwen cleared her eyes with an unsteady hand. "Allen always said he was born out of time. He acquired first editions of all the great explorers. Lord Burton was his favorite."

Derek leaned in so close his hand holding the lens touched the frame. He gave it thirty seconds. No more. Then he straightened and did his best to keep his voice steady. "I need to know how this came into your possession."

"What you see here arrived as a parcel from Syracuse."

"Syracuse, as in Sicily."

"Correct." Gwen touched the drawing's tattered border. "Allen included a brief note, telling me to keep it safe. Six weeks later, we received notice from the Italian police that he had died. His body was never recovered." She took a very hard breath. "We performed last rites over an empty grave."

He kept his voice as gentle as possible. "What exactly did Allen say in his letter?"

"It wasn't a letter at all. Just a few sentences, telling me to preserve this at all costs. Preferably in a safety deposit vault. Allen urged me not to tell Bernard. He knew of his father's habits, of course. Allen said if things ever became truly dire, this would restore our fortunes."

Trevor's gaze switched back and forth between Gwen and the frame, utterly flummoxed. "I suppose I could locate a collector interested in an unfinished and unsigned—"

Derek cut his boss off with, "Can I keep this for a couple of days?"

Chapter 3

As Derek escorted Gwen back to her car, she asked, "Do you have any idea why Allen would put such value on an unsigned and unfinished painting?"

Derek found himself liking her. Gwen Freeth held herself well for a lady whose world had come crashing down. Derek had spent enough time in grief groups to know the difference between someone after attention and a woman close to the edge. He would not offer hope until he had a chance to check things out. So all he said was, "I think maybe it's what the painting represents."

"And that is?"

"Let me have a couple of days to do some digging. In the meantime, you should offer Trevor something to sell."

"A commission for the merchant prince."

"Trevor's standing in the arts community is his most important asset. To represent the Freeth collection would be a major coup." He hesitated, then added, "Plus there's every chance we will need him on our side."

"I'm sure I can find something that will tame your colorful friend." She started to slip into the car, then stopped and asked, "Our side of what?"

"One day," he replied. "Two at the most."

Derek held her door, shut it softly, and stood watching as she pulled away. His thoughts took the form of what he hoped to be telling her in their next meeting. That Gwen's late son had found a missing treasure.

Logic held little sway in the world of treasure dogs. Derek had personally come to know many of them. They would invest years on a great deal less than what Gwen had offered him that morning.

Everything that happened now, once the lady drove down the sunlit avenue, was aimed at confirming what he already knew. Down in his gut. Where it mattered most. At least, to the sort of people who shared his new passion.

Soon as he reentered the shop, Derek called the law firm in San Luis Obispo and asked to speak with Gwen's attorney. The secretary took his name and asked him to wait. Three minutes later, Megan Pierce came on the line. "I was wondering if you'd call."

"You're the first name on my list," Derek replied. "Seeing as how you picked me out of the barrel."

"You're welcome."

"Is there any chance you could spare me a few minutes? I've got a fresh load of questions and almost no answers."

"Where are you now?"

"Trevor's place. Santa Barbara."

There was the sound of turning pages. "I could give you half an hour at one. You can buy me a sandwich."

"A three-course meal with wine would probably be more in line with what I owe you," Derek replied. "But your research probably told you I'm holding on to my home by my fingernails."

"A sandwich will do," she said. "Please be on time."

When asked, Derek usually said he was originally from Denver. But Colorado was only the place where he had graduated from high school. His father had been a freelance engineer doing seismic searches for water, oil, and soil quality in tunnel digs. His work had relocated them seven times before Derek's mother divorced him and moved back to her hometown. Derek had played football and run track, and his sports had supplied him with a full ride to Pepperdine.

At age sixteen, an inheritance had granted Derek the means to take a summer abroad. That first afternoon in Amsterdam, while most of his fellow students were off getting their taste of a legal high, Derek had entered the Rijksmuseum, stood before the first Rembrandt he had ever seen, and fallen in love.

From that point forward, his life choices had

all been about turning his dream into reality. Building a career around the artists that gave form to humanity's transformative periods. Showing how they created art from political turmoil and bad rulers and plagues and fiefdoms and lawless realms. Explaining how these artistic wonders still held a vital importance in today's world.

Pepperdine's art history department was second to none. He stayed there for seven and a half years, long enough to complete his doctoral thesis and find a new love in teaching undergrads. Derek met his future wife six months after landing his teaching gig at UC Santa Cruz. Erin's home life had been even more fractured than his own—parents divorced soon after she was born, mother remarried three more times, building her world on alimony and glitz and false friends. Early on Erin developed a loathing for everything her mother deemed more important than love and a stable home life.

Erin worked as a freelance CGI cartoonist, but her true passion was bringing art into the lives of underprivileged kids. They moved to Miramar because it was more or less midway between Santa Cruz, where Derek lectured, and San Luis Obispo, where Erin worked with the local school system. Neither of them had expected, not in their wildest dreams, that the central coast town would become the place they had been looking for all their lives. A haven against the world. A refuge where love could grow. For as long as they both shall live.

Outsiders often dismissed San Lu as blue collar. Which was true as far as it went. But locals knew the place also held a great diversity of people and flavors. The old country song said it best. People who chose to call San Lu home never forgot who brought them to the dance. They might own huge vineyards or organic farms or one of the burgeoning local industries. But their hearts remained firmly grounded in reality.

Derek thought the law offices of Sol Feinnes perfectly suited their central coast clientele. The building was relatively new, yet fit right in with the old mission structures that fashioned the city's beautiful heart. The high-ceilinged reception area was pleasant and without glitz of any kind. The main walls held paintings and photographs in desert shades of ocher and amber. Derek spotted two oils by a regional artist whose work also adorned his Miramar shop. The floor was Mexican tile framed by broad-plank beams, and these covered by hand-loomed carpets. The furniture was leather and rough-hewn wood and very comfortable. Derek gave his name to the receptionist and was informed that Megan was running late. He chose a seat, took out his phone, and sat staring at it. Knowing he needed to make the call. But unable to punch in the numbers.

"Derek Gaines?"

He rose to his feet. "That's me."

"Megan Pierce." She watched him pocket his phone. "Did I interrupt a call?"

"It can wait." Years, if need be.

Megan Pierce was a dark-haired beauty in her early thirties, with a sharpish edge to her clothes, her movements, and her voice. "What's in the bag?"

"Line-caught tuna on wheat with sprouts, lettuce, and mustard," Derek replied. "Havarti on rye with the same plus tomato. All organic."

She opened the door to a corner office. "I like both. Go halfsies?"

"Snapple green tea or vitamin water?"

"Tea." She waved him at a chair facing the outer windows. "I'm overdosed on coffee but I could use a caffeine kick."

They laid the meal out on a small table forming a T-shaped extension from Megan's desk. She rolled her office chair around so as to face Derek across the narrow surface. He had the impression this was a common practice, a busy and successful young attorney accustomed to filling every available minute.

Three bites into their meal, Derek was still sorting through his questions, trying to decide which should come first, when she dabbed mustard from the side of her mouth and announced,

"I didn't go into the search blind, if that's what you're thinking."

Derek nodded. "I wondered about that."

"You were probably also asking yourself how a member of Santa Barbara's rich elite got hooked up with a lawyer in San Lu."

Derek liked her already. "Where did you do time? I mean, before here."

"Los Angeles. Kirin and Klaufstein." Speaking the name left a bad taste in her mouth. "You know them?"

"The name. Sure."

"That's right. You spend a lot of time hob-nobbing with the Getty crowd."

"I used to. Not anymore."

"Only because you insist on staying away. That's according to Evelyn Hardy. Remember her?"

"Difficult lady to forget." Evelyn Hardy was one of the Getty's senior directors. She was also the lady Derek had been happy not to call. "That was a different lifetime."

"Evelyn said to tell you there's an opening on her staff, and it's yours for the asking."

Derek had the distinct impression that Megan was building toward something. She tried to hide it, but he had become good at reading secret tells. It was a crucial element in dealing with the people his new passion had brought into his orbit. Seeing when they were about to shift into

26

a higher gear. Or lie. Tells were important to knowing the difference. Vital.

His gut told him the lady did not lie. Which meant . . .

"I have information that I would like to share with you." She interrupted each word with a tight little space. As if the act of speaking them aloud required punctuation. "But I can only do so if you take me on as your legal representative."

"I can't afford a lawyer," he replied. "Erin's illness left me with a mountain of debt."

"I know all that. You lost your university pension when you quit. All your savings went toward caring for your wife." Again there was the careful diction. Like she was presenting a difficult issue to a judge. Doing so with a cautious and measured pace. "My fees have been covered."

"By who?"

Megan remained silent. Unmoving. She did not even blink.

Derek would not like to play poker against this lady. "All right. I would like you to become my attorney."

Megan rose, walked around her desk, and took a manila folder from the pile of documents stacked on her credenza. She returned to her seat and offered him the file and a pen. "Read and sign all three copies and initial the places marked with the yellow arrows."

Derek didn't bother reading. Either he trusted the lady or he was probably lost. He signed.

She gathered up the pages, cosigned, tapped the pages into order, handed him a copy, then pushed the file to one side. "I'll tell you what I know. Then I'm hoping you can answer some questions of my own."

Derek nodded slowly. Not because he understood. Because his suspicions had been right.

This was all about treasure.

Chapter 4

"Sixteen months ago, I was contacted by Allen Freeth, who asked me to represent him. His first words to me were, 'Don't ask me how I obtained your name, because I can't tell you.' I met the late Mr. Freeth exactly once. He waltzed in and handed me four things. Your name and address, an envelope of cash, an item, and instructions." Megan studied Derek across the narrow divide. "Can you guess what his instructions were?"

"If Gwen Freeth were to contact you, put us together."

"How exactly did you come up with this?"

"Finish your telling and I'll explain."

"There isn't much left to tell. The item in question is yours. The cash is to cover your legal expenses. That's the lot." She showed him two palms. "Now it's your turn."

"The tactic Allen used is called a double-blind. It's standard practice among treasure dogs."

"Treasure." She drew out the words. "Dogs."

"Allen told his mother to ask your help in locating someone to take up his quest. He used you to hide the next clue."

"He knew someone was after him?"

"Not like you're thinking. Not necessarily. Allen

might have simply been worried that other treasure dogs were on the same trail."

"But now he's dead."

Derek nodded. There was certainly that. "May I see what he left you?"

Megan studied him a moment longer, then rose and walked to her wall safe. She spun the dial, twisted the handle, and drew out . . .

The slender envelope held just three items. A plastic key-card and metal key with a number engraved on its surface. And the copy of a rental contract for a safety deposit box. In a Miramar bank. Naming Derek as co-owner.

Derek saw the way she studied the items. "You haven't seen this before?"

"He asked me not to open it. How well did you know Allen Freeth?"

"Not well at all. But I guess you could say we had mutual friends." He slipped the items back into the envelope and rose from his chair. "I'll be in touch."

Derek drove from the law offices to the Miramar shop. He spent forty-five minutes following up on phone messages, talking with clients, arranging a valuation. He arrived home just after six, debated going for another bike ride, then set it aside. It wasn't the ride. It was what he was trying to put off. Just as long as he possibly could.

He worked out on the free weights in his

backyard, releasing the tension and stress from an unexpectedly strange day. He neither liked nor disliked his standard routine, running the small shop and being there for Trevor whenever his boss needed a hand. Taking time for his bike and his workouts. Seeing his new friends. Even going on the occasional date. Paying his bills. Running his triathlons three or four times each year. His life was filled with busy days. Safe.

And when he could, when there was an opportunity like this one, Derek slipped into his new secret role. Evaluate newly found treasure. Seek to establish provenance. Bring the sellers into contact with the world of money. Keep both at arm's length. Because the rich had no interest in getting to know the kind of people who spent their lives on the edge of legality. Out where danger lurked.

Which was precisely what Allen Freeth offered him.

And to do that safely, Derek needed allies he could trust with his life.

Which was why, at twenty minutes past seven that evening, Derek called the Getty and asked for Evelyn Hardy.

Evelyn was known as a nighthawk. Aged somewhere in her late fifties, Evelyn lived for her work and the LA scene in equal measure. Her habits were tolerated because she was, quite simply, one of the world's finest museum curators. She never arrived at the Getty until noon. If a meeting was scheduled for the morning, Evelyn did not attend. This was known in the trade as Evelyn's Law. The world rotated without her until Evelyn was good and ready.

When she answered, he said, "It's Derek."

Hearing his name was good for a pause. "Is it really?"

"Really and truly."

"Forgive me for needing a moment to stop my head from spinning. How are you?"

"Doing okay." He had worried what it would be like, speaking to Erin's bridesmaid. After four long years. Truth be told, it was just a conversation. Derek felt the band of tension gradually ease. "Actually, I'm better than that."

"I've heard you had started walking the dark side. Shame on you."

For people like Evelyn, anyone who dealt with the sale of precious art was classed as an almost-enemy. "That is both true and not true."

"I'm not talking about your working for Trevor."

"I know that."

"How is he, by the way? Still married to his clocks?"

"More than ever."

"Well, there are worse ways to fill the empty hours, I suppose."

"I spoke with Megan Pierce today. She said . . ."

"That I need your services. Good. When can we meet?"

"Would tomorrow work?"

"You do realize there will be a lot of tears and embraces, your showing up here after all this time."

He took a long breath. "I know."

"Wait just a minute." There was the sound of clicking keys. "I have a meeting at one that can't be put off. I'll give them an hour and not a minute more."

"Thank you, Evelyn."

She sniffed. "Shame on you, messing up my makeup like this."

He breathed again. Missing all that never would be again. "See you tomorrow."

Chapter 5

The next morning, Kelly Reid entered the Los Angeles headquarters of Christie's at a quarter to nine. As far as Kelly was concerned, Christie's LA had the perfect location. The two-story white-on-white building stood on Camden like a block of vanilla ice cream, with Chanel and Hermès and the Beverly Wilshire Hotel and Rodeo Drive for neighbors. Parking her car and walking the sidewalk was a daily kick. As was knocking on the entrance, smiling a hello to the morning guard, glancing at the rooms holding the latest collection, climbing the polished granite stairs, using her pass on the glass doors, and making her way around the central bullpen. She smiled at the woman now occupying the cubicle where she had labored for two and a half years. Every employee in the bullpen, seven women and four men, watched her passage.

Her office was the smallest lining the northern and western walls. She did what she had done every morning since her promotion four and a half weeks ago. The new junior vice-president of Christie's LA raised the exterior shades that had blocked the previous afternoon's setting sun. She lowered the interior blinds so as to grant herself a moment's privacy. She seated herself behind the polished rosewood desk with its gilded legs. She leaned back. She sighed.

Paradise.

Twenty-five minutes later, Kelly was lost in the intricacies of designing the catalogue for their autumn gemstone and jewelry auction. The centerpiece was a double-page presentation, six photos in all. The item was a French Empire necklace of white gold, holding thirty-one diamonds totaling twenty-six carats. This formed the backdrop for a central pendant, an eighty-seven-carat vivid yellow diamond.

When her boss entered Kelly's office, she assumed it was to continue the discussion they had started three days ago. The temptation was to assign the necklace to Marie Antoinette. The last queen of France before the Revolution had owned one of the largest gemstone collections in history. Without such a provenance, their top jewelry expert had estimated the item would sell for between seventeen and twenty million dollars. But by bonding the necklace to the late French aristocracy . . .

Stratosphere.

Higher. Near-earth orbit.

She greeted her boss with, "I don't see it happening. I want it. You want it." She lifted the mock pages. "But every time I put the queen's name on the page, I hear laughter from New York to Tokyo."

Jerome Summers was a handsome man in his mid-thirties. His athletic build was perpetually decked out in a very expensive wardrobe. Jerome was also addicted to all things English. Some people assumed Jerome Summers had obtained his position as head of Christie's LA through some vague connection to the landed gentry. Jerome did nothing to dispel the myth. He was actually from a middling Baltimore suburb, raised by a single mom working as a legal secretary. Jerome's three years in England and a master's degree in art history from Cambridge had come by way of a Rhodes Scholarship.

Kelly often wondered if his background was why he now took such evident pleasure in the tailored Savile Row suits, the hand-stitched Church broughams, the bright silk ties with matching pocket kerchiefs, the gold watch by Garrick. Late into a well-oiled evening, Jerome had once claimed to have spent his happiest former life as a minor earl. He was married to a woman he had met at university, had two sons approaching university age, and never strayed. Recent rumors of troubles on the home front changed nothing—much to the dismay of office ladies who possessed what Kelly called a speculative eye.

There was another side to Jerome. Almost a different man entirely. This Jerome was why Kelly considered him to be the finest boss she had ever worked with. Totally dedicated to his work. Unquestionably brilliant about the auction trade. Jewelry, artwork, antiques, on and on the list went. Worldwide, Christie's held between thirty and forty major auctions each year. Global revenue topped six billion dollars. Jerome was one of the senior executives who strategized over when and where and how their largest auctions and private trades would take place.

He was, quite simply, a master at obtaining the most from every sale. This was how Christie's had survived in the cutthroat world of global auctions for almost three hundred years. Because of people like Jerome.

It was Kelly's dream to one day join their ranks. Not yet. She still had a huge amount to learn. But she thought she had what it took to become a company director. One day. What was more, so did Jerome.

She almost loved the man for the confidence he showed in her abilities, and her potential.

Today she faced her boss's hard side. Brilliant, cunning, and worried. He shooed away his assistant and shut Kelly's office door a little too firmly. He crossed the room, seated himself, and drummed the arm of his chair. He stared at the sunlit shade to her windows. Seeing nothing.

"Something the matter?"

He nodded slowly, as if coming to an internal decision. "I need you to do a favor for me."

"Anything."

"Derek Gaines just called."

"I'm sorry, I don't—"

"An old friend. We had a falling-out. It's the first time he's been in touch since . . ." He waved that aside. Later. "Here's a name you will know. Gwen Freeth."

"The recently widowed. Possessor of a legendary collection. And broke." Kelly cut off her computer screen, giving this her full attention. "I thought she shot us down."

"Us and every other major house." A few more taps, then, "Derek claims to have the inside track on the disposal of her collection. Or part of it, anyway."

Her boss's tension slipped across the desk and began infecting her. "The way you're acting, there's a price."

Jerome had still not looked her way. "There probably is."

"You don't know?"

"What I know is . . ." Jerome reached into his pocket, pulled out his phone, touched a number and then the speaker phone, and set it on her desk.

She listened as a stranger's voice said, "Jems, it's Derek. I doubt you're any more interested in small talk than me. I'm heading down your way. Gwen Freeth has assigned me a task. It will probably require the assistance of a major house.

If you want in, meet me. Two o'clock, Evelyn's vault, the Getty."

Jerome pocketed the phone. "Now you know as much as I do."

"You want me to go in your stead?"

Her boss did not respond. Jerome's expression showed a sorrow and vulnerability that unsettled her.

Kelly disliked entering into such a potentially huge project with so much uncertainty. The problem was, Jerome was not someone she could press. The man loved his secrets. It was part of what made him so successful. Kelly had seen him eviscerate people who tried to pry out confidences.

Still, she had to try. "Jerome, this really isn't much to go on."

His response was slow in coming. "Derek is too honest for his own good." Jerome cleared his throat. Again. "The year before you arrived, Christie's LA was one of two finalists to handle the sale of a late Constable."

"I never heard about this."

"Because we didn't land the sale. Derek insisted the work was by a follower of Constable. The Sotheby's expert disagreed. I fired Derek, and he went public. There was a scandal of the first order."

"Was he right?"

"The only answer that matters is, we lost the sale."

Kelly remained silent. Waiting.

Finally Jerome conceded, "Sotheby's was finally forced to concede that Derek had been right all along. But that's not the issue."

Kelly nodded. "You were the one who brought Derek in as outside consultant."

"And that decision almost cost me my job. Which is why I can't be personally involved in whatever he's bringing to the table."

"Jerome, I'm happy to help."

Jerome tapped the chair arm. Once. Twice. Then he pushed himself to his feet. "I owe you."

"No, Jerome. You don't. Not now, not ever."

He turned and left the office. Still without actually looking at her.

Chapter 6

One of the reasons Kelly was so comfortable with Jerome was that she had lived all her life with a mother who showed the world two distinct faces. Even in her fifties Giulia Reid maintained a statuesque beauty that turned heads in a city where lovely ladies were, quite literally, everywhere. Giulia showed the world a vivacious, magnetic air. She doted on Kelly's younger sister and her three children.

Kelly's own relationship with her mother was something else entirely.

Since childhood, Kelly had been the one to bring out her mother's Sicilian side. Rarely did Giulia actually grow angry. Even so, Kelly knew her mother maintained an almost constant *potential* for rage. She could feel the cauldron simmer from time to time, when Giulia did not get her way. But the lid had only come off in the final dread days of Kelly's failed marriage, when Kelly had refused to take back her ex, give him yet another chance, love him despite everything. The resulting battle had been enough to frighten them both.

By contrast, Kelly's nature was uniquely like her father's, the English gentleman. Analytical by nature. Standing at a distance and politely dissecting the situation.

Which was what she did now.

The employees of Christie's LA had reserved spaces in a multistory parking lot shared with other offices and shops lining Wiltshire and Rodeo. She slipped into her car, a late-model BMW 5 Series, and started the engine. The day was heating up, and the AC wash was welcome. She waited for the car to cool, then cut down the fan and placed the call.

Her contact was a semiretired studio executive, whose string of megahits had left him wealthy enough to be counted among Christie's major clients. Kelly also considered the man a friend. They saw each other at exhibitions and events. She called him whenever a major item was coming up for sale. Giving him what was offered to a rarified few clients, the option of acquiring a piece before it even reached the stand. Such actions allowed him to keep things very discreet, very hidden. For such buyers, anonymity was worth paying well above the odds.

Brian Beschel answered with, "I don't get this sort of runaround from my biggest stars."

"I have no idea what you're talking about."

"The sixteen messages I left with your offices. The texts. The pleas."

"You have done no such thing."

"Well, I meant to. But things have been crazy

around here. Doesn't mean I'm not interested in whatever you're selling."

"At this stage, it's just a possibility. A whisper I've heard."

"Must be big, this whisper."

"It could be. Is there any chance we might be overheard?"

He liked that. The first to know a true secret. The one on the inside track. It deepened his voice, like he had suddenly revealed a ravenous streak. "I'm sitting in my office with the door locked, staring at an empty space on my wall."

"The Freeth collection."

A pause, then, "I knew Bernard. Not well. We competed on several items."

"You know Bernard recently passed away."

"And the widow Freeth is drowning in debt. I know. You have a handle on the sale?"

"Not yet. But maybe."

"I want in."

Kelly nodded to the lot's concrete wall. She had been right to make this call. "I'm leaving for a first meeting. And I'm going in blind. I need your help."

"You'll give me the inside track?"

"When I know, you know."

"Tell me what you need."

"Derek Gaines. Jerome has heard Derek is the link to Gwen Freeth and the sale of her collection. I'm scheduled to meet him in just over an hour. I have no idea who Derek is, why he's involved, or what might be happening here."

"Give me twenty minutes."

"Brian, wait."

"Yes?"

"No one can know about this conversation." She spaced the words. Emphasizing them with soft intensity. "Including Jerome."

He gave that the pause it deserved. "I'm your man."

Kelly cut the connection and reversed from her space. The conversation with Jerome had unsettled her. She had never seen her boss so troubled. But at least now she had an ally on her side. Someone who had a vested interest in keeping things quiet.

Kelly had just exited the 405 when her phone rang. Brian Beschel announced, "I have some preliminary information."

She heard the honk of a truck's horn. "Where are you?"

"Headed into the Universal lot. We're partnering with them on a couple of new projects. I've been asked to handle this personally."

"I'm sorry to have bothered you—"

"This isn't a bother, Kelly. This is a thrill. Where are you meeting Dr. Gaines?"

"The Getty."

"Now that is very interesting."

44

"Tell me why."

"Derek Gaines met his late wife at the Getty. Erin Gaines was a commercial artist working freelance. But she also taught art appreciation in the regional high schools. Several times each year, she organized bus trips for her top pupils."

Kelly put on her blinker and pulled into an empty parking space. "And Derek?"

"He was considered one of the Getty's top outside evaluators. The source I contacted called his knowledge encyclopedic."

She watched the rainbow flow of passing vehicles, but in truth saw almost nothing. "You say, he *was*."

"Far as my source could say, he hasn't been back to the Getty since his wife died. That was four years ago."

Kelly felt the electric current grow in her middle. It was a rare moment, yet one she had experienced often enough to recognize. Far below the realm of conscious thought, she confronted the reality just beyond her field of vision.

She was approaching that most incredible of moments.

A new find.

A headline event. One with the heft to create waves around the world of museums and galleries and serious collectors.

It had never happened to her before. Not personally, when she was the one directly responsible.

But she had been involved in several. Each time she shared a faint taste of what she now experienced. The incredible high of a history-making event.

Brian broke into her thoughts with, "Hang on a second, let me pass through the studio gates." She heard Brian greet someone, then, "Okay, I'm back."

She did her best to keep her voice calm. Steady. "I'm still trying to get a handle on the man himself."

"Which was exactly what I told my team." Brian's voice held a gravelly edge. Kelly suspected the studio chief was struggling with his own adrenaline rush. "They came back with two more items. Don't know if either are important."

"Tell me."

"Since his wife's death, Gaines has become a real fitness freak. Last year he competed in the Kona Ironman."

"I've heard of it somewhere, but . . . ."

"They had to explain it to me as well. The Hawaii Ironman is a legend among fitness fanatics. Invitation only. Course is, hang on. I wrote it down . . . four-kilometer swim. This is in open ocean, mind. Then a hundred-and-eighty-kilometer bike ride including a climb up the central mountains, followed by a forty-two-kilometer run."

She tried to fit that around her impression of a

fired college professor and failed. "Two things."

"I don't know if it's even worth mentioning. Just a rumor they picked up. Apparently Gaines has started helping treasure hunters bring their finds to market. Establishing provenance, that sort of thing."

The electric tremors grew too strong to hide away. "Can your people shoot me the file they've developed, and a couple of photos of our guy?"

"No problem." Brian almost growled the words, "Whatever is bringing Gaines back to the Getty, it has to be important. Can we meet when you're done?"

"Jerome expects me to report in."

"Then after."

"I suppose, sure." She owed him that much.

"Maybourne Hotel, rooftop bar. Seven o'clock work for you?"

Chapter 7

The line of cars waiting for space in the Getty's underground garage stretched down the entrance drive and crowded the narrow approach road. Navy-suited security waved their walkie-talkies in the air, trying to turn back newcomers. Some drivers rolled down windows and showed the guards printed passes they had arranged online. Others merely shouted. Which was fairly typical for the city. Nobody could do irate like a wealthy Angelino.

The security who approached Kelly's car was a middle-aged Latina who perspired heavily in the midday heat. "If you don't have a pass, you need to turn around. If you have a pass, it's still a thirty-minute wait. Maybe more."

"I have an appointment with Dr. Derek Gaines."

"Okay. Sure." She lifted the walkie-talkie and said, "Derek's guest is here." The radio squawked in response. The guard asked, "Your name?"

"Kelly Reid."

"Yeah, it's her." She used her radio to point at the entry. "Head into the garage, give them your name."

Kelly did as instructed, sweeping past the quarter mile of fuming vehicles, and entered the shadows.

A second guard walked over, this one male and massive. "You Derek's guest?"

"That's me."

This guard waved to the glassed-in office, and a second barrier marked VIP ONLY lifted. "Find an empty space and take the monorail. Derek says he'll meet you at the main entrance."

The museum was reached via a monorail that climbed the eastern slopes through a forest of pine and palm and hardwood. The train was packed, the tourists excited and chattering in a dozen tongues. Families and couples crammed the windows, shot photos, pointed, exclaimed. Kelly was one of the few people who remained seated. She spent the journey scrolling through the information gathered by Brian's team.

As they pulled into the upper station and she stowed her phone, Kelly wondered just how active Brian remained within the studio system. This was not the peripheral summary she had expected. Brian's researchers had done an incredible job of putting together a review of Derek Gaines and his work and his life. All in the space of thirty minutes. Less. This was the sort of in-depth work she would expect from an active studio executive, preparing for the make-or-break meeting with an agent or star, the deal that could green-light their film. And do so in no time flat.

Not a retired guy playing at consultant on the occasional project.

And something else. A minor point that Brian had failed to mention.

Derek Gaines was one very handsome man.

All but one photo were dated from before he lost his wife. Kelly studied the only recent picture, taken two years back at some event where he was receiving an award. Derek's features had become more tightly sculpted than before, probably the result of his extreme level of fitness and training. The lighting was too harsh, the man's smile almost pained. As if he would have paid good money to be somewhere else. Even so, he was most definitely a head-turner.

The Getty was fronted by a broad plaza and steps curved like waves. Kelly had always considered the grand entry a work of art in itself. She and her father had started coming here when Kelly was still in high school. The fact that this was her first visit in two years might have been good for a crying jag, if she allowed herself to dwell on the bonds between now and everything that had come before.

But she didn't have time for any of that, because there he was.

A trio of stone benches merged into the wall forming the stairs' balustrade. Derek Gaines sat on the middle bench, a large leather artist's portfolio propped against his right leg. A hundred teenage kids in matching school T-shirts joined him along the wall. They chattered with a gaiety that was infectious. Almost everyone who passed smiled their way. Kelly heard them speaking Italian, and almost smiled herself. There were few people on earth who could do effervescent joy like Italians.

Derek's response set him apart. He stared at the kids with an expression that just turned him ancient. He did not look sad. Not really. The kids unearthed something deep as a grave. Kelly recalled how his late wife had brought students here. He observed them with the gaze of a man who had endured a thousand hard years.

Kelly climbed the stairs and kept glancing his way, safe because he was clearly expecting Jerome. She did not really think through her response, the way she intended to introduce herself. Kelly felt a tenuous bond forged by the worst of her own bad days, back when the hours were little more than shadows threatening to consume her.

So she walked around to where she stood slightly behind him, and waited as the four Italian adults gathered their charges and led them indoors. Only when the courtyard grew silent did she step forward and say, "Dr. Gaines, good afternoon, I'm Kelly Reid."

He jerked to his feet, surprised at being caught unawares. "Jerome isn't coming?"

"No, I'm happy to say he's not." She seated herself, set her purse by her feet, gathered her hands in her lap, and launched straight in. "I know there's a history between you two. And probably sometime soon I'll need to hear what it is. But not now. I'm too overwhelmed. . . ."

She stopped and clenched her teeth. This was absolutely absurd. She was acting . . . like an *Italian*. So caught up in trying to draw this man back from the brink, create some sort of link between them . . .

And here she was. Fighting for control.

What a silly, stupid thing to have happen.

She took a hard breath and stared at the crowd emerging from the next monorail. The words were there in front of her, scripted in the golden air. "I need your help. You see, this place holds a special significance. So special I haven't been here in almost two years."

Slowly Derek lowered himself back to the bench. She glanced over, relieved to see his gaze had cleared. He said, "Join the club."

She nodded. But in truth it was mostly in acknowledgment that her instincts had been correct. This was a distinctly Italian segment of her personality, trusting in the illogical and the instinctive. "My father was a very quiet man. He could go days without saying a word. My mother detested that about him. She is very Italian, and had a hard time putting up with his lack of verbal response. Just the same, I think his extremely British nature was how they managed to survive as a couple."

She watched the museum's front doors flash with reflected sunlight as they opened and closed. "The closest I ever felt with my father were the hours we shared walking through art galleries. He loved his art, his books, his study. He was an aerospace engineer, but he never went in for what his coworkers considered important, the sports and the television and the beer. For him, the easy hours were spent poring over art books and preparing for the next place we'd visit."

Derek's voice was easy now, freed from the dark depths, or so it seemed to her. "Where did you live?"

"I was born in Baltimore, but we lived all over. His work moved us to the San Fernando Valley when I was fifteen."

His eyes were a remarkable mix of deep blue and the gray of evening smoke. In dimmer light they probably looked almost black. "And the Getty?"

"My father was the bond that held me to my family, just as he forged the link with my nearly impossible mother. He was proud of me and my work at Christie's. My mother pretended to care, but it was really because Dad urged her. Mom's only real measure of life is family. Dad was different. He knew how much I loved

53

my job, how I even loved my little cubicle. He considered all the hours I put in a worthy price to pay. Because I was chasing my dream. And for our times together, we always had this place. Until . . ."

When she went silent, Derek leaned in closer still, almost like he was going to draw the words from her. And waited.

"Until he died. That very same season, I learned my husband had made infidelity a second profession. And then I came up here for a different reason." She had to turn away. The sympathy was too strong in his gaze. The desire to weep anew flooded in strong as a cry of help. "The week of Dad's funeral, and again the week after my divorce, I came up here every day. And I haven't been since."

She just sat there, raw from the confession, but knowing with a Mediterranean's certainty she had done right. She had no idea how long they sat there. Long enough for the pain to ease, the sense of being close to a man she might actually enjoy getting to know . . . It warmed her.

Derek rose to his feet. "Why don't we get started."

Chapter 8

Derek recognized one of the guards outside the main doors, but the crowds were so thick it was easy to pretend he had not noticed. Crowds filling the vast lobby area formed a tidal rush of sound. The year before the coronavirus crisis, the Getty welcomed almost three million visitors. Most of the foyer staff were different from the friends he and Erin had made here. The young woman staffing the information desk was unknown to him. Derek gave his name and asked her to let Evelyn know they had arrived. He then led Kelly across the main courtyard and into the second building, the one containing art from the seventeenth and eighteenth centuries. Thankfully these rooms were not overly crowded. The worst crush was to be found two buildings over, in the Impressionist wings. Even so, the clamor was enough to mask anything he wanted to say.

He stopped by the glass wall fronting the interior courtyard, waited for a pair of Dutch families to pass, then said, "I need to know that whatever we discuss remains between us."

She did not need to think that over. "That won't happen. Sorry. Jerome—"

"Jerome can be trusted with any secrets you and

I uncover. I am speaking about people beyond our inner circle. Anyone else you share this with, I have to okay first." He gave her a moment to object, then continued. "If I can convince you and Evelyn that we are on the trail of a world-class find, Jerome will agree with my need for compartmentalizing who knows what."

She studied him a long moment. Derek found it very easy to wait. Kelly Reid was not merely attractive. She possessed a magnetic quality that was almost electric in its power.

Her name belonged to some California variety of the English rose. Instead, he confronted a woman who looked almost Arab. Onyx eyes held a trace of an angle, pushed upward by high cheekbones. Her lips were full, her features feminine and yet holding a bird of prey's intensity. She was, in a word, stunning.

Finally she said, "If Jerome or I can't live with this, I will inform you."

Her words emerged like a formal contract. Until that moment, Derek had been unsure whether he should trust this woman. He found it hard to see beyond her beauty and potent allure. It was the first time in years he had felt drawn to a lady. "That will do for now."

As they entered the first hall, he asked, "What is your specialty?"

"Late Romantics, early Impressionists. Recently I've focused on Post-Moderns because they form so much of our work." If she was aware of the attention cast her way by virtually every male who passed, Kelly Reid gave no sign. "Can I ask some questions of my own?"

"Of course."

"You've gone in for treasure hunting, is that true?"

"Art treasure. And the answer is both yes and no. I leave the hard work to others. At least, I have until now." He took it slow, pausing before a couple of late-Renaissance painters. "Treasure dogs are by and large a scruffy lot. Most buyers wouldn't come within a hundred miles. I've focused on helping them establish provenance and make contact with potential buyers."

"Which is vital on two levels. If you can prove a heritage, the value skyrockets. And maintaining secrecy over how a questionable item was located can be crucial." Kelly seemed completely blind to the crowds flowing around them. She was dressed in a blouse and jacket of blue-gray silk with trousers one shade darker. Matching pumps. Small Chanel purse slung from one shoulder. No rings on strong-looking, tanned hands. Derek wondered if there was a sports scholarship somewhere in her past. She asked, "Something has changed with this particular item?"

"This is a first for me. Always before, I'm the guy who's brought in after the hunt is over."

"When the treasure dogs are back in the corral."

"Exactly." He liked that too, how she could read the situation so clearly, and speak in a manner that indicated she was there with him. "This time, I'm being asked to lead the hunt."

"So now the question is, can you trust me in the same way." She nodded. "What can I do to help you make up your mind?"

No pressure. No typical auctioneer's open-faced greed. Just two people embedded in the moment. Searching for answers. He liked that a lot.

He pointed to the next room. "There's something I want to show you."

He led her into the next chamber. The lighting was excellent, the paintings displayed in as close to perfection as was humanly possible. Derek had always marveled at how the buildings and even the hilltop focused both light and attention upon the artwork on display. He said, "We're here because of a painter named Michelangelo Merisi da Caravaggio. Considered one of the most admired artists in history. His work finished off the Renaissance and ushered in the Baroque." Derek pointed to the painting they faced. "To understand Caravaggio, we need to start here at a self-portrait by Raphael. Caravaggio despised Raphael. He rejected everything to do with the theatrical compositions that formed virtually all art up to that point. Instead, he developed a style based upon the common humanity of his subjects."

Derek gave it to her fast. There was no need for Kelly to remember, or even fully understand. He was simply laying the groundwork. This was nothing more than a preliminary first step. He told himself this granted him more time to decide whether or not to trust her. But internally he knew that to be a myth. Just bringing her into this room, sharing his compass heading, meant he had already crossed over the line.

He was committed. He just wasn't ready to admit it yet.

He guided her over to one painting. "*The Supper at Emmaus*, for over a century attributed to Caravaggio. Now it is assumed to have been painted by a follower. Not a student. We know that because Caravaggio had none. He considered other artists to be his rivals, even enemies. But by the time of his death in 1610 at age thirty-eight, his style was already transforming the art world." He hesitated, then added, "Some scholars still dispute this painting's origins. I'm one of them. I personally think this was Caravaggio's last painting. There are too many elements of his unique style to be otherwise."

Kelly was nodding in time to his words. "Sure, I get that. Like a building designed by one architect and finished by another."

"Exactly. Caravaggio murdered a man over a bet, then spent the last four years of his life on the run. It's entirely possible he had to flee before finishing this work. I think his last benefactor recognized its brilliance and paid another artist to complete it."

"Brilliance," she repeated. "Explain that."

"The standard tactic for artists of that era was to gather together a group of admirers and form a school. Caravaggio never had a pupil and despised imitators. Even so, his concepts of naturalism and light were so powerful they became central elements to the entire Baroque movement."

Derek stepped to the next painting. "*David with the Head of Goliath*, on loan from the Borghese in Milan. Thought to be one of the artist's last completed works."

She studied it a long moment, then murmured softly, "The light."

"He was known to paint with just a single lantern in his studio, emphasizing the light-and-shadow composition that came to be known as chiaroscuro. This method sharpens and obliterates areas, leaving large empty spaces on the canvas, concentrating action and isolating the main figures." He watched her lean in closer still, liking the intensity of her focus. "All these things are common practices today. In Caravaggio's era, the shift away from formal settings and careful lighting was explosive. What's more, he modeled saints and apostles on peasants, another first. His paintings show the rough features and dirty feet of normal people. Legend has it that he once used a drowned prostitute as the model for Mary on her deathbed."

She stayed as she was, inches from the canvas. When she finally straightened and faced him, Derek could see the same electric light in her gaze that he felt churning through his gut. "You know what I'm going to ask."

He nodded. "The answer is, I don't know."

"Yet."

"Right."

"But you think . . ."

"Maybe," he conceded. "Just perhaps."

"And the widow Freeth . . ."

"Not her. The son. Allen. Recently deceased."

She studied him a long moment. "Because of a painting by this artist?"

"I have no idea. But I think, maybe. Perhaps."

She turned back to the painting. And continued to study it until Derek glanced at his watch and realized, "We're late for round two."

Chapter 9

Derek led Kelly into the secret kingdom. Beyond the Getty's public face existed an entirely separate realm. The art and treasures on display were only a small fraction of everything the complex possessed.

The main entry point for this second dominion was via the museum library, which could only be accessed through reinforced glass doors. Derek showed his ID to the electronic eye, wondering if it still worked after four years.

The doors slid open and a woman's voice spoke through the security intercom, "Welcome back, Dr. Gaines."

"Thanks."

"Have your guest press her visitor's badge to the reader, please." When Kelly had done so, the guard said, "Ms. Hardy is waiting for you in the main vault."

"Thanks."

They crossed the library's main lobby, and up ahead the lower-level elevator opened to greet them. Once they entered, Kelly motioned to the blank metal framing the electric reader. "There aren't any buttons."

"The guards have to grant you access," Derek replied. "In or out."

"I've heard about this place for years. I thought maybe it didn't actually exist." Kelly rocked on her toes. Just like a kid. "This is so cool."

As the doors chimed open, he hoped Kelly's attitude might help make peace between the two women. But he doubted it.

Evelyn Hardy was tall and thin and English to her very core. Her style of dress could only be described as severe tweed. Her frizzy graying hair was held rigidly in place with antique tortoise-shell combs. Silver reading glasses dangled from a vintage Cartier necklace. Her attitude was as stern as her clothes. Then there was Evelyn's other side.

Her knowledge of art, especially paintings, was encyclopedic. She was supportive of people who shared her passion, be they collectors or academics or the artists themselves. She was loyal. She was caring. She had a way of making her friends feel like they were the center of Evelyn's universe. They in turn forgave her for her occasional bouts of being opinionated, offensive, and difficult in the extreme.

As the doors opened, Evelyn stood behind Judith Raimy, her number-one restorer. Both women were bent over an easel by the opposite wall. Evelyn lifted her finger in Derek's direction and bent in closer to the canvas. "Give me a moment. I need to ensure Judith does not utterly demolish this perfectly decent work of art."

"I'd do a much better job if you'd stop crowding me."

Evelyn shifted the swivel stand holding the magnifying glass over a trace. "You missed a spot by his ear."

"I haven't missed a thing. . . ." She jerked the glass back. "Do you *mind*."

Evelyn sniffed. "The attitude I must put up with these days."

Judith changed brushes. "You took the words straight out of my mouth."

Evelyn straightened and came rushing over. Today's tweed was autumn brown, and the long skirt made a soft *thwock-thwock* as she moved. "Shame on you, you bad boy, making me wait so long."

It was strange how the woman's embrace took him back. The strength in her arms, the fragrances of old perfume and cigarette smoke and paints. The last time he had been held by this woman had been at Erin's gravesite.

Derek gently released himself and took a step back. "Hello, Evelyn."

She must have seen something in his gaze, for the sympathy and concern in her gaze vanished, to be replaced by her customary aloofness. "I suppose you might as well greet Judith. Otherwise she'll blame me for monopolizing you and stay in a huff for ages."

The younger woman waved a brush over her

shoulder without turning around. "Take the job. Start tomorrow. She's become absolutely insufferable."

"And you, young lady, are within a hair's breadth of being sacked."

Judith swiveled around long enough to mouth the word, *Insufferable.*

Derek motioned to the woman standing beside him, "This is Kelly Reid."

"Reid. Reid." Evelyn fumbled for her glasses. "I know that name."

"Actually, Dr. Hardy, we've met."

"Really." She lifted her nose so as to peer through the lenses. "And when might that have been?"

"You attended the launch of our spring sale," Kelly replied. "The early Modernists."

Which turned Judith back around. For once the restoration artist shared Evelyn's look of shock. Judith said, "You work for Christie's?"

Evelyn stepped away. "Really, Derek. Bringing one of that lot down here? You go too far."

"We need to talk."

"What could this one possibly have to say that justifies her presence?" When he remained silent, her voice sharpened further. "This is what you've lowered yourself to, consorting with the dark side?"

Derek was still trying to come up with a response when Kelly spoke. "I've admired your work for years, Dr. Hardy. This is such an honor, I can't begin to tell you." If Kelly was even aware of the older woman's hostility, she gave no sign. "I based my master's thesis on your book about the Realist movement."

Evelyn studied her intently, then motioned toward Judith and her canvas. "Come tell me what you see. Judith, you may go to lunch."

The restorer rose from her stool and took a half-step away. "Not on your life."

Derek watched Kelly approach the easel, then halt about three steps away. A long moment. A step closer. More study. She reached for the stand holding the glass, her fingers searching blindly. Judith stepped forward and brought the metal within reach.

"Thank you."

Derek liked being able to stand there beside Evelyn, watching the lady in action. He knew there was a dual purpose to this test. It was not just about Kelly's knowledge of the subject. What they sought even more than expertise was the woman's heart. Was she passionate about the *art*. Or was it only about the *value*. The *money*. The *sale*.

He realized Evelyn was watching him now. Her gaze was knowing, as if she managed to pierce his skull. See how important it was for Kelly Reid to pass Evelyn's test.

Kelly demanded, "There was no signature?"

Judith answered. "None."

Kelly swiveled the glass in a smooth arc, running around the canvas's borders. "Nothing beneath the frame or on the back?"

"Not a name, not a date," Judith confirmed.

Kelly shifted the glass away. Took a step farther back. "Well, it definitely belongs to the late Barbizon school. Probably a student of Daubigny."

Judith glanced at Evelyn, who merely frowned. The restorer asked, "Not Daubigny himself?"

"No."

"You're sure about that, are you."

"I am. Yes." The painting was of a woman in a pale ivory frock standing isolated on a riverbank. The subject was surrounded by bare-limbed trees and the brown foliage of winter. Kelly pointed to a skinny columnar fir rising to the right of the woman. "This is probably a tribute to the leafless birch Daubigny painted into his *Springtime*, finished in 1857." Kelly studied it a moment longer, then decided, "I would attribute this to Daubigny's son Karl. A number of Karl's early works were so similar in form and quality they were almost indistinguishable from the father." Another moment, then, "I would date this around 1878. Karl is said to have taken his father's death very hard. The winter scene, echoing one of his father's most famous paintings of spring . . ."

When Kelly went quiet, Evelyn pressed, "Yes? Finish your thought."

"It's a fitting tribute to the great man, and would explain the absence of any signature. Karl sought to emulate his father. He wanted no credit. He painted this as an act of remembrance." Kelly took a hard breath and wrapped her arms around her middle. "It's magnificent."

Judith looked at her boss and made round eyes. Evelyn said crisply, "Very well. You may stay."

Chapter 10

The Getty vaults contained a series of high-ceilinged concrete chambers. Big enough to hold entire exhibits in the long preparatory stages before they went on public display. They formed a windowless empire, one dominated by Evelyn Hardy.

She led them to the offices lining the far wall. Derek faltered only once, when he saw the three-by-five notecard stenciled with his name still taped to what had once been his office door. Evelyn must have expected his surprise, because she said, "I positively refused to give up hope."

The office's only furniture consisted of a narrow desk and battered office chair with a squeaky wheel, a trestle table, four folding chairs. Just like he had left them, back before his world imploded.

He stood in the doorway, remembering. The way Erin had transformed their shared lunches into picnics so joyous she drew in guards and receptionists and even Evelyn on occasion.

The walls she insisted were reserved for the rainbow of paintings she taped there, all products of her favorite pupils, her stars of the future universe. The three lonely easels where he was permitted to attach his work. The magnifying glass on its swivel stand, focused on the whitewashed cement. The strong fluorescents illuminating all the empty days.

The chairs where they had sat and held hands and wept together, the last time she had felt like making the trip down. Insisting that he not clear the place out alone. Urging him to come work here full-time. Build a new life without her. Find a future . . .

"Derek?"

He forced himself to enter. Only then did he realize Judith stood ready to reach for him, should his strength falter. Judith was a hefty woman in her late forties with no fashion sense whatsoever. One of Erin's closest friends. A heart as big as the largest Rembrandt canvas. Bigger.

Derek cleared his throat. "What I am about to show you, it has to stay strictly between us."

Evelyn protested, "Really, Derek. That's all rather melodramatic."

It was the perfect response. As if she had managed to read the script of his aching heart, and knew precisely what to say in order to draw him away from the brink. He lifted the leather artist's portfolio and said, "One man is quite possibly dead because of what I want you to see."

The news silenced her.

"All I have at this point are questions. But the answers are coming. I feel it in my gut. And it's telling me that they could mean trouble and triumph in equal measure."

"Well, I for one have always had the greatest respect for your middle section," Evelyn said.

Judith added, "I'd give anything to be part of an adventure. Escape this boring dungeon. Just for a little while. Life has been awful since you departed."

Derek liked the light in Judith's eyes more than he could say. "Shut the door."

Derek unzipped the portfolio and drew out the picture. "Yesterday Gwen Freeth made an appointment with Trevor. She asked specifically to meet me." He used specialty clamps with felt-covered faces to attach the picture to the central board. Then he stepped back, allowing the three ladies to move in close. "When we met yesterday, Gwen said her late son had sent this from Italy. With it was a note claiming it would restore the family's fortunes."

Evelyn's nose was within inches of the canvas. "I thought the Freeths were rich."

"Past tense," Kelly said. She rolled the magnifying glass on its portable stand over to where she could inspect the right side. "Her late husband ran up an astonishing assortment of debts."

Evelyn glanced over, her expression sour once more. "No doubt your lot were among the vultures circling overhead."

Derek watched Kelly stiffen, but she did not respond.

Instead, from the director's other side, Judith said, "Evelyn."

"I'm just saying."

"Play nice," Judith said. "Else I'll make you go stand in the corner."

Derek saw Kelly's shoulders relax somewhat. He went on, "For the moment, I want us to focus on one possibility. I've had a day and a night to come up with two other options, and sooner rather than later we'll need to discuss those as well. If for no other reason than to discount them."

It was Kelly who turned to him, her eyes shining. "This is him. Isn't it."

He liked how she was the one who first shared the electric current. "I think so. Yes."

Evelyn looked at Kelly.

But Kelly remained locked on him, and her gaze fed the electric worms burrowing in Derek's chest. She said, "The hands. The use of shadows." She did not ask a question. It was a statement. Hard and tight as her gaze. "And those faces. The structure, the raw nature of their expressions—"

"Sweet heavens above!" Judith almost erupted. "Will someone *please* tell me what is going on?"

Kelly remained locked on him. Waiting.

It was Evelyn who said, "You truly believe this to be a lost Caravaggio?"

Judith rewarded that with a swift intake of breath. She looked away from the canvas long enough for her gaze to skip from Kelly to Evelyn to Derek. Then back to the canvas.

"Here's what we know." Derek took another step away from the board and the painting and the women. "Caravaggio was the Baroque version of an artistic bad boy. He was forced to flee Rome, the center of his growing fame and fortune, because he murdered another man over a tennis bet. This wasn't some isolated incident. He had been in and out of trouble for years. But this time he crossed the line. The authorities could no longer overlook his action. A warrant for his arrest was issued. He fled in the middle of the night, a few steps ahead of the marshals."

The three women all followed the same pattern. Tight focus on him, occasional glances back to the unfinished painting. Intent.

"He went south, keeping barely ahead of his pursuers. Caravaggio fled from one Italian kingdom to the next. By this point, his fame was such that almost every ruling family would be more than happy to give him shelter, so long as he painted, and as long as they didn't get in trouble themselves. From that point until his death four and a half years later, Caravaggio lived on the run. Naples, then Malta, Calabria, Bari, Naples again. And finally Sicily, where he stayed until a few months before his death. Caravaggio left

Palermo and headed north, a frantic chase that ended with his death in 1610, age just thirty-eight, in the Spanish-ruled fortress town of Porto Ercole in Tuscany."

Kelly suggested, "He had bounty hunters on his trail. It's the only thing that makes sense. The Italian kingdoms maintained a fragile peace at best. The authorities in Rome represented only one of four different global factions, all of them pressing for domination. Only independent soldiers of fortune could have tracked him across such a landscape. They carried letters of marque, probably from both the king and the pope—"

"All right, you've convinced us." Evelyn had lost her crisp irritation. She was involved now. What was more, Jackson was certain Kelly had been accepted into the fold.

Only the work's central two-thirds was completed. The surrounding canvas was yellowed with age. The three central figures showed a male in formal court dress standing behind a chair holding a woman and a newborn infant. The man looked down upon the pair with a tragic affection that shone through the centuries. The chair holding mother and child was typical Baroque, high-backed with an embroidered fabric that was matched by the stained-glass window in the rear wall. The portrait's only illumination came from a standing candelabra and the window showing the silhouette of a woman and a white dove flying toward heaven. Both the candles and the window were behind the man's right shoulder. The illumination shone upon just one side of the faces. Shadows crept forward from the painting's opposite side, almost as though they prepared to swallow the mother and child. Devour them.

Kelly almost whispered the words, "They're dead, aren't they."

That turned the other two women around. Evelyn said, "Explain that."

"The plague swept through southern Italy every few decades," Kelly said. "Look at how he watches them. He doesn't just love them. He's saying farewell."

"That's so sad," Judith murmured.

"You can't know that," Evelyn said. Again, no heat.

"It would explain a lot," Derek said.

"Such as?"

"Several of Caravaggio's later works were completed by other artists. He arrived in a new principality, and was commissioned. He painted until the marshals or mercenaries caught up with him. Then he fled. The painting's owner hired someone else to complete the work. Only not this time. Why?"

"Because neither the patron nor his family are complete," Kelly said, mourning with this stranger. Joined to a tragedy from five hundred years ago. "Because the painting is fine just like it is."

Evelyn simply watched her. Silent.

"There's something else," Derek said. "There has never been a sketchbook identified as belonging to Caravaggio. In his era, that's unheard of. It's another way the artist stands apart." He stepped forward and pointed out faint charcoal lines extending from the completed center, made almost indistinct by time's passage. "And here is the answer."

"He sketched directly onto the canvas," Evelyn said. "How remarkable."

"We have always assumed this was a tactic invented by the Impressionists," Derek said. "And yet here is evidence that an artist used the same method four hundred years earlier."

Evelyn pursed her lips. Breathed in and out. Nodded to the painting, an almost formal farewell. Then she walked over and seated herself at the central table. "Places, everyone." When the others had settled, she said to Derek, "I assume you have worked through your next steps."

"I have. Yes."

"Very well. Let's hear it."

"I need a valid reason to go to Sicily," he replied. "And money. And your help in keeping me alive."

"Keeping *us* alive," Kelly corrected. "You're not going anywhere without me."

Chapter 11

"I'm not sure that was a good idea," Jerome said. "Involving Brian Beschel at this stage."

The Maybourne was a palatial hotel that stood in sedate splendor beside the Beverly Canon Gardens. Kelly's rooftop table was shaded by a massive square parasol. Beyond the bar's boundary, a lone woman swam smooth laps, slicing the pool's dusk-clad waters into ribbons of gold and russet. The bar was filling with the after-work crowd. She recognized two of Christie's wealthy patrons. At a table tucked slightly away from the rest, three studio executives hosted an A-list actress. There were worse places, Kelly reflected, to bring her boss up to date.

She replied to her phone, "You were the one who sent me off without a full briefing. I need you to give me carte blanche on this. Either I handle it as I see fit, or you take over. Which may actually be the best way forward."

"No. I can't become involved."

"Jerome, if I do this, it will be as your executive. You are involved and so is Christie's."

"And the painting?"

"If we can work up a solid provenance, Christie's will share the sale with Trevor."

"I don't understand."

"Which part?"

"Why does Derek need a travel budget and a trustworthy team to prove provenance?"

"Because," Kelly replied, "he doesn't think the painting in our possession is the prize."

Soon as she finished the call with her boss, the rooftop manager approached. "Mr. Beschel apologizes, but he has been held up." He indicated the waiter hovering a step back, holding a frosted bucket. "He hopes you will accept his apologies, and enjoy a glass of vintage champagne while you wait."

Kelly thanked the manager and watched the two of them enter into the orchestrated ballet of opening the three-hundred-dollar bottle and pouring her a glass. She waited until they had departed to lift the slender goblet and toast the gathering dusk.

When Brian showed up an hour and seventeen minutes late, Kelly was only midway through her second glass. She had limited herself to tiny sips now and then, savoring the refined flavor, the miniature bubbles almost chuckling as they went down. She had ordered a selection of tapas, and two empty plates still littered the table as the manager ushered Brian over and waited while he settled into his chair and said, "Bring us another plate of whatever the lady's had here."

"Certainly, Mr. Beschel. Coming right up."

"I'm so sorry, Kelly. This afternoon just exploded in my face."

"Don't apologize. I've needed this time more than I can say."

"The meeting with Derek Gaines went well?"

"The meeting," Kelly replied, "was incredible."

Brian's phone buzzed. He pulled it from his pocket, checked the readout, shook his head. "These people."

"Answer it if you need to."

"What I need is for a senior executive to take on some of these issues and handle them." He nodded to the waiters as they set down the tapas and filled his glass. "Could I possibly interest you in changing jobs?"

"Kind of you to offer, but I'm happy where I am."

"I am serious, Kelly."

"So am I."

"Well, keep me in mind if the itch strikes." He cut off his phone, slipped it back into his pocket, and picked up a tapas. Ate the sliver of air-dried beef on black peasant's bread with pickle and dab of mustard. Nodded approval. Drained his glass, let the hovering waiter fill it, then asked that they not be disturbed. He gave the night and the stars and the rooftop aerie a long look. Settling.

Brian was dressed in California chic, a blue-gray jacket of some fabric that shimmered in the candlelight, probably silk and linen. Navy dress shirt opened at the collar. Gold Rolex. He took another tapas and stretched out his legs. Kelly was more than happy to wait. The night was splendid. Her story was one that deserved his full attention. When he was ready.

Finally he pulled the bottle from the bucket, refilled his glass, waved it in her direction. When she refused, he settled it into the ice, leaned back, and said, "So tell."

But Kelly only managed half of her story before Brian held up his hand and ordered her to stop. She asked, "What's the matter?"

"Where's the painting now?"

"Derek took it back with him. He wants to inspect—"

"Can you get him down again tomorrow?"

"I suppose, sure, but Brian, you haven't heard what he claims to need."

"Which is?"

"For starters, a budget large enough to finance a team going to Sicily. And no, he won't give up the painting. He is urging Gwen Freeth to do nothing until provenance is clear."

To his credit, Brian did not reject her out of hand. "Can I get right of first refusal?"

"Possibly. But I can't guarantee . . ." She stopped because he had his phone out. "What are you doing?"

"Booking you into my calendar." He shook

his head. "Thirty-seven new messages. These people. Okay, how does seven tomorrow morning sound?"

"Fine for me, but Derek can't possibly make it down in time."

"Where is he?"

"Miramar Bay."

"Where?"

"A town on the central coast."

"Must be nice." He scrolled through his schedule. "Okay, so let's make it for six tomorrow evening. We'll need to meet at the studio headquarters. You know where that is, right?"

"Of course."

"I'll make a reservation for your Dr. Gaines to stay here tomorrow night."

"Here, as in, the Maybourne?"

"Think he'll like it?"

"Derek claims he's barely managing to hold on to his home. I think he'll flip."

"Flipping is good. Soften the guy up."

"To do what, exactly?"

But Brian was already on his feet. "Let's save that for our next meeting." He kissed her cheek. "Remember what I said about a job."

"I thought you were retired."

"If only." He motioned for the check, started away, then turned back to ask, "How much of this money does our guy intend to pocket himself?"

Kelly felt extremely foolish having to admit, "I didn't ask. But I think . . ."

She stopped when the waiter appeared at Brian's elbow. He glanced at the bill, handed over his credit card, and asked, "You think what?"

"I don't think Derek expects to keep anything beyond covering his expenses. To be frank, I don't think the issue even crossed his mind."

"I've known a few people like that. Not many. One or two. So caught up in their work they treat money as an irritant."

"I don't know Derek well enough to say anything for certain. But that's my first impression."

He signed the bill. "Be on time."

Chapter 12

The northbound traffic out of LA was so heavy that evening, it turned the freeway by Long Beach into a parking lot. Derek did not arrive at the Freeth residence until a quarter past eight. When the gates slid open, he drove his pickup across the graveled forecourt and parked by Trevor's Infiniti. He rose slowly, his body stiff from the drive, and made his way to where Gwen and Trevor stood by a central pool. He dreaded having to sit through Gwen's idea of proper etiquette, doing what needed doing, then driving another two hours back home.

His approach was halted by his phone's ring. He checked the readout and said, "Sorry, I have to take this."

Kelly Reid greeted him with, "I may have a handle on your requirements."

He turned his back to the pair. "That was fast."

"It's not a done deal. But I've met with the longtime client you said I could approach. He is definitely interested."

Once again, Jackson hoped he had been right to okay the contract. "There is no provenance, Kelly. None whatsoever. He needs to understand this going in."

"Brian Beschel is the kind of collector who is used to dealing with maybes."

Derek knew he needed to be sharp. Totally focused on what was happening. But just then his thoughts sparked like disconnected fragments in his weary brain. "And you trust him."

"I have worked with him on four different acquisitions." They had been through this in the Getty vault, but evidently Kelly saw nothing wrong with repetition. "But what we're attempting here, it's taking things to a totally new level."

Derek nodded to the golden light. That described his own situation with pinpoint accuracy. Always before he had held such work at arm's length. He came in, he put his stamp on the item, he estimated its value, when possible he worked up a provenance, he made introductions, he stepped away. All this, the maneuverings, the risk, the hunt, he left in other people's hands.

"Derek?"

"Thinking." He rubbed his face with the hand not holding the phone. "I don't know what to say."

"Well, I'm not going to pull your team and a travel budget out of a hat." She sounded impatient now. Pushing with polite firmness. "You asked me to help and this is me trying to do my job."

"Okay. So what next?"

"We meet with him tomorrow evening. He's booked you a room for tomorrow night at the

Maybourne Hotel." She sounded genuinely excited. "This is going to be fun."

The steep slopes inland from Santa Barbara and Montecito were home to some of central California's richest people. Owners gathered here for the relative privacy, the anonymity, the jaw-dropping views. Estates rarely appeared on the open market. Sales took place on a cash-only basis. For many of these residents, their idea of a wild night out was to chopper or limo down to LA, take in the dinner or party or concert or film launch, then ride back in time to watch another semi-perfect sunrise.

Compared to some of the palatial estates where Derek had valued works of art, Gwen Freeth's art deco home was almost plain. The single-story residence was white stucco with clean lines and walls of reflective glass. Derek walked over to where Trevor and Gwen stood by a small reflective pool, staring at the sculpture planted at its heart.

Trevor greeted him with, "Well?"

Derek did not need to take as long as he did, examining the sculpture. But the sense of weary disconnect remained, and there was a vague comfort to be found in studying the artwork. "Medardo Rosso."

"I wasn't sure," Trevor said.

"Neither was the auctioneer who sold my late

ne'er-do-well the piece," Gwen said. "There was no provenance. Apparently they found it in a snow-covered Canadian garden."

"Then your husband got a steal," Derek said. The sculpture showed a young girl's face emerging from the granite base, lovely and yet unfinished. It reminded Derek of a flower frozen at the moment when the bloom first appeared. "I would date this around 1910, when Russo was mimicking Rodin's structural concepts."

Gwen studied him. "You don't sound well."

He had no choice but admit, "I'm exhausted. A very long day."

"But successful, I hope."

"I hope so too."

Gwen led them inside, then halted in the entryway and gazed at the object that adorned the table opposite the entrance. "Of all the pieces in Bernard's collection, this has always been my favorite."

"It's your collection now," Derek said.

She shook her head, a tight gesture, almost a shudder. "Not for long, if my accountant is to be believed."

Trevor murmured, "Oh my dear sweet word."

The item was actually three separate pieces. The central object was a clock. Or rather, a gilded sculpture supporting a clock. Two crouching lions of what appeared to be solid gold held up a base of marble and blown glass. Winged cherubs of gold and silver held a clock whose diamond-studded face was the size of a dinner plate. A woman, or goddess, looked down in approval and poured what appeared to be emerald petals from an alabaster urn. To either side rose candelabra held by more gilded cherubs.

Trevor's hands trembled as he pulled white cloth gloves from his pocket. "May I?"

"It's yours, if you want it," Gwen replied softly.

He lifted the central object by its base, nodded, set it carefully down again. Inspected the face of the clock. "I forgot my glass."

"Bernard's is around here somewhere."

"No need. No need." Another breathless inspection of one candelabra, then Trevor straightened. All business. "Well, it's obviously Napoleon Third. Second Empire. But you already know that."

Gwen wrapped her arms around her middle and did not reply.

"The decorative flourishes are quite simply exquisite. All of it is handmade, of course. And it bears the signature of that era's most famous sculptor. Jean Jules Salmson was known to have worked on several designs for the royal jewelers, Raingo Frères, that's their name here on the clockface. They brought in several top artists to create such ornamental items for the royal family."

Derek asked, "Why unique?"

"Because none of the Salmson jeweled articles

have survived, or so I thought until this very moment."

"Maybe his signature is faked?"

"Not a chance." Trevor was definite now. "Salmson's elements are all over this. The flared base, the ormolu and gilt applied to marble, the exquisitely carved central figures. His signature is merely icing on the gilded cake." Trevor hugged himself as well, but for a different reason. "How on earth did you come to possess this?"

Gwen impatiently cleared her face with both hands. "I'd rather not get into that."

Trevor glanced over. "Of course. Forget I asked."

They followed Gwen into the main parlor. The Freeth collection was, in a word, exquisite. But Derek was too weary to give the items on display their proper due. He joined Trevor on an ivory sofa facing the glass wall and the western vista. Gwen settled into an Eames chair to their right. "I suggest we dispense with trivialities and get down to business. Before the young man here keels over."

"I'm okay," Derek replied.

"*Okay* is not the word I would use to describe anything about your state," Gwen replied. "Running on fumes, more like."

He nodded. "Business, then."

"The insurers have prepared their official valuation." She pushed a slender file across the table. "This represents every item I possess."

Trevor started to reach for the file, but Derek leaned forward and shook his head. Once. Trevor's fingers remained outstretched. The file was a magnet drawing him toward his shop's largest-ever sale. But Derek held his boss's gaze until Trevor settled back. Sour. Trevor said, "I suppose we can use their numbers as a base."

"Not just yet," Derek said.

Gwen did not appear to hear him. "After leaving your shop, I endured two horrid meetings, first with the accountants and then Bernard's bankers." She looked around the room, resigned to saying farewell. "Given what they've said, it appears unlikely that I will be able to keep my home."

"Let's not get ahead of ourselves." Derek drew from his pocket the envelope from Megan Pierce. "After you left our shop, I met with the attorney who gave you my name."

Trevor demanded, "Why am I only hearing about this now?"

"Trevor."

"What?" But something in Derek's gaze caused his boss to back off. Even more miffed than before. But at least silent.

Derek went on. "There are two possible reasons for the attorney to have chosen me. The first is, I can be trusted as an evaluator. In that case, my job is done." He described his meeting in the

89

Getty vaults, and the ladies' unified response. Then he waited.

Gwen was connected now. "I don't understand."

Trevor said, "That makes two of us."

Gwen said, "You and your friends are certain Allen uncovered a lost Caravaggio?"

"As certain as anyone could possibly be at this point. Yes. We are."

She studied him a long moment. "What precisely are you not saying?"

"If you want, this painting represents a substantial deposit on your future. Yes, okay, you may lose everything here. And declaring bankruptcy may be your only course of action. But the Caravaggio is not included among the assets you'd be losing."

Trevor said, "The *supposed* Caravaggio."

Derek kept his gaze on Gwen. "For the moment, I think we should assume this painting is real."

Gwen asked, "How much is it worth?"

"There will always be detractors who question its provenance. Even so, I am fairly certain I will be able to establish a clear point in the artist's history when this painting was made. Once that happens, Christie's will happily take it to auction. Kelly estimated the value, even in its unfinished state, at between two and three million dollars. I agree."

Gwen frowned. "I don't understand."

Derek nodded.

Gwen continued, "Allen's note was very precise. He did not say, this would pay for my future after losing everything I cherish. He said, this would restore our fortunes."

"Right." Derek slid the envelope across the table. "Which brings us to the second option."

Gwen opened the envelope and drew out two items. "A safety deposit key and pass card."

Trevor rose, stepped around the table, and examined the card with her. "Why a bank in Miramar Bay?"

"Because it was intended for me all along," Derek replied. "Allen set up what treasure dogs call a double blind. He told you to use Megan, he told Megan to suggest you use me, he left the key and card with her."

"But *why?*"

"That's the first question we have to answer."

"You obviously have suspicions."

He shook his head. "Not tonight. I'm too tired."

She rose from her chair. "In that case, I suggest you settle yourself into Allen's residence. We turned the garage apartment into a place where he could be fully independent, but still part of our family. Such as it was."

Derek rose, but did not follow her. "Gwen."

"Yes?"

"The clock."

"Oh. Of course." She waved a vague hand in Trevor's direction. "Take it."

Derek went on. "Trevor needs to receive formal assignment as your agent for all future sales. Whether or not you go through with this, this public announcement will elevate his status."

"To the stratosphere," Trevor said weakly. "And beyond."

She did not even look back. "Prepare the documents, Trevor."

Trevor remained planted on the sofa. "I am speechless with gratitude."

"Wait, Gwen. One more thing," Derek said.

"What is it now?"

"How long did the bankers give you before . . ."

"Two weeks." She held herself erect by strength of will alone. A vibrant and intelligent woman brought low by multiple blows. "If I haven't put things in motion within the next fourteen days, they will take matters out of my hands. Now come along."

Chapter 13

Derek helped Trevor carry the clock and candelabra to his van and wrap them in protective
blankets. Derek stepped back and stared at the
starlit sky, enveloped in waves of fatigue. "The
store in Miramar—"

"Forget the store. I'll send Heather up tomorrow." Heather was his part-time assistant, a
retired florist, glad for the occasional hours.

Gwen's footsteps scrunched across the gravel.
She said to Trevor, "Don't sell the clock. Not
until we're certain."

Trevor glanced at the three wrapped bundles.
He started to protest, but instead looked over at
Derek. "Help."

Derek said it for him. "Trevor can put a sky-
high price on the item. Double the market value."

"My front window is begging to hold this
treasure," Trevor said.

"That will allow him to declare to the world
that he represents your collection."

Gwen's gaze glinted brightly in the night's
illumination. "Will one of you please stop
dancing around the topic and tell me what you
mean?"

"If you take it back, you should agree to pay

him what he might have realistically obtained from the sale," Derek said.

Trevor added, "It would only happen if the real treasure is located."

Gwen said softly, "The *real* treasure."

"Enough to pay off your debts," Derek said. "It means Trevor can be assured of payment for the role he will play."

"His *role*," Gwen said. "In the *future*."

"Exactly." Derek glanced at his boss. "My guess is, we're going to need him."

"Very well." Gwen started back to the house. "I'll leave you to work out the details."

When Derek turned back, Trevor was smiling. "In case you were wondering, now is the time when you make your utterly unreasonable demands for payment."

"I probably should," Derek replied. "But all I want is a good night's sleep."

Derek woke to sunlight pouring through the eastern A-frame windows. The apartment was too large to be called a studio, more like a loft sectioned by gentle suggestions of walls and broad single steps. It was a lovely place, the sort of home that a mother might use to entice her wandering son back whenever he was within reach.

It was also completely clean. Sterile.

The walls held a number of lesser artworks, original sketches and numbered prints. The furniture was pale wood, mostly Swedish modern. Of the man who had once lived here . . .

Nothing.

At least, nothing that even suggested what the late Allen Freeth had done with his time. The closet was stacked with boxes containing expensive-looking clothes. Otherwise the place was empty. No safe, no hidden compartment, no files, no maps, no messages.

Derek showered and dressed in his clothes from the previous day. As he started down the stairs, his phone chimed with an incoming message from Kelly, saying she'd meet him at the hotel in a little over five hours. He responded, then went in search of coffee and the lady of the house. In that order.

He found Gwen seated on the rear veranda, a book opened in her lap. She greeted him by pointing to an envelope on the table beside her. "Key to the house and garage apartment, pass codes for the gates and the alarms. I want you to come and go at will."

"Gwen, I don't know what to say."

"You are welcome." She closed her book and set it on the table. "Coffee and breakfast things in the kitchen. Help yourself."

The kitchen was simple and as elegant as the rest of the house. The west-facing wall held glass sliders that pushed open to merge into alcoves. There were two dining tables, one between the cooking island and the glass, and another outdoors on the patio. He poured himself a coffee and added a bowl of fruit and carried them back outside. "I've never had money. Never felt the urge or the need to go out and buy. Own. Possess."

"Lucky you."

He shrugged. "But your home, it's something else."

"Thank you. I think so."

"Can I get you a refill?"

"You're a dear." She handed him the mug. "Just a touch of milk." When he returned and settled into the chair opposite hers, she went on, "Bernard was always after me to take on staff. Whatever for? One of the nicest things about this place is the privacy. Why allow someone to come in and disturb our peace on a daily basis?"

"I'm with you."

"I love to cook. If we have guests, we can bring in a server, a chef, whatever. They come, they do their job, and the next morning I wake up and come out here, and love my isolated refuge just as much as the very first day. Perhaps more."

The morning light revealed a woman of remarkable control. Gentle strength, intelligence, and something more. He could not name it, but felt drawn to her just the same. "Thank you for letting me stay last night."

"I don't mind telling you, it was good to have

a man over the garage again." She smiled to the sunlit vista. "I wish you could have known Bernard. Now that he's gone and the vultures are circling, all everyone talks about are his failings. And he certainly had more than his share. I'm not playing the grieving widow here, glossing over the man's flaws. He could be the ultimate louse."

When she went silent, Derek offered, "Then there were the good days."

"So many, and so good. Bernard was a man of passion. He loved life. He loved good wine. He loved art. He loved the sea, though he was the worst sailor who ever wrecked a friend's boat. He loved . . ."

Derek finished softly, "He loved you."

She smiled to the sea and the blue sky and the wind. "Yes. He did."

"And Allen?"

"Allen." Another determined smile. "Fierce. Stubborn. And frail."

He nodded. "That's how I remember him."

"When did you meet my son?"

"Eight months ago. UC Santa Cruz hired me to take the place of an ailing professor. After my first lecture, Allen stopped by, shook my hand, said he'd heard good things. He told me he was on the hunt for missing artworks and might have need of my services. I gave him my details. A couple of weeks later he stopped by the shop. We talked about Baroque artists, mostly Italians.

Caravaggio's name came up, but only in passing. That was the last I heard from him," Derek recalled. "He looked sick."

"Allen was born with a condition known as hypertrophic cardiomyopathy, or HCM. The heart muscle, or myocardium, is abnormally thick on one side, usually the left ventricle. It causes the heart to work far too hard. Stress can be a killer. A number of men in Bernard's family had died early due to heart failure. Now we know why."

"I'm so sorry."

"Bernard was always after him to take it easy. Allen had no intention of doing so. Which led to some monumental father-son battles. Almost as many as they had over Bernard's business dealings."

Derek watched her intently, trying to understand what had the woman so, well, *cheerful* was the word that repeatedly came to mind. As if she was discussing the long-ago events of some family friend, rather than the loss of her husband and son. He came up blank.

Gwen went on. "As a child, Allen was bright and inquisitive and loved adventure stories and science fiction, which I suppose in some respects are one and the same. He never became the teenage rebel, never did drugs, he had his friends and he didn't study as hard as he should." She shook her head. "Some of the problems our friends have with their children, you can't imagine."

"Actually, I can. My late wife taught high school."

"Dreadful, nightmarish problems." She studied the swooping drop and the shimmering Pacific. "Allen the man remained fascinated with treasure and explorers and pirates and the whole world of lost artifacts. Bernard fought it, as I said. He wanted his only child to take care of his health, to rest easy, to share Bernard's passion for collecting. Allen wasn't having any of it."

"And you?"

"I never stopped loving my little boy. He was such a joy to be around, so full of life and enthusiasms. When he began talking about these lost treasures, he would become so *alive*."

He took that as his cue. "There's something we need to discuss."

"There are any number of things we must talk about."

"This can't wait. I still think you should seriously consider walking away. You have a painting that is not officially part of your collection. We hold off on any sale until after your current situation has been fully unraveled. You pocket the proceeds, you start a new life, and—"

"No," Gwen said. Firm and definite. "No."

"There are risks. We both know what happened to Allen may not have been an accident."

"What about the risks now? Staying here in this

house, watching the clock count down to losing everything? Or rather, I would, but Trevor has my favorite clock in his window."

"Gwen . . ."

"What?"

He could name the harsh light in her gaze. The almost frantic determination to stay the course. He knew it because he shared it. And had for four long years. "I like you very much."

"Are we done talking nonsense?"

"For now, at least. And it's not nonsense. I want you to join me for opening the safety deposit box. And Trevor. But it will have to wait until after I get back from Los Angeles."

"And now?"

"Allen's apartment. It's as impersonal as a hospital room."

"That's how he lived. For a man who loved the hunt, he had no interest in collecting. I suppose it was Allen's way of dealing with his lack of tomorrows. That or simply rejecting his father's rather pompous attitude to his collection."

"And research, notes, records, maps . . ."

Gwen was already shaking her head. "Allen kept everything in his head. He called his mind the only truly safe repository."

Derek checked his watch, rose to his feet. "I better get going."

She inspected his rumpled form. "To LA? Dressed like that?"

"I don't have a change of clothes. And no time to go home."

Gwen rose to her feet. "You just come with me."

Chapter 14

Gwen led him into the garage apartment and began sifting through the boxes containing Allen's clothes. Derek was a couple of inches taller than Allen, but the trousers were cut in the Italian manner, which meant they were almost long enough. Their waists were almost identical. The shoes were several sizes too small. The shoulders of Allen's dress shirts were too narrow, but the knit shirts fit well enough. The material was some ultra-expensive blend, cotton and silk and something else. Derek suspected maybe cashmere. He felt guilty trying them on.

Gwen inspected him, then left and returned with a pair of cuticle scissors and cut the threads holding up the trouser cuffs. She stood, looked him over, and decided, "You could almost pass for the newly rich."

"I feel like an imposter."

She offered him the day's first smile. "That shirt looks poured on. Don't be surprised if the lady you're meeting takes one look and swoons."

"I've only met her once, but my impression is, Kelly Reid is not the swooning type."

"Maybe she just hasn't had a reason."

She took him back into the house and started

working her way through boxes at the back of her late husband's dressing room. The wood-lined chamber was larger than Derek's bedroom and smelled of cedar and polishing wax. The odor was faint, drifting in the still air like a ghost. Gwen pointed to the leather suitcases stacked on the top shelf. "Pull down that satchel."

"A plastic shopping bag is all I need."

"I can't believe you even suggested such a thing."

"If I didn't know better, I'd say you were enjoying yourself." Derek watched her expertly fold the garments and stow them. "Gwen, I only need enough for tonight."

"You're doing me a favor. I should never have held on to their things for so long. What's the name of your hotel?"

He scrolled back through Kelly's messages. "Maybourne Beverly Hills."

"I believe Bernard has stayed there. Which means it is very nice indeed." She studied his form. "You need belts."

"I can use—"

"Don't even say it." She opened a drawer in the central console. "Here, take these."

One was brown, the other black. Both were crocodile or alligator, both with gold buckles. "These probably cost more than my truck."

"How do you feel about silk underwear?"

"Now you're making fun of me."

"Perhaps a little." She pulled on another handle and the entire section of wall rolled out smoothly, revealing rack after rack of shoes. "What was your shoe size again?"

"Eleven and a half."

"Bernard wore elevens." She took three pairs from the lowest shelf. "These were a bit large and hardly ever worn."

He tried on a pair of black tasseled loafers, so supple he could have rolled them up like socks. "They might as well have been made for me."

"Then they're yours." Another drawer, and six pairs of socks were added to the pile. "Jacket?"

"I don't do jackets."

"Allen loathed them as well. In any case, Bernard's would be far too large in the middle region." Another drawer, this one stacked with V-neck sweaters. She bundled up four or five, then pointed to the case. "Start packing. I'll be in the kitchen."

When he emerged, she was on the phone. "Thank you, Alice. Yes, he's on his way now. Derek Gaines. Yes, I promise I'll stop by next week." She cut the connection and said, "Down the main road, the little shopping center on your right just before you enter town. The hair-dresser's—"

"Gwen, no, it's too much. . . ."

She pressed at the air between them. "Who is it you're meeting with?"

"Her name is Kelly Reid."

"And she is . . ."

"Some executive."

"With Christie's. And you're going because . . ."

"She asked me to."

Gwen swiped at his arm. "You sound like a pouting nine-year-old. She is trying to help you put together a safe way to travel to Sicily. Isn't that what you told me? Derek, dear, you are entering into a new dimension of wealth and power. You must dress the part, and you must *look* the part." She fished in her pocket and reached out. "I want you to wear this."

"This" was a solid gold Rolex. "Not on your life."

"It's just a loan." She shook it hard enough for the band to rattle. "Bernard liked them to slide around his wrist, I never did understand why. Try it on."

Reluctantly he accepted the watch. "Maybe a little tight."

She stopped him from arguing further by grasping his arm and steering him toward the front door. "One more stop and you're done."

"Gwen. No."

"Just hear me out."

"It's not happening."

"I certainly won't insist. But I think you should at least consider what I have to say."

They stood just outside the middle of three double garages. Daylight cut a shadow in front of where Derek stood, strong as a blade. "It won't make any difference, but go ahead."

"This Christie's executive has arranged a meeting with one of her clients. Someone so rich and powerful they can finance sending you and your squad to Europe."

"You've already said that."

"Hush up and listen. These sort of people are approached every day by people wanting money, a job, a chance. Supplicants will say anything, *do* anything, to get what they want." Gwen pointed at the pearl-gray Bentley Continental parked next to her own. Derek thought it resembled a metal beast watching him from its shaded cave. "Arriving in Bernard's car is the sort of statement that could make all the difference. It says to them, your connection to my family, to this mystery and the painting, and whatever else is out there, this is *real*."

He looked at her and realized, "You're enjoying this."

"Well of course I am. You should see your face. As if driving a Bentley to Los Angeles is a dreadful prospect."

"It's not me."

"They don't know that." She dangled the keys. "Think of it this way. Once this horrid episode is done, you can climb into your ratty little truck and put all this terrible experience in your rearview mirror."

The slopes above Montecito were lined with stone walls and high-security fencing and blooming jacaranda trees. The mall was exactly where Gwen had said, a lovely cluster of cedar-shingle shops sheltered by hardwood trees. The hairdresser was a matronly woman in her sixties with the smile and eyes of a born flirt. She pressed him for the names of films he had acted in, and refused to believe Derek was just a university professor. "You can teach me anything you like," offered the tall Latino working at the next chair over. The hairdresser did not speak again until it came time to refuse his payment, insisting that everything was taken care of. Gwen again.

Derek grabbed two breakfast tacos from a neighboring diner and ate them in the car, coming to terms with the machine. The controls were bewildering at first, and several of the options he could not figure out. Not that he would ever be putting this beast into Sports Mode or Track Mode, whatever they were. When he was finished, he bundled up his trash and carried it to the nearest wastebasket. A trio of ladies in designer fashion watched his every move, and were still standing there as he pulled away.

The drive south was the most luxurious guilt trip Derek had ever taken. He drove the freeway for the third time in two days. The first section around Carpinteria was nice enough. The PCH dissolved into the eight-lane freeway because the distance between the ocean and the cliffs was too narrow for both roads. A train moved in alongside his lane and tracked his progress, past La Conchita and Faria and Dulah. Then the two highways split again, and soon after, the central coast beauty became smothered by the Ventura sprawl.

He had made this trip hundreds of times. But never like this.

Clients of the Miramar shop included any number of sports-car enthusiasts. Derek had always enjoyed listening to their conversations. They discussed their machines with the same happy passion as avid art collectors.

And that, Derek decided, was the best way to describe this metal beast. Art on wheels.

He had once heard a Bentley enthusiast describe his ride as a Ferrari with manners. Only now did he understand what the man had meant. The ride turned the roughest segments silky smooth. Freeway noise was reduced to some faraway whisper. And then there was the power. Twelve cylinders, six hundred horsepower. Enough to ram him back in his seat, just shifting into the passing lane.

On the approach to Thousand Oaks the traffic gradually slowed to a standstill. Derek exited the freeway and took the 23 to the PCH. South on the oceanfront highway to Sunset, then up through Topanga.

Abruptly he was struck by how much fun he was having. How distant all his empty days seemed.

Derek pulled into a parking space and sat there, tasting a word as if he was thinking of it for the very first time.

Happy.

His body still hummed slightly from the drive, his mind's eye filled with images of flashing cars and sunlight on concrete and the soft rumble of trucks.

Happy.

He felt as though he was sampling some foreign elixir.

Chapter 15

The Maybourne, Beverly Hills's newest ultra-luxury hotel, maintained an old-world flavor in its public rooms. Kelly was seated in a side lounge that served no other purpose than to offer visitors and guests a comfortable place to hang out. Such elegant spaces were all but erased from most modern hotels, even five-star establishments, because they brought in no revenue. If a patron wanted to sit down, they had to pay for the privilege, or so the reasoning went. The Maybourne was different.

Once the uniformed waiter had greeted Kelly and learned she waited for an arriving guest, he left her alone. The furniture suited the high-ceilinged room, with its painted beams and Spanish-tiled floors. The chairs were carved from oak and lined with hand-embroidered cushions. The calfskin sofas would have been right at home in a Mexican *castillo*.

The tables lining the outside patio were filled with chattering patrons. But Kelly had this room to herself. She phoned her boss, told him she was waiting for Derek, summarized her next steps, and waited.

Jerome let the silence hold for a time. But her

unspoken request finally pressed him to say, "Derek and I roomed together through all four years at Pepperdine. We were both scholarship kids. Our friendship saw us through a lot. After graduation I headed to Cambridge and Derek started on his doctorate. I came back in time to be Derek's best man." Jerome's words slowed, like they were being forcibly extracted. "His late wife had been diabetic since childhood. Erin had all sorts of related health issues. Right through their married life, she suffered from one crisis after another."

"We were talking about Derek."

"We still are. When Erin got sick that last time, all I knew was what Derek told me. He simply said Erin was having another bad spell, he was taking unpaid leave to tend to her, she was angry over being a burden, she felt like she had become a drag on his professional career." He stopped. Then added, "They had a couple of bad fights over him leaving the university position. I knew that too. It just tore Derek up, but he refused to go back to work."

Kelly felt as though the story was unfolding before her eyes, a tragic script written on the walls of this almost-empty room. "You offered to help."

"They were getting hit from all sides. Of course I offered. Plus we needed that evaluation."

Kelly opened her mouth. Breathed in and out.

Wondered at having friends like this. And a wife so concerned over her husband's professional life she was furious at the sacrifices he made. For her. Kelly yearned for somewhere dark and secret. Where she could weep over all the wrong moves littering her own past.

Jerome went on, "Derek was the ideal choice to help with that particular collection. The seller had basically bought everything he had on whims, his and his wife's. Provenance was solid on some paintings, others had nothing whatsoever. They had trusted a dealer they considered one of their closest friends. They bought on his say-so. You know the type."

"I know." It was one of the hardest parts of her job. Working with clients who had followed the advice of unscrupulous agents. People who put themselves up as experts, but who actually knew very little. "They thought they were sitting on a fortune, and Derek told them differently."

"And nothing was proven. Our in-house expert claimed Derek was wrong."

Kelly continued to read the invisible script. "You refused to countenance Derek's opinion. You fought. He went public."

"Without warning me first. Being part of a potentially illegal transaction hit Derek at the wrong moment." Another silence. Then softly, "Like you said, Derek went public. I lost the client. The Christie's board threatened me with dismissal. Derek and I had our shouting match. The next day, Erin was gone."

"Oh, no."

"I didn't even know she had died until three weeks after her funeral. We haven't spoken since."

"Jerome, I'm so sorry." Then something caught her eye out the front window, a glint of sunlight off an arriving Bentley. She watched as a very handsome man rose from the car, handed his keys to the valet, and insisted on carrying his old-style leather valise himself. He was buffed, polished, and had features sharp as cut-crystal. . . .

Kelly gasped softly when she realized who it was.

"Kelly?"

She managed, "Derek is here."

"Keep me posted. But handle this on your own. Do that for both of us. Me and my former best friend."

Chapter 16

Derek was signing the registry form when Kelly stepped up and scanned him from tasseled loafers to new haircut. He said, "I can explain."

"Hey, everybody needs an outlet. Professor by day, rich playboy by night. It has potential."

Derek accepted the room key, waved away the bellhop, and picked up the valise. "There are so many things wrong with that statement I don't even know where to begin."

She pointed down a side hall. "I'm in there having coffee. Care to join me?"

"Give me ten minutes."

His room was big and lavishly appointed, with a small balcony overlooking the Beverly Canon Gardens. Almost every park bench was filled with well-dressed people enjoying the afternoon. Derek left the balcony doors open while he showered. He dressed in the same outfit, closed the doors, and went downstairs.

The lounge was almost empty. Waiters scurried back and forth, serving outdoor tables lining the hotel's wide veranda. Kelly was seated in an alcove beyond the bar, toying with her spoon. As Derek crossed the room, he thought she was the portrait of a sad and solitary lady.

When he slipped into the chair opposite, she asked, "Can I get you anything?"

"Coffee would be nice."

She snagged a passing waiter, ordered coffee for two, then went back to playing with her spoon. "I don't know you at all. And this is really none of my business. So if you tell me to back off, I will."

Derek had no idea where she was headed, so he decided to remain silent.

She took that as an assent, and continued, "I think you need to repair your relationship with Jerome."

Derek was still working on a response when the waiter returned. Kelly's gaze remained locked on her little spoon. Soon as the waiter departed, she went on, "He's told me some of what happened. I got chapter one before we met at the Getty. Chapter two came just before you pulled up. Nice ride, by the way. It suits you."

"Kelly—"

"Both times as Jerome shared bits of your story, all I could think was how lucky you two are, to have a friend like this."

"Were," Derek quietly corrected. "How lucky we once were."

"Your entire adult lives, right up to the moment when the world struck at your weakest. Jerome's pressure on you to go against your judgment, your wife's death . . ." She shook her head, very

115

slowly, back and forth. "I can't imagine what that must have been like for you."

The words had a very strange effect. His normal reaction to the memory was low-grade agony, like heat from the remnants of a massive blaze.

Not today.

Derek sat and studied the woman, her lovely features aged by far more than someone else's battle. "Why does that make you sad?"

"Because when I had my own low moment, there wasn't a friend like Jerome I could turn to. My father was gone. My mother . . . She has always taken my ex's side. Not even my divorce changed that. Still to this day she wants me to give him another chance." She looked at Derek then, her dark gaze hollowed by old pain. "It was a terrible event, and it happened at the worst possible moment. Things were said. Awful things. Both of you could have handled it better. And that doesn't change what you had, who you were. Who you *are*. Jerome probably won't ever take the first step, much as I think he wants to. Which means you have to be the better man."

Derek waited through several long breaths. "Are you done?"

"Pretty much."

"I will think about it. Seriously. Whatever happens . . ."

"Yes?"

"Thank you, Kelly."

She studied him. "I'm trying to remember the last time a man was grateful for my telling him he was wrong."

"Oh, is that what you just did?" He released a smile. "I take it all back."

Ten minutes later, as they left the lounge, Kelly was still coming to terms with Derek's response. The simple fact that he was willing to even consider such advice said a lot about the man.

Not to mention this new and improved version of Derek Gaines handing his parking ticket to the valet. In exchange for the keys to a Bentley.

She liked this new buffed and polished Derek, dressed in his borrowed finery, drawing glances from the jaded Beverly Hills crowd. She liked even more how he asked, "Do you want to drive?"

She was tempted, really. But decided, "Some other time." The Bentley speedster was the color of old pearls. She thanked the valet holding her door and slipped into the ivory interior. "What year is this?"

"No idea." He started the motor, and revved the engine like a kid. "Does it matter?"

"What is your normal ride?"

"Ford double cab." He put the car in drive and started forward. "Where to?"

"We're meeting at Brian's Studio City offices.

This time of day, we're probably best staying off the freeway."

"You're the boss. Which way?"

"Let's head up Sunset and see how it goes."

Traffic was heavy but moving, so Kelly left them on Sunset. That was the last either of them spoke until they were on the descent out of the Hollywood Hills. Then Kelly asked, "Are you hungry?"

"Starving."

"Why didn't you say something?"

"I figured we didn't have time."

"Not for a sit-down restaurant. Not for the kind of place a guy driving a Bentley probably expects."

"Knock it off with the Bentley guy stuff. What did you have in mind?"

"There's a great Pacific Rim street vendor up ahead."

"Sold."

She pointed to an upscale strip mall where a trio of rolling vendors were serving a cluster of after-work customers. "Park anywhere."

One of the tables opened up just as they approached, so Kelly told him to go grab it. She ordered a double portion of stewed chicken with an orange and chili glaze, spicy lamb with spring onions and sesame seeds, sticky rice, and then added an order of the Laotian-style meat salad known as larb.

He watched her carry over two full bags, helped unwrap the dishes, and said, "This is a feast."

"I always order too much."

He tasted the chicken and actually moaned. "Unbelievable."

"There's an app you can download, it tracks the best vendors." She watched him scan the people waiting in line, the cars, the growing shadows. "What are you thinking?"

"This is Erin's kind of place." He tried the lamb and hummed his pleasure.

"Tell me about her. One thing." She couldn't believe she had actually said it. If it had been possible she would have dragged the words back inside, almost the instant they emerged. But the easy camaraderie didn't fracture. Instead, his gaze softened, like it was mirroring the late afternoon shadows.

He took another couple of bites, then said, "We met at the Getty. You already know that. First time we talked, I was completely hers. I like to think she felt the same, maybe not as strong, but that she was . . ."

"Connected," she offered. Liking how easy their conversation was. And thinking that if she was going to grow close to this man, she needed to accept that Erin was probably going to stay the unseen third figure. Kelly had no idea how she felt about that. Actually, she couldn't even believe she was having this sort of internal conversation. About a guy she scarcely knew. But there was something about Derek Gaines, an air of boyish simplicity that defied his looks and his ride . . . Something.

Derek took another bite, his smile as soft as the light in his gaze. "We went out on a couple of dates, I was totally smitten, I mean, just over the moon. On our third date we took a sunset walk. . . . Have you ever been to Miramar?"

"Never visited the central coast. Go on with your story."

"There's this coastal path, it runs between the road and the shoreline, almost three miles of graveled lanes and little wooden bridges over the rocky bits. We were about halfway down when Erin said she needed to warn me. She said that she was a lady of the emerald tide. And she would never change."

"What does that even mean?"

He nodded, easy with her now. Two friends sharing a private time in the midst of traffic and people and wonderful food. "Along the central coast you have these protected coves where there's a true in-between world. Part ocean and part shore. They're called tidal pools. All sorts of creatures make this place their home. At sunrise and sunset, when the ocean's calm, tidal pools take on the most amazing color. The rocks and the sea and the pools all shine like polished emeralds." He seemed to be studying the line of parked cars, but Kelly had the distinct impression he saw none of his surroundings. "What she meant was, she wanted nothing more than the simple life. I've never met anyone who was less concerned with money or possessions. She dressed like your typical schoolteacher, conservative and proper. But it was all a mask. Erin was a born gypsy."

Kelly slipped back in her chair. Reveling in the quiet familiarity. "And you?"

Derek looked down at his food, and toyed with the remnants of his meal. "That is an interesting question."

She did not mind him taking his time over responding. In fact, it only added to the evening's spice. As did feeling relaxed enough to offer, "You loved her enough to let her shape your existence."

He took a final bite. Set down his fork. Thinking.

"You were this hunk of a professor, climbing the university ladder, making a name for yourself. And you shaped your world outside the classroom around what made your wife happy." There was no reason why saying those words should make her eyes burn. Or cause her throat to constrict with old sorrow. None whatsoever.

"Other than that bit about the hunk, you have it exactly right." Derek lifted his gaze and his smile both. "How did you know?"

It was both wonderful and exceedingly hard, feeling this close to the man. Kelly rose from the table and began gathering the remnants of their meal. "We better go."

Chapter 17

Derek had twice served as a consultant on documentary film projects based in the valley. Studio City had always struck him as a blue-collar town. Only here the factories, the billboards, the talk in bars and cafés, everything was about making movies.

The Trademark Films building rose in the middle of an otherwise tawdry mix, shining in the late afternoon light like a bright new penny. Its neighbors were a sixties-era office building, a warehouse-size soundstage for rent, and a parking garage. Kelly directed him into the car park, and over to where he had a side view of Trademark. Derek cut the motor and asked, "Our guy runs this?"

"Brian Beschel. It used to be his very own fiefdom. Two years ago he sold out, then retired."

"What can you tell me about him?"

"Brian got his start doing rom-coms for Hallmark. He gained a reputation for being on time and under budget. His projects were almost always in the channel's top ten for audience draw. He graduated from there to low-budget features, mostly romance, a few dramas and comedies. He financed most of his projects in-house, and gradually built up a sizeable reserve. Then he did a series for CBS that became a global hit. Syndicated all over the place. He used that to begin making major star-driven feature films. Then came a pair of series for Netflix, both of which have gone through multiple seasons. Two years ago, Viacom bought him out. Brian retired. Said he was going to focus on his other addiction."

"Art."

"I've helped him with four purchases. Three more he wanted but lost to people willing to pay above their true market value. He was one of my first clients. I mean, me personally. Brian is tough but fair. I like him." She hesitated, then added, "I thought I could trust him, you know, to keep things quiet."

"What changed?"

Kelly related the meeting she'd had the previous evening.

Derek gripped the steering wheel. Feeling as though he needed to steer his way through unseen shoals. "That doesn't sound like a retired guy to me."

"No. It doesn't."

"So what are you thinking?"

She stayed quiet for a time. When she spoke, the cadence was slower. Thoughtful. "The deal that cemented our relationship was a small oil he'd located at a regional house in Modesto, almost a garage sale. I worked on it after hours, my own time. I was certain he'd found an unsigned work by Abram Molarsky. You know him, right?"

"Late American Impressionist. Sure. Molarsky was known not to sign paintings he wasn't totally satisfied with. Were you right?"

"Nothing totally definite. But I was sure. More importantly, so was Brian." She smiled into the dimming light. "When I warned him I could be totally wrong, Brian said he'd spent his entire career gambling inside the film and TV markets. Starting projects that take two, three, sometimes four years to complete. Betting that audience tastes would mesh with his finished product. He said taking a risk on this artwork fit the story of his life."

Derek nodded, following her now. "You thought he would gamble on this. Take a first option in return for giving us the money. *His* money. Personally."

"Right."

"And now?"

"Something's changed. I have no idea what. But meeting here, at the office he's not supposed to have anymore . . ."

Derek waited until he was certain she would not say anything more. Then he reached for his door. "Let's go see."

Derek retrieved the artist's portfolio from the Bentley trunk and followed Kelly into the offices of Trademark Films. Typical for an LA entertainment company, the lobby's receptionist was a very alert security guard. The sharp-eyed Latina checked Kelly's name on her computer, said they were expected, and used a passkey to open the elevator and light up the top floor.

Kelly was dressed in a caramel-colored top with gold buttons along her left shoulder, slacks one shade darker, matching pumps with cork heels. A slender pouch of chocolate leather, not a purse nor a briefcase but something in between, hung from her right shoulder by way of a gold chain looped with a leather strap. Derek caught Kelly's eye in the elevator door's reflection and said, "You look really nice."

"Funny. I was thinking the same thing about you."

"Gwen said it might help if I dressed like I belonged."

"Remind me to thank her when we meet."

The doors pinged open and they entered a large well-appointed penthouse lobby. A matronly woman dressed in what to Derek's eye looked like a Chanel suit was already on her feet. "Good evening, Ms. Reid. And your associate is . . ."

"Derek Gaines."

"Of course. I'm Gayle, Brian's assistant. He is expecting you. Right this way, please."

They followed her down a central corridor, past two conference rooms whose occupants clustered worriedly around a series of easels. Derek thought they were arguing over cartoon illustrations. Kelly evidently saw Derek's confusion and explained. "Storyboards. They use them to target weaknesses in a project's story, and to show the director's perspective on the shoot."

Derek said, "I thought Mr. Beschel had retired."

The woman stopped before a set of polished double doors, knocked, and said, "So did Mr. Beschel."

Chapter 18

The setup inside the executive office halted them both in mid-stride. Derek asked, "What's all this?"

"I have no idea," Kelly replied. "What's going on, Brian?"

"Come in, have a seat, and I'll explain." He was seated behind a desk of polished Brazilian granite. Legs of carved mahogany. A work of art. "This your guy?"

"I . . . Yes. Derek Gaines, meet Brian Beschel."

Three other people were standing to either side of the chief. He motioned to the man in the corner by the windows, his arms crossed. A tight expression, narrow features, late fifties, as carefully groomed as Brian. Not angry, at least, Derek didn't think so. He was the analyst. The man who stood back from the arena's dust and carefully monitored the action. Brian said, "Rick Sessions is my CFO." He then pointed to the pair to his right. "My top documentary cameraman is Noah. The soundman, what's your name again?"

"Shimmel, Mr. Beschel."

"Which means 'horse' in Yiddish," Noah said. "But it also means 'to listen.' This for a soundman. Funny."

Two low-back chairs were placed about three feet apart. They were surrounded by a forest of equipment. Two square spots were supported by metal tripods, both shaded by adjustable metal leaves. A larger rectangular light hung overhead and between the chairs and the desk. Two padded mikes hung like metal fruit over the chairs. Brian asked, "Where do you want them?"

"Let's have the lovely lady on the left." Noah stepped forward, a slender geek in his thirties with merry eyes. His T-shirt advertised a Baja bar. He used a viewfinder to adjust the lights as Kelly eased herself into the chair. "Shimmel, you're on."

As the soundman stepped forward and attached a battery mike to Kelly's collar, she said, "I asked you a question, Brian."

"Just a second," he replied. To Rick, "What do you think?"

"So far, so good. Might as well have the cosmetician work on them."

Noah shifted the light on Kelly's face. "In that case, ask my second cameraman to come in. I'll have him shoot a few close-ups."

Brian lifted his gaze to where his assistant stood in the doorway. "He still out there?"

"Right where Noah planted him."

"Have the guy join us."

Shimmel had a pianist's hands, long fingered and very pale. He smiled as he attached Derek's mike. "Not how you were expecting to spend your evening?"

"Hardly."

He handed Derek the battery pack. "Slip the wire inside your shirt. Fit the pack into your rear pocket."

The makeup artist was a slender woman in her forties. She stepped in front of Kelly and cocked her head to one side. Brian said, "Well?"

"The lady is a pro with the makeup brush," she replied, revealing a light Scottish lilt. "A touch of fresh powder, maybe a bit of rouge—"

"I hate rouge," Kelly said.

"But this isn't about you, dear." She pointed over her shoulder. "It's what the camera likes. Rouge will make you sparkle."

"Rouge it is," Brian said. "And our man?"

"Oh, this one's special, he is." When she settled his hair in place, Derek smelled old cigarette smoke on her hands and clothes. "I'd make this one up to be a bit of the rough trade. A buccaneer in Bond Street's finest, if you like."

"Go for it." Brian could just be made out beyond the lights. "Okay, here's the deal. I'll front you a million dollars."

"We don't need anywhere near that much," Derek said.

"Who knows what you'll need? You're going after whatever it is that maybe got the other investigator killed. You don't have any idea what's out there waiting. Cash on hand may be the make or break to this project."

Derek nodded slowly. "Point taken."

"So, like I said, a million bucks should cover all costs and incidentals. And it's yours on two conditions."

"Brian . . ."

"Hear the man out," Rick said. "This is for real."

"As real as it gets," Brian agreed. "We're thinking there might be a docudrama in this."

"Lost art," Rick said. "Murdered treasure hunter. Grieving widow. A great beginning."

"We don't know how Allen died," Kelly said.

"Doesn't matter," Brian said.

"He died like we say he died," Rick agreed. "At least as far as our drama goes."

As the cosmetician finished with Kelly and shifted over to Derek, Brian said, "We're using this conversation as a test. We'll show it to the station execs, see if it's a go. And one more thing. The painting, when we're done, it's mine."

"I can't possibly—"

"Christie's gets one estimate. I get another. We meet in the middle."

Kelly's voice turned scalpel sharp. "This is Christie's decision. Not yours."

"Don't forget Trevor," Derek said.

Brian leaned forward, drawing his angry features into full illumination.

But before he could speak, Rick said, "Brian. Give the lady a chance." When Brian remained grimly silent, Rick asked, "Noah, you ready to shoot?"

"Rolling."

Shimmel said, "Sound's good."

Rick pointed to Kelly, who said, "If we can obtain solid provenance, this will be the first new Caravaggio identified in over a century. Even in its unfinished state, every museum on earth will come begging."

"And the price will skyrocket," Brian growled. "Because of the publicity *my* program generates."

Rick said, "The man's got a point."

As Kelly started to argue, Derek reached over, touched her arm, then said, "It's not about the painting, and it never was."

Brian kept his gaze locked on Kelly. "Unpack that a little."

"First you give the lady her due. Then I explain."

To his credit, the chief looked at his CFO. Rick said, "If they can prove provenance—"

"When," Kelly corrected. "The more time I spend around this, the more certain I become."

"They didn't murder the Freeth kid for a fake," Rick said. "With provenance, your shot at the artwork is gone. Not to mention any docudrama. Unless you sign her now. So play nice with the lady."

Brian said to Kelly, "Right of first refusal."

"Agreed."

Rick said, "And if there is an official Interpol claim that arises from the search?"

"The artwork will stay in your possession until the official requests are sorted out," Kelly said. "At no cost."

"So long as you agree to let the Getty do a special exhibition," Derek added.

"Which will identify you as primary source," Kelly said. "Your name above the title. Isn't that what Hollywood fame is all about?"

Brian looked at his CFO again. Only now he was smiling. "Three minutes into this, and already I'm being tag-teamed."

Rick asked Noah, "You get this?"

"Oh yeah. We're rolling."

Brian lost his smile. "Okay, Professor. You're on."

Chapter 19

They brought in an easel from one of the conference rooms. Derek unzipped the portfolio and clipped the unfinished painting into place. He kept his back to the others as Noah and his assistant lit the easel. He said softly, "Can you give me room to pace?"

Noah glanced over. "Say again."

"I hate standing still when I talk."

"Oh. Sure thing." Noah pulled a roll of masking tape from a thigh pocket, tore off a strip, checked the lights, then bent and applied it to the carpet. Moved over about seven feet, holding to the space between the easel and the desk, and laid down a second strip. "Can you stay between these?"

"No problem. Thanks."

"Nada." To Kelly, "Mind if we swing your chair over a bit?"

While the lights and Kelly's chair were adjusted once more, Brian stepped over and inspected the painting. "Beautiful work."

"It is indeed."

"Needs cleaning up."

Kelly said, "The Getty's top restorer has itchy fingers, waiting to get her hands on this."

Rick said, "We need to film that."

Derek warned, "It will be as exciting as watching paint dry. Literally."

"We'll only show a few moments of the entire process," Rick explained. "Reveal the before and after. It'll be the director's and editor's job to add excitement."

"You're talking like this is already happening," Kelly said. "Don't forget Christie's has a say in all this."

Brian demanded, "Do you want the million or not?"

"Yes," Derek said. "The money plays a crucial role in what comes next."

"So don't expect Christie's to have more than a whisper of a say." Brian waved a hand, taking in the easel and the painting and Derek. "Now tell us why your idea of what comes next could be interesting."

"The autumn of 1969 was a bad time for Sicily. The local government was in shambles, rife with corruption and choked by factions who fought constantly. The government in Rome was not much better. Italy suffered through five national elections in two years. Five different leaders from three different parties. Normal civic routines became frozen. Government employees went months without their pay. Morale within the police and military was at an all-time low."

Derek had never been able to sit and talk, not

for more than a few words at a time. Standing in one place only worked when he could grip a podium and force his restless energy under control.

It did not matter that he was restricted to tiny steps, tracking back and forth between the two strips of tape. Moving slowly. Keeping his hands relatively still. This was the first time he had lectured in almost two years. Part-time teaching gigs had gradually waned. His name and reputation faded, and chances to earn the extra money through lectures went to desperate post-grads. He had almost forgotten how much he loved the work.

"Sicily is rocked by its worst crime wave since the end of World War Two. The island suffers from a constant onslaught. Murder, corruption, kidnappings, and one thing more."

Derek stopped and faced the camera head-on. "Theft. More than six thousand works of art and treasured artifacts were stolen. Museums, state offices, regional government buildings, churches. Six thousand articles. Most were never recovered."

He resumed pacing. "We need to assume some things about Allen Freeth and his last trip. Why did he go to Sicily? It can't have been this painting. He already possessed it. He was not a specialist in art, hunting down the painting's provenance would have been impossible. He was after something else. Something so big, so potentially explosive, he went even knowing that he might not survive the journey."

Derek stopped and stared at the canvas. Waiting.

As if on cue, Kelly said, "The note."

"Exactly. Allen sent the artwork to his mother with the note that it would restore her fortunes. But he knew his father had run up a huge debt. A mountain of liabilities. Allen's family was bankrupt. This one painting, even if its provenance could be proven beyond a shadow of doubt, wouldn't come close to balancing the books."

Kelly was with him now. "The painting is a clue."

"More like, the tip of an iceberg."

"What exactly are we talking about?"

"Treasure."

Kelly asked, "So how do we know the painting came from Sicily?"

"We can't," Derek replied. "Not without making the trip."

"But you think you know."

"I do. Yes. Actually, more than think."

"Tell me."

He pointed to the window in the left-hand corner. "The answer is right there."

"A stained glass window? There must be thousands."

"Hundreds of thousands." He could stand still no longer. "But this wasn't a window in a chapel."

"How do . . ." Kelly breathed. "They were *dead*."

Derek swiftly ran through his suspicions that the mother and child were dead when the painting was made. He pointed out the encroaching shadows, the man's tragic expression versus the surreal peace portrayed on the pair. He finished with, "Caravaggio painted this using a family room as the backdrop. Perhaps an audience hall, but more likely a bedroom. A wealthy family of strong faith. So strong the widower insisted that this window with the dove be included. Illuminating the fact that even here, in this dark hour, there is hope. An eternal chance of being reunited. Beyond the earthly veil."

Derek paced through two more tight rounds. Long enough to hear what he thought was a soft sniffle. This from his supposedly hard-hearted auctioneer. He had never liked Kelly more than now. Finally she said, "So we go to Sicily . . ."

"Just the three places where Caravaggio resided. Palermo, Messina, Syracuse."

"And ask about a sixteenth-century manor . . ."

"With this." Derek pointed to the stained glass window. "Find this, prove the owners at that time were patrons of Caravaggio, and we have our provenance."

"Wow." Then, "Which leads to my next question."

"Perhaps the most important question of all," Derek agreed. "At least to us."

"Assuming what we suspect is actually what happened. Allen's death in Sicily wasn't an accident."

"For our safety, it's important that we move forward assuming he was murdered," Derek agreed.

"Then how do we avoid the same fate?"

"Two things."

"Two very important things."

"Crucial," Derek agreed. "First, we're not going alone. I asked for a team. You've given me . . ."

"A film crew," Kelly said. "I didn't like that prospect. Not at all."

"Me either."

"But now it sounds fabulous."

"I thought you would feel that way."

"And the second reason?"

He turned to face her. She was wreathed in a glow far stronger than what could have been formed by just a few television lights. "We're not traveling to a dangerous country to ask questions about missing treasure. That would be worse than stupid. It could get us killed."

She breathed the word. *"Provenance."*

"That's all we're after. A Hollywood film crew, a senior executive of Christie's, and a consultant to the Getty Museum. Making a very public search for the truth behind an unsigned painting. One we're certain was done by Caravaggio."

"So the missing treasure . . ."

"Either it finds us, or we come back empty-handed," Derek replied. "Safe. And simple."

There was a moment's silence, then Brian said, "Cut."

Chapter 20

Derek used the executive bathroom and gave his face a quick wash. The adrenaline rush was wearing off now, and the makeup crinkled his skin like a mask. When he emerged, Rick Sessions, the numbers guy, escorted them back to the elevator. He pressed the down button and said, "I thought that went well."

Kelly said to Derek, "You were great."

"Thanks." He rubbed his forehead. "A full Ironman doesn't leave me this tired."

Rick smiled. "You'll get used to it."

Kelly asked the numbers guy, "What happens now?"

"You and I need to meet tomorrow morning. Start putting the details down in black and white."

"Derek needs to be there too."

"You handle that without me." When Kelly looked ready to argue, he added, "I have to get back. Day after tomorrow, you need to come up. So do Noah and Shimmel."

"I'll make the arrangements," Rick said. He held the elevator doors open as they entered, then asked Kelly, "Do you have an entertainment lawyer?"

Kelly straightened. "What? No!"

Rick was totally somber. The power behind the throne, accustomed to wielding the knife. "Get one." He stepped back, letting the doors shut. "Today."

When they arrived back at the parking garage, Kelly scooped the Bentley's keys from Derek's hand and walked around to the driver's door. They drove back to the hotel in silence. Kelly stayed off the freeway, pushing the car fast. The night was cooling, the air a pleasant wash through Derek's open window. He sat with eyes half-closed, listening to the motor's growl as they climbed into the hills and then descended. When they pulled into the hotel's forecourt, she halted well away from the entrance and declared, "That was fun."

"The showdown in Brian's office or the drive?"

"Both." When the valet started over, she waved him off. "You okay?"

Derek lifted one hand, rocked it back and forth.

"You were great in there." When he remained silent, she said, "A Caravaggio for your thoughts."

"Funny."

"I thought so."

He kept his gaze on the hotel's entrance. A steady stream of the rich and beautiful headed inside. "This is a universe removed from my life."

Kelly used the steering wheel as a lever and

shifted around. "Your wife loved simpler things." She gave that a beat, then added, "And now you're afraid of losing her."

Derek looked over. It seemed as though he was able to study her from a vast distance. Disconnected from her, the car, the night, even from his own words. "No. She's gone."

"I meant—"

"I know what you meant. And that's not it. Erin is *gone*. And I've spent four years following the same routine I started after the funeral. A sort of frantic game of extremes. This manic dance of exercise until I was too exhausted to think straight. Competing with other guys who were as focused and crazy as me."

She did that thing with her gaze, showing him two bottomless pools that glistened dark and beautiful in the light. "It's not crazy."

Derek turned back to the night.

"Manic, okay, maybe a little. But at the time, it was important. You developed a routine that helped you handle the impossible. What's crazy about that?" Kelly waved a hand at the hotel. "And now you're shifting gears. The meeting tonight, this hotel, it's an open door. Nothing more. You can do this and go back to your old life, or start a new course."

Derek felt the distance between them evaporating. Her words were a binding force now. Drawing her and the night into sharp clarity.

Kelly went on. "The question you need to answer is, what do you want?"

"Scary."

She nodded. "Tell me."

"I mean, it's scary that I have no idea."

She turned away from him. Pursed her lips. "I know what my father would have said."

"Which is?"

"Sometimes the best you can hope for is to ask the right question."

"He sounds like a wise man."

"Wise enough to handle my mom." She offered the night a sad smile. "Most of the time."

Derek reached for his door, then stopped.

"What?"

"Are we becoming friends?"

This time, the smile was real. Full-on. "Funny. I thought we already were."

Chapter 21

That evening Kelly went out with other people from the trade. They were a mobile bunch, some acquaintances and a few she would class as almost friends. They met at least once a month, their numbers as fluid as the night and location. Tonight, it was a nearly seedy place on the Hollywood stretch of Sunset, a bar set up as an old-timey dance hall. They occupied the largest table on the upstairs balcony, directly opposite the stubby downstairs stage. A remarkably good band played hits from the seventies and eighties. Their crowd was noisy and young and intelligent and flash. Kelly nursed a single drink and smiled at the swirling conversation and took very little in. The day was with her still, a potent mix of fatigue and nerves and unexpected events. Mentally she replayed Derek pacing by the easel, as comfortable under the lights as any professional actor. The man's features were carved into various dimensions of craggy shadows by the lights. Though his voice remained calm, his excitement had remained a palpable force. She felt it still.

A sudden burst of laughter drew her attention. Seated directly across from her were two men, both of whom she had dated. And more. They were handsome, sharp, and highly appealing in a Teflon sort of manner. Kelly found herself comparing them to Derek, the stranger she could not get out of her head.

The woman seated to Kelly's right was assistant manager to a Beverly Hills art gallery, a lady on the rise. She leaned in and said, "Where are you tonight? I know for certain you're not here."

Because the woman was as close a friend as Kelly had in the business, she replied, "Sicily."

That stopped conversation at their side of the table. "What?"

"I leave in a few days."

"For real?"

"As real as it gets."

"Dare a girl ask why?"

"You can ask, but I can't answer." Kelly decided she had enough. She stood, gathered her things, and said, "Catch you on the flip side."

Her Santa Monica condo was two blocks off stylish Montana Avenue. She left the lights off and opened her balcony doors. The air was cool, fresh with the faint hint of salt carried by a light breeze off the Pacific. These nights were why she had gone into serious debt, taking on this apartment. So she could stand here on the balcony, breathing the tangy air, listening to the faint laughter and music rising from the nearest cafés, and feel like she had arrived. Like she belonged.

After a time she returned inside, locked the doors, and entered her bedroom. As she prepared for bed, Kelly found herself thinking back over the days and nights that had brought her here. In the midst of divorce heartbreak, Jerome had assigned her a tricky job, guiding a trio of terrible clients through the sale of their estates. Preparing the catalogue and the sale had been all-consuming. Kelly had often wondered if her boss had been aware just how desperately she needed a set of responsibilities that would fill her every waking hour. She had spent six and a half dreadful months working on the project, from signing the clients to the auction. Most nights she had not returned to her awful furnished studio on the wrong side of Pico Boulevard until the wee hours. Seven days a week, her only breaks coming from the hours she gave to lawyers and mediation and the divorce court. Three days after the divorce became final, she had stood at the back of the main hall at Christie's, so burned out that the auction and the applause and the accolades had all just washed over her. Jerome had rewarded her with a promotion and a bonus, and that had led to her standing here. In the master bath of this beautiful home. Hers and hers alone.

Kelly studied her reflection as she brushed her hair. Only it was not her image that captured her.

She took such pride in the attitude that she had forged since the divorce. The perspective that had made LA home. All the labels she had come to apply to herself. Ever since she had learned through bitter defeat the true meaning of big-city love. What an awful, embarrassing, destructive joke.

So she had changed. Reframed her world around a new design. Became what the city demanded. Ms. Independent.

Ambition certainly played a big part in who she was now. Building on what had helped her survive the crushing of her romantic dreams. A job she adored. A boss she trusted and liked. She lived her life one day at a time. Taking what she wanted or needed from others. Giving what she could afford, what she could offer without risk. Nothing more. Not ever.

She set down the brush, but remained standing there, staring into the mirror. Only now she saw Derek. The man who had been forced to restructure his life. Just like her.

But in his case, Derek had been guided by a lost love. Such simple words.

His faint shadow-reflection offered Kelly that remarkably gentle smile. Such an immense difference between them, illuminated by the memory of his smile.

She slipped into bed, turned off the light, and lay staring at images that floated by her ceiling. She found herself thinking back to their first meeting on the plaza fronting the Getty, how she had fed a hurt and lonely man the lines she thought he needed to knit together his empty moment. At the time, she assumed she was playing a role. But now, the darkness reflected back a different truth. That she had used the moment to confess. Not to him, to herself. She certainly had not meant it as such. And there was no logic to the idea, saying words to a stranger that she'd carried all this time. Revealing a need she had hidden from herself. There was no other reason for why she had to wipe away the tears. Or how sad she felt over all the wasted evenings.

Chapter 22

Derek's hotel room was spacious and breathlessly quiet. He slept deeply and woke as usual just before six. He dressed in running clothes and headed downstairs. He poured himself a coffee from the lobby urn and drank it outside, stretching and watching the dawn strengthen. When he was ready, he set off for his first-ever run through Beverly Hills.

The previous day's thermal layer was history. Six o'clock on a weekday, traffic was light and the air almost clean. He started with a loop through Beverly Flats, enjoying the mix of small businesses and relatively modest houses. Derek then ran the length of three upscale shopping streets, Rodeo and Beverly Glen and Canon, enjoying the brief flashes of wealth on window displays. Then he crossed Sunset and entered the high-rent district. Beverly Hills proper.

Back when he first started teaching in Santa Cruz, dawn runs had been his way of laying a foundation, anchoring himself to the region and its energy. From the moment his shoes met the asphalt, however, this morning was different. Derek knew he would never belong here. He simply wanted to explore the jungle while the predators still slept.

He returned to the hotel, stretched, showered, and dressed in another of Gwen's outfits. Then downstairs for a leisurely breakfast. When it was time, he walked the two and a half blocks. He had not been back to Christie's West Coast since the blow-up with Jerome. The week of Erin's passing. The only time he had left her side during those dread final days.

Just approaching the ice-white cube brought back a flood of memories. The absolute conviction he had been contracted to give provenance to a pair of well-executed fakes. Jerome's refusal to even consider the fact that Derek was right. Their first argument. Derek's warning, which in their second and final argument Jerome claimed he had not heard because Derek had not cautioned him. The article on the front page of the LA *Times* weekend art section. And then the final public blow-up.

A lot to carry with him as he entered the building.

A bright and lovely young woman approached, as perfectly presented as the art adorning the walls. "Welcome to Christie's. Can I help you?"

"I'd like to speak with Mr. Summers."

The name was enough to brighten her further. "Do you have an appointment?"

"I don't, no."

"Mr. Summers is extremely busy. Can I ask your name?"

"Derek Gaines."

Thankfully, she clearly had no idea who he was. "I'll see if Mr. Summers is available."

A guard stepped forward to take the receptionist's place. Other gray-suited guards were visible in each of the viewing rooms. Derek had no trouble with waiting there by the front doors. He had always enjoyed his visits to Christie's. The ground floor had been created to disappear, leaving just sunlight and art. Even the frames blended neatly into the background. Having an exhibition here was as clear a declaration as could possibly be made that the artist had entered the commercial stratosphere.

He took a catalogue from the reception desk and leafed through the pages. The exhibition was entitled *Four Centuries, Four Seasons*, and contained the art of three private collections. The catalogue's first page declared this to be a private sale, meaning prices had been set and were not open to negotiation. Such non-auction events happened every now and then, but rarely on this scale: The catalogue's initial pages contained winter landscapes by Monet and Van Ruysdael, a spring garden by Vonnoh, a bowl of fruit by Maurice de Vlaminck, and yet another summer landscape by Monet. Prices were not stated in the catalogue, as in, if one needed to ask, one could not afford. To create such a collection was a signature event, a statement to everyone involved in the global art world that Christie's occupied the highest possible position.

Jerome Summers, head of Christie's LA, announced his arrival by asking, "Spot any more fakes?"

Derek tasted several responses, and decided on silence. He merely turned the catalogue's page.

Jerome waved off the guard, stepped forward, and said, "I'm sorry. It was a knee-jerk reaction to the surprise of finding you here."

"It takes a big man to apologize." Derek shut the catalogue. "I always thought of you as that."

"Full of himself."

"No, Jems. Big ideas, big ambitions, big dreams, big knowledge of your field." Derek studied his friend. Jerome was the same, only more so. Tailored suit, perfectly coiffed hair, LA tan, sharp gaze. "You wear your success well."

"Thank you for coming." Jerome hesitated, then asked, "Why are you here?"

"Kelly said I should make this step. She was right." It was his turn to pause. "I had mostly hoped you wouldn't be in. Or come downstairs. Then I could tell her I tried."

"I almost didn't. Come down, I mean."

"Why did you?"

In reply, Jerome waved him toward the first gallery. "Come have a look."

Each room was given over to a season. Derek was so gripped by the masterpieces on display he found it wrenchingly hard to shift from winter to spring. "This is phenomenal."

"I fought tooth and nail for the collectors to let me have this. And do it as one event, rather than as three independent shows."

"You were right, Jems. And showing them as seasons is brilliant."

"The egos involved almost did me in." Jerome inspected a countryside at dawn by Jules Breton. "You'd have thought I meant to steal their collections."

"You did what it took. And you won."

"No one will ever know how much it cost me."

"Does that matter? Really?"

They entered the autumn display, and momentarily had the room to themselves. Jerome said, "Kelly told you to come because of this new project?"

"No. Well, yes, I assume that was partly the reason. The way she put it was, a friendship like ours is too rare to lose it over one argument."

"One thermonuclear event, more like."

Derek nodded. "For what it's worth, I apologize unreservedly. There were a dozen ways I could have handled it better."

Jerome faced him squarely. "You cost me, Derek. A lot. You almost cost me everything."

"Again, sorry."

Jerome almost smiled. "I heard somewhere that it takes a big man to apologize."

They stood there, two men trapped in the amber of lost seasons. Finally Jerome said, "Let me show you around."

They gave the exhibition another twenty minutes, then stood by the little bar in the back room while the receptionist made them coffees—double espresso for Derek, latte for Jerome. They played ten minutes of catch-up, mostly about Jerome's two kids, both teens now, both great but also enormous pains. Jerome avoided speaking about his wife, which Derek took as a bad sign. He also did not ask about Derek's life, and Derek did not offer. Another time. Perhaps. Then Jerome's assistant arrived in a breathless rush, reminding him that his new clients had called to ask where he was. They shook hands, Jerome left, and Derek gave the paintings another few minutes. Adjusting to this latest transition. Then Kelly called, and Derek used it as an excuse to walk outdoors. The sunlight was strong as a blade, but pleasant just the same. It fit Derek's mood.

Kelly asked, "Where are you?"

"Your place."

"Excuse me?"

"Christie's. I went to see Jerome. You were right."

"Give me a minute to pick myself off the floor."

"You told me I should do it, Kelly. Why are you surprised?"

"Well, let's see. You waited four years. Then I made a suggestion—"

"Order from on high, more like."

"Don't interrupt. So I say you should do this, and the next morning, you're off doing it. Does that sum things up?"

"I'm still not clear on why this is such a big deal."

"And I'm trying to remember the last time I told a guy how to run his life, and he does what I say."

"I thought we were almost friends. Isn't that what friends do, listen to advice?"

"Are you actually smiling?"

"Not a chance."

"That sounds like a smile to me."

"Okay, maybe a tiny one." He crossed the street and started up the rise leading to the hotel entrance. "Why are we having this conversation?"

"I've just finished round one with our entertainment lawyer. You need to hear what's being proposed."

"I want you to handle that."

"You're not interested?"

"Of course I am. Especially if this will help me keep my home. But there are a hundred other things I need to worry about." He handed the valet his parking ticket and turned away. "Besides which, doing deals was never my strong point. Whatever you work out, I agree to. In advance."

A silence, then, "I suppose this isn't too bad a floor to keep picking myself off of."

Now he was really smiling. "I'm headed north."

"I still say we need to meet."

"And I need to check in with Gwen Freeth. Then take care of something important."

"More important than me?" She paused. "I can't believe I just said that."

"It sounded pretty unreal, I agree."

"So. Moving on. You said at Brian's I needed to come up."

"With the film crew. Right. Tell them to travel separately. You need to stop in Santa Barbara and pick up Gwen."

"I'm sorry, what?"

"Gwen Freeth. You need to get to know her."

"Derek . . ."

"What?"

"You can't keep planting me on the floor. It hurts."

"I have no idea what you're talking about."

"You're going to have me meet alone and unsupervised with a major new client, whom you probably haven't even bothered to sign up yet."

"Trevor's preparing the contract. But that doesn't . . . I thought we were friends."

"Well, we better be, is all I can say."

"Are all our conversations going to be as confusing as this one?"

"Maybe." A pause, then, "I've always wanted to visit the central coast."

"You're starting at the top. Miramar is . . . special."

"You want to show me your world?"

"Absolutely." There was no reason why the prospect should add yet another zing to his morning. "I can't wait."

Chapter 23

Derek arrived at the gates to the Freeth home two and a half hours later. He pressed the buzzer several times, but the house remained still, silent. He used the passkey, let himself in, and parked the Bentley in the garage. Derek entered the house, cut off the security alarm, then found pen and paper in the kitchen and wrote a note to Gwen. He detailed what needed to happen the next day, her driving to Miramar with Kelly, and opening the vault with the camera crew in attendance. He left it on the front table where the clock had formerly resided.

He reset the alarm, let himself out, transferred his cases to the pickup, and left. Heading north.

The pickup's many defects were on sharp display now, things he normally noticed only when a warning light went on. He kept his truck in good condition and serviced it regularly. But it was nine years old and had over a hundred thousand miles, and normal wear and tear were evident everywhere he looked. He had bought it secondhand because Erin had loved the big rear seat, ready for all the friends she wanted to bring along. She loved riding with her bare feet propped on the dash and window open, singing her way through a hundred beautiful trips along the Miramar coast. A thousand.

He took the Vandenburg exit and drove through the town that serviced the air base. Six miles further west, Derek turned north onto a narrow country road. Just beyond the nature preserve, he pulled into a graveled parking area holding a dozen or so cars. He cut the motor and sat there awhile, remembering other times. How excited she would get, bouncing in her seat like a kid, leaping out the instant he parked. Screaming for him to get ready, come on, stop dawdling, the tide would change without them if he didn't hurry. Then singing her way along the trail, finding wonder in every step. Loving him. Loving her.

When shadows began blotting out his memories, Derek restarted the pickup and drove away.

Chapter 24

The next morning, Kelly pulled up to the Freeth gates at ten minutes to eight. Gwen Freeth stood by her front door as Kelly drove around the circular drive and parked next to the garage. She gave the central pool and sculpture a long look, then said, "When I make my way up the ladder, this is where I'd like to land." She offered her hand. "Kelly Reid. A pleasure, Ms. Freeth."

"Call me Gwen. Is Trevor not joining us this morning?"

"He left for Miramar hours ago."

Gwen pointed to the garage. "Shall we take my car?"

They did not speak again until they passed San Luis Obispo and headed north on the smaller county road. The silence was easy, pleasant. The Bentley's passenger seat enveloped Kelly in luxurious ease, inviting her to leave the big-city tension behind. Gwen drove with a confidence and speed that bordered on reckless. "When did you meet our young man?"

"I'd never heard of him before this week."

"First impressions," Gwen said. "Go."

"I like him."

"That's hardly any help. I'm still trying to

fashion a reason why my son pointed me in his direction."

"My boss is Jerome Summers."

"Him I know."

"He and Derek have been friends since college. They had a falling-out . . ." Kelly waved that aside. Later. "It's why I'm sitting here and not Jerome. When he assigned me this project, he described Derek as being too honest for his own good."

"Interesting."

"I thought so." Kelly waved her hand a second time, only now it was taking in the car, the trip, the lady seated beside her. "For me to be in this position, traveling alone with you, defies every unwritten rule of the art world."

"Explain that, please."

"Contacts are everything. Especially at this point, where we are looking at a possible new find, or . . ." She hesitated.

"Or my being required to sell my collection." Gwen spoke with the casual manner of someone coming to terms with her fate. "Which Christie's would no doubt be delighted to cover."

"Thrilled beyond words."

"And yet Trevor is to play a role in all this. If or when it happens."

"Right. But Derek doesn't have you under contract, I know because there hasn't been time. And yet he tells me to stop by and travel up with you. Why?"

"Because he trusts you."

"Because he wants us to be a team. He told me last night that you wanted to be a part of this investigation, if that's what we find waiting for us inside your son's safety deposit box. Derek hasn't asked for payment, he hasn't claimed a commission. . . ."

Gwen slowed and glanced over. "Why does that make you sad?"

There was no way she was going to share what she had been thinking. About standing before her bathroom mirror the previous night, brushing her hair and seeing all the bad moves and empty relationships and hard decisions silhouetted in the glass. "My boss calling Derek honest doesn't go nearly far enough. I wonder if the man is even capable of telling a lie."

"Funny," Gwen mused. "I've asked myself the very same thing."

Kelly swiveled in her seat, using the motion as a chance to clear her eyes. "Derek is having trouble making payments on his house."

Gwen kept glancing over. "He drives an absolute wreck of a pickup."

"He's made for the ivory tower of university research. But he's been fired from his position."

"For taking time to care for his dying wife."

"He's been offered a position at the Getty."

"Really? I'm a patron, and I've heard nothing about this."

163

"The head of restoration made the offer while I was standing there beside him. But Derek doesn't want to leave Miramar."

Gwen nodded slowly. "His wife."

"I'm not sure that's it. Well, sure, at least partly. But it's more . . ."

"Tell me."

"Derek isn't made for the big city. He's . . ."

Gwen kept nodding. "It's not just that he's honest. He's an open book."

"That's it exactly." She swung back around, and spoke the words a second time. "I like him."

"That makes two of us."

But she wasn't done. "I trust him."

Gwen breathed. "It's been a long time since I've managed to apply that word to a man."

"Tell me about it." Kelly smiled. "Did you ever watch that show, *Lost in Space*?"

"My son adored it. Adventuring around the galaxy, a new planet every week? It was made with Allen in mind."

"I feel like the robot, what was he called?"

"The Series 1A Model B9 Rodney Class, or something like that." This time Gwen wiped her eyes. "My son begged us for one every Christmas for years. He placed it at the top of every letter he wrote Santa."

"He's standing right there in front of me," Kelly said. "Waving those stupid arms and shouting, 'Danger, Will Robinson. Danger.' "

Chapter 25

Trevor started complaining before he slipped into the booth opposite Derek. "I was waiting hours for you to phone me back. I hate waiting."

"Sorry." The previous evening, Derek had only turned on his phone when he entered his home. By that point, Trevor had called seven times and texted ten. Derek texted back, suggesting they meet for breakfast at the diner on Miramar's main street. "There was something I needed to do."

"More important than telling me how it went in Los Angeles?"

"Yes." Derek greeted the waitress standing by their booth and ordered. "Three poached eggs, brown toast, black coffee."

"I'll take the same, but make mine tea." When she left, Trevor started in again. "That doesn't go far enough and you know it."

"I drove over to Wall Beach."

Trevor did not merely go quiet. He became so still he might have become frozen in place.

The Santa Ynez River marked the end of the Vandenberg Air Force Base's northern perimeter. Beyond that was Wall Beach, and then a nature preserve where more than half the world's population of snowy plovers annually migrated to nest. The preserve ended by a rocky enclave that stretched some thirty miles, cliffs etched and sculpted by eons of Pacific force. The tidal pools lining this shoreline were some of the finest on earth.

Trevor asked, "Was that wise?"

Derek nodded to the waitress as she deposited their drinks. When it was just the two of them, seated in the sunlit booth, he said, "Truth be told, I have no idea. I didn't make it past the parking lot. Just the same, it felt right to at least try."

"You went to tell Erin goodbye." Needing to put the name out there. As if she was not already a presence in their booth.

"No, not really." He sipped the steaming mug, trying to dislodge the knot in his throat. "It's time I stop holding on to the life we had."

They did not speak again until they finished eating. Then Derek said, "I need to get to the bank. The studio is sending up a cameraman and sound technician. I spoke with the bank manager last night. He's a cycling buddy. He's agreed to let us film as Gwen opens the safety deposit box."

"Wait, what?"

Derek swiftly filled him in, at least the bare bones of what had happened in LA. "Trademark Pictures owns the rights to film as a documentary whatever we find. Brian Beschel has a right of first refusal to the Caravaggio. Your shop and Christie's split the commission."

Trevor showed genuine surprise when Derek started to slip from the booth. "That's not nearly enough!"

"Gwen and Kelly should be here in a few minutes. They'll give you the details."

Trevor rose with him, but only so he could move in close and whisper, "In case you hadn't noticed, I'm still waiting for your terms!"

"I agree to whatever you think is right."

Trevor studied him a long moment, then slumped back into the booth. Defeated. "And here I spent hours last night preparing for battle."

Derek patted his friend's shoulder, and spoke words that had waited four long years. "Erin always said you were one of the good guys. I wish I could tell you what it meant to have you there after she was gone."

Chapter 26

Kelly had seen Trevor Coomes at numerous events where high-end gallery owners gathered. He had also attended a number of Christie's auctions, identifying himself as the official representative of a confidential bidder.

A common practice among second-rate galleries was to set up a dummy corporation that served as their entree. They made a few lowball offers, but such auctions were really nothing more than opportunities to troll for clients. Auction houses referred them as lampreys, after the suckerfish who survived by attaching themselves to sharks.

Trevor Coomes was not like that.

His main gallery in Santa Barbara was known for the quality of its product and the strata of society it served. Also, Trevor was himself a passionate collector. Which indicated a solid level of personal income. Kelly had watched him bid on a pre–Revolutionary War mantel clock with avid desperation. When he lost to a Boston museum, the man had been devastated. They had never spoken, but Kelly already had reason enough to like him.

Trust, however, was another thing entirely.

When Kelly followed Gwen into Miramar's

Main Street Diner, she found herself approaching a man in severe distress. She hung back, uncertain what to do or how to respond. They were, after all, here to film the opening of a safety deposit box. Plus there was the aftereffect of her conversation on the drive north. Gwen's easy manner had successfully masked an ability to probe deeply. She still felt bruised.

Gwen slipped into the window booth opposite the gallery owner and said, "What's wrong?"

"Nothing." Trevor made a feeble motion, shoving unwanted memories off the table. "We should go."

"We're not going anywhere." Gwen slid over and gestured for Kelly to seat herself. "Trevor, I'm not asking you again."

He slumped back. "This morning Derek talked about Erin."

"What about her?"

"I . . . Nothing, really. He hasn't spoken her name in years. It just . . ."

Gwen reached across the empty table and took his hand. "Look at me." When Trevor lifted his tragic gaze, she went on, "You care about Derek. What's more, you know him. At a level that's impossible for us. And yet we're about to enter into something that might, just might, have gotten my son killed." She gave that a beat, then, "Do you see where I'm going with this?"

Trevor dropped his gaze. Sighed. Nodded.

"Trust is a vital component of our moving forward. I want to be a part of this. But I also want to *understand*. I'm carrying two questions here. One is, why did Allen bring me into contact with this man? And two, who is Derek Gaines? I don't mean, the expert on art. I mean, the man."

"I can't help you with the first. I'm wondering the same thing."

"So let's set that aside for the moment. But as for the second . . . Tell me about Derek's heart."

Kelly huffed a soft breath. The question was as potent as it was gentle. Gwen heard her, glanced over, and smiled as if she approved.

Trevor said, "Erin was everything to him."

Kelly recognized the pain in the man's gaze. "She was your friend too?"

"Confidant. Friend. The sister I never had."

"Give us one image, something that will help us see her. And them together." When Trevor started to turn his wrist and bring his watch face into view, Gwen covered it. "Please."

Trevor's words started as a whispered rush, soft as a breaking wavelet. "We scattered Erin's ashes in the tidal pools north of Vandenberg. Derek tried to go back there yesterday, for the first time in four years. He made it as far as the parking lot."

Kelly and Gwen both gave that news the silence it deserved.

"Those pools were Erin's happy place." Trevor

smiled at Gwen's hand still covering his wrist. "She called them her very own art gallery. Every time she came back, she brought me a gift. Starfish, glass vial of multicolored sand, coral, cuttlefish, oyster shell, even three small pearls. She always said the same things. 'I saw this work of art and thought of you.' I keep them on my mantel. Derek spent the memorial standing there by my collection, studying them. Missing his Erin. It broke my heart."

When Kelly was certain Trevor would say no more, she started. "I'm in the middle of negotiating with the film group. Derek's refused to become involved. He just told me to handle it."

"Same thing with me this morning when I said we needed to work out his share of any commission." Trevor showed them open palms. "See what I mean? This is Derek being Derek."

"This won't do," Gwen snapped. "It won't do at all."

"This goes beyond honesty," Kelly agreed. "The man doesn't seem to care."

"He cares about losing his home," Trevor said. "But when it comes to money matters, the man might as well be blind."

Gwen took the bill from the waitress. "We'll see about that."

Chapter 27

Derek met Trevor and the ladies in the lot fronting a small city park. Shimmel miked them up, tested the sound, then Noah pointed them up toward a lovely shopping street. Kelly had always planned to visit the central coast. She had any number of friends who raved about the region's natural beauty, the light, the empty spaces.

A Pacific mist drifted in the still air, spicing the day with salt that tasted much purer than anything she had known while standing on her Santa Monica balcony. The same day, same ocean, but here everything seemed different. The light filtered through a thousand trees, hardwoods mixed with pines and palms, transforming the park into a green prism.

The bank was housed in a three-story building of Spanish stucco and dark beams. The manager stood in the awning's shadow, smiling at Derek's approach. Middle of the day, middle of the week, center of Miramar's shopping street, they attracted quite a crowd when Noah started filming outside the bank's entrance. Kelly held back, watching Derek chat with Carl Reese, the bank's manager. They definitely made quite a pair. Carl might be wearing a suit and tie. Derek was dressed in what Kelly assumed was another of Gwen's outfits, tapered sports shirt and pale gabardine trousers, loafers without socks. But standing there facing each other, smiling while the manager pretended not to be thrilled over what was happening, she could see how the two of them stood out. Not overly tall or big, their muscles not bulked up. Just the same, their level of fitness was almost frightening. This is what the human body is capable of. The utter absence of flab, the taut conditioning evident in the lines of their faces, their necks, the way they held themselves. Easy and tight and balanced. Derek motioned her forward, introduced her to Carl, and Kelly shook a hand solid as a concrete slab.

Downstairs in the vault Carl stood beside the guard as Gwen presented the vault pass and they all signed in. Carl wished them success with whatever the heck they were doing, and left.

The guard walked them down the long row of narrow security boxes and halted by the last section. These were much larger, big as the drawer to a full-size filing cabinet. He used his key to open the top lock, waited while Gwen inserted hers, then stepped away.

When they were alone in the vault, Derek said, "Gwen, do you want the honors?"

"He left this to you. Do it."

"Noah?"

"Trevor, shift slightly to your left, you're in

173

the light . . . Gwen, can you turn twenty degrees toward me, no, don't move your position. Good. Now Kelly, step over behind Derek. Okay. Rolling."

Derek said, "Here goes."

He swung open the vault door. Leaned in. "Oh my."

"What is it?"

He reached inside. "Treasure."

The oversize safety deposit box held three items.

Each was wrapped in old burlap and tied with twine, as if purchased in some third-world street market. A handwritten note had been slipped under the twine. Just a few words scrawled in faded blue ink, enough to identify the article. The handwriting was almost illegible, at least to Derek. But when he showed the first slip of paper to Gwen, she struggled for control, swallowed hard, then said, "My son wrote this."

"Tell us what it says."

" 'Emerald necklace, perhaps worn by Constantia when exercising power as representative of her son the emperor. Fourth century.' "

Someone gasped, but Derek couldn't be bothered to see who. It might even have been him. "Scissors."

Kelly searched her purse and came up with a pair of cuticle scissors. He pulled white cotton gloves from his rear pocket, slipped them on, cut the twine, unrolled the burlap, and revealed . . .

The oversize gold links were crudely carved, each about the size of a marble. The metal held a reddish tint that suggested Middle Eastern in origin. The color of early gold often revealed its source, as the purity was rarely above ten or twelve carats. Which meant almost half the material was something other than gold. Middle Eastern and North African gold artifacts often contained heavy amounts of copper.

There were fourteen emeralds in all, thirteen about the size of Derek's thumbnail surrounding a central one twice their size. One side of each had been sanded flat and then carved with faces.

Kelly reached into her shoulder bag a second time, and came up with a black velvet coverlet, the standard method for displaying jewelry. Derek said, "The lady came prepared."

"That's my job." She slipped on her own gloves, then adjusted the item until every face lay flat. "Twelve disciples, Jesus, and . . ."

"The reigning emperor would be my guess," Derek replied. "Constantine."

"Of course."

Noah said to Derek, "Step back just a little, your shadow is on the item."

"Sorry."

They waited while Noah came in for a close-up. When he retreated, Derek said, "Time for round two."

" 'Diptych, ivory covered with gold leaf," Gwen read. "Central figure is male and wears Roman robe of royal office. Signifies Constantine, first Emperor of Byzantium. Fourth century.' "

The word *diptych* came from the Greek roots *dis*, meaning "two," and *ptykhe*, meaning "fold." Originally, this referred to writing tablets used in ancient Rome, folded to keep the inscriptions clean. In the late fourth century, the diptych became a way to display religious stories or honor saints. Such items became increasingly important as Christianity spread among the common people, the vast majority of whom could not read.

The ivory was tinted almost yellow with age. The carvings held the same sharp-edged crudeness of very early icons. The left-hand leaf held a Cross made from gold and crushed gemstones, probably sapphires. The right image was of a man whose hair was carved red gold.

Noah said, "Show me the cover."

Derek held the heavily carved exterior for the close-up, hoping his hands did not tremble.

The third item took their breath away.

" '*Globus cruciger*,' " Gwen read. " 'Solid gold. Rubies and diamonds. Seventh century.' "

The term meant, literally, "cross-bearing orb." It had become a symbol of religious and earthly power with the Byzantine emperors, and represented their power over both the world of man, and the world of the church. The fist-sized globe weighed over a pound. The cross was probably gold as well, but Derek couldn't be certain because of how it had been blanketed with gems.

Noah said, "Close up."

This time Derek needed to say, "Somebody else hold it. My hands are shaking."

Giving the item to Kelly meant he could take a small step back and examine the others. Kelly's face shone with the adrenaline-stoked thrill of a true collector. She might be working for the world's greatest auction house. Her career might be determined by how much she added to the Christie's bottom line. But at the deeper level, beyond what the world demanded of her, she stared at the items with something akin to ecstasy.

Trevor shared Kelly's awe. But he also looked worried. Derek liked him for that. He was able to look beyond the treasures on display, and see the mysteries they represented. Centuries of bad moves and blood. So they could shine under the lights in the Miramar bank's vault.

Gwen simply looked sad.

Derek stripped off his gloves, reached over, and took hold of Gwen's hand. Just letting the lady know another person shared the question central to this moment. Because without a doubt, these treasures represented the hunt that had killed her son. There was no question any longer.

The chances that Allen Freeth had accidentally drowned off the Sicilian coast were now reduced to zero.

She met Derek's gaze, and took strength from whatever she found there. She straightened and asked, "What now?"

Chapter 28

As they left the bank, Gwen asked Kelly if she'd care to join her and Trevor for lunch. "Love to, but not today," she replied. "I've got a dinner back in LA. Family."

"Before you go, grant me one moment of your time." Gwen led her over to where Derek spoke with the film crew. Gwen drew him a few steps away and declared, "I want in."

"Then you're in."

"Just like that? No attempt to pat me on the head and tell me to go count my marbles?"

Kelly liked Derek's smile more every time he revealed it. "I will never, not in a billion years, try to pat you on the head."

"Derek—"

"Gwen, you're as much a part of this hunt as anyone. But you can't come with us to Sicily."

"I can understand that."

He said it anyway. "We are not declaring to anyone how this painting came into our possession. Or suggesting in any way we are attempting to restart Allen's quest."

"I like that word. *Quest*," she said softly. "Allen would too."

As Derek started back to where Noah waited,

she then added, "I just wish I knew how to say thanks."

"Give me back my life. That's thanks enough."

Kelly phoned Brian as she was leaving Miramar. His secretary said Brian was in a meeting and asked her to hold. Three minutes later Brian demanded, "How did it go?"

"We have a story. A big one."

"We."

"Excuse me?"

"That's what you said. *We* have a story. Which is good. I like having my team on board." A voice spoke to Brian, something about people waiting. "I have to get back. Breakfast tomorrow?"

"Absolutely."

"Did you sign with the attorney Rick suggested?"

"We have a handshake deal in place. Papers to follow."

"Cafe Vida in Palisades Village. Seven o'clock. See if your lawyer can join us." He cut the connection.

Kelly spent the rest of her return journey giving Jerome a run-through of her time in Miramar. The drive up and back with Gwen, the diner, Derek, the bank, the filming . . .

The treasures.

Jerome asked, "Where are you now?"

"Just passing the 405 turnoff. Heading east on the 101."

"Can we have dinner? There's a lot still to discuss."

"Jerome, I'd love that. But I'm due at my mother's."

He caught the flat way she had shaped those two words. *My mother's.* "Something wrong?"

"Not really. Well, yes, but it's nothing . . ."

"Tell me."

"My sister will be there. It's a sort of monthly ritual. Having the two of them gang up on me."

"Why on earth would they do that?"

"My sister is happily married, two wonderful kids, I love them to death. But when she and Mom get together, it turns into this lovefest for the life I don't have."

"That's ridiculous."

"When it comes to family and kids and husbands, my mom is bedrock Italian. If that makes any sense at all."

Jerome knew all about Kelly's wayward ex. He had to. Since he had helped her through the awful months. "Why don't I join you?"

"Jerome, that's so nice. But I couldn't possibly—"

"Your family needs to hear just what an amazing woman you are. Consider it payback for renewing my contact with Derek."

"You'll hate it."

"On the contrary. I will relish the chance to burnish your image. Let me come."

Toluca Lake was a quiet backwater, an island of luxury in San Fernando Valley's crowded asphalt sea. The lake itself was fed from one of LA's last remaining natural springs. The surrounding neighborhoods were sheltered beneath centuries-old hardwoods and perfumed by a myriad of flowering shrubs and trees. Frank Sinatra had lived there. Bing Crosby. WC Fields. William Holden. Stars who sought a refuge from the Hollywood jungle.

Kelly's father had been an engineer with Pratt & Whitney. The year she had started junior high, he had been appointed vice president of the LA division and relocated them from Phoenix. She had loved the house and her LA life from the very first day. Their home was a modest Spanish-style stucco built in the twenties, located at the end of a tree-lined cul-de-sac. Big yard, two cedars, and a trio of ancient cherry trees whose pinkish-white petals had been announcing spring's arrival for over a century.

Kelly's father had retired the year before her high school graduation. He remained the quintessential English gentleman until the day his second heart attack took him away. Richard Reid was soft spoken and modest and dressed like he starred in a fifties-era sitcom. For years after his retirement, he still wore a tie almost every day.

He was a man of quiet passions, a lover of good food, his daughters, wine, art, and his wife above all else. He had lived long enough to walk both his children down the aisle.

Soon after Kelly discovered her ex was sleeping with virtually every available woman, Kelly's father died in his sleep. Departing this life as politely as he had lived, a quiet man who never made a fuss about anything.

In the period surrounding her divorce, Kelly had often wondered what her father had truly thought of her ex. Richard had always been unfailingly polite, even cordial, to both his sons-in-law. But he had also shown that same polite British mask to a boss he had despised and mistrusted. Kelly had been in love, and her mother thought Kelly's ex walked on water; whatever concerns or negative opinions her father might have harbored remained hidden to the very end.

Kelly pulled up in front of the house and did what had become a habit since her divorce. She tried to armor herself against the emotional assault to come.

When it came to family, Giulia Reid demanded full, total, unquestioning loyalty.

Something Kelly had never been very good at giving.

When Jerome pulled up and parked behind her BMW, Kelly was staring at the branches of the biggest cherry tree, where a swing had once hung.

Every spring she and her sister would wait for the day when the first blossoms began to scatter over their front lawn. Their father would swing them hard and high, one and then the other, while petals fell like a spring snow over their heads and shoulders. Times like this, she missed him with an ache that pierced her bones.

Jerome tapped the glass, then opened the passenger door and slipped inside. "You okay?"

Kelly balanced the air by the steering wheel with her right hand. So-so.

He followed her line of sight to the house. He had last been here for her father's funeral. "Anything I should know going forward?"

It was the same question he always asked when meeting clients. And the perfect question for this hard moment. Inviting Kelly to take a step back. Look at this with the objectivity that helped to make her so successful at her job.

"You remember my sister."

"Yvonne, right? Sure. Two kids?"

"Three now. All girls. Mom expects her to bring at least one of them to these dinners. It's her way of reminding me how disappointed she is with everything I do. And am."

"Your mother still hasn't accepted you were right to leave the louse?" That had been Jerome's name for her ex since the very first revelation. The louse.

"She probably won't ever be. Mom thought he

was the perfect catch." Kelly started to say that was one reason why she had allowed herself to be swept off her feet. But digging up that particular grave never got her anywhere but sad.

Jerome shook his head. Still watching the house. "That's just nuts."

"Family is everything to Mom, and always has been. It's the lens she uses to judge the success or failure of her daughters' lives." Logic said Kelly had no reason to defend her mother. Even so, she went on, "Plus my divorce followed Dad's death by just a few months. A terrible time for everyone."

"I remember the louse playing the dutiful son-in-law at the funeral."

"He basically shepherded Mom through the entire service." Kelly tasted old bile. "And apparently was so overcome with sorrow he got it on with my former best friend. In the garage."

Jerome did his best not to laugh. "A real class act, that one."

She reached for her door. "We might as well get this over with."

"Kelly, wait." When she settled back, he went on, "My wife and I are separating."

"Oh, Jerome."

"Things have not been great for a while. Actually, longer than that. Years. We stayed together for the kids. But our youngest is fifteen now. An LA fifteen."

She knew his boys. "Totally independent."

"Right." He shrugged. "The other night she said it was time. I couldn't find a single solitary reason to object. I moved out last weekend."

"I'm so sorry."

He found it easier to watch the house. "Thing is . . . I've always thought you were a very special lady. And I'm not talking just professionally." He looked over. Nervous now. "Do you think there's any chance for us?"

Kelly found herself recalling the comics from her childhood. When one of the characters got whacked upside their head with a bladder and the sound went *"Yang-ang-ang-ang."* Exactly how she felt.

Jerome did his best to smile. "Surprise."

"You can say that again."

"Bad timing?"

"No, well, actually, I have no idea."

He nodded. "I've wanted to say something for a long time. Months. Years, really."

"Wow."

He opened his door. "Just think about it, okay?"

As Kelly approached the house, she was captured by the distinct impression that had accompanied her since laying her father to rest. *Same cover, different book.*

One story about her former home had ended, another began. In the new one, Kelly's place in this house had been redrawn. She had become the outsider, the permanent disappointment.

Even so, today was different.

Jerome's bombshell left her feeling slightly disconnected from her own feet. She walked the front path, wondering what she was going to do or say. How she felt. But all these elements were beyond her. How could she not have known he had feelings for her? Did all the Christie's staff know? Had they assumed this was how she had won her promotion? Did they laugh at her behind her back? The questions kept crowding in, so fast and so many she felt almost sheltered. Both from the house's occupants and from needing to come up with a response.

How did she feel about Jerome? Just then, it wasn't the question. Rather, how had she *not* known how *he* felt? That was the mystery to cap her long and exhausting day.

As Kelly reached for the front doorknob, Jerome asked, "Mind if I make a suggestion?"

"Go right ahead."

Yvonne must have heard their car doors close, because her face appeared in the side window. Jerome only had time for three words before Kelly's sister opened the door. "Follow my lead."

Yvonne was four years younger than Kelly. Since early childhood, the two sisters had treated each other with the sort of polite disinterest they might have shown a neighbor. They had so little in common it was ridiculous, at least to Kelly. Yvonne had her father's looks, the sandy straw hair and willowy strength and gray eyes and skin that burned easily. But when it came to the elements that mattered most, Yvonne was very much her mother's daughter. Family formed the bedrock of Yvonne's existence. She was a highly accomplished graphic designer, and remained enough in demand that she was able to become an at-home consultant after her second child was born. But for Yvonne, the work was secondary. Something fun that brought in extra income and would someday pay for her three children's education. What mattered most, the one focal point of her entire existence, was family.

When it came to appearances, Kelly might as well have been cloned from her mother. Dark saturnine eyes and hair and complexion, tall and shapely and fierce when riled.

Then there were the other traits. The characteristics that would have been fine in the son they never had. The factors of which her late father had been so proud.

Passion for her work. Ambition toward her professional standing. Determination. Focus upon the outside world. The ability to walk away from a man who had scarred her terribly . . .

And so forth.

Yvonne balanced her youngest on her hip. The

little girl sucked her thumb and inspected the two of them with a solemn gaze. Yvonne stared at Jerome in confusion, then said, "Don't I know you?"

"Jerome Summers. Your sister's boss."

"Sure, now I remember. Kelly, did you say anything? Because Mom—"

Jerome interrupted with, "I'm not staying. Kelly is just back from filming and we urgently need to speak before she leaves for Europe. I'll only be a few moments."

Yvonne accepted Kelly's quick embrace, then stepped back, clearly confused by this man's appearance. Kelly could almost see the gears working in her sister's brain. Sorting through the unexpected words she had just heard. *Filming. Europe.*

Drawing attention away from the child in Yvonne's arms. The ingredient that made Yvonne the center of their mother's universe.

Yvonne said, "Well sure, I guess . . ."

"Thank you so much, that's so kind." Jerome playing the coldly polite manager. "Kelly, is there somewhere we might perhaps talk . . ."

"Of course." She started toward the parlor. "Sis, would you tell Mom I'll be a few minutes?"

They left Yvonne standing there in the foyer, the baby she so proudly used as an unspoken rebuke almost forgotten.

The formal living room remained pretty

much as it had been during her teenage years. Her father's easy chair positioned by the front window, the ivory damask covers on the sideboard, the crystal vase holding flowers from the back garden, the framed prints on the side walls. Kelly seated herself on the sofa next to Jerome and asked softly, "What now?"

Jerome waited until Yvonne had retreated into the kitchen to say, "You look exhausted."

"Six and a half hours on the road, the meetings, the filming . . ." Not to mention the continuing aftershocks. "I'm so tired I can't think straight."

Jerome's response was halted by Kelly's mother appearing in the doorway leading to the dining room and kitchen. Yvonne was tucked safely in behind Giulia's left shoulder, baby still on her hip. Kelly observed their arrival through the same lingering fog of astonishment. She watched Jerome rise from his seat, walk around the coffee table, and approach the ladies with hand outstretched. "Jerome Summers, Mrs. Reid. My sincere apologies for foisting myself into your family gathering. But your daughter and I have urgent matters that simply can't wait."

Giulia Reid avoided taking his hand by wiping her own with the dish towel she held. "My daughter said something about . . . Europe?"

"Indeed so, madam. Kelly's expertise and growing fame in the international art world requires her to leave for Sicily tomorrow."

"How is it, I wonder, that I only hear about this now?"

"This new project only developed yesterday." Jerome spread his arms. "Which is how I come to be here."

"I see. My daughters and I were about to dine. You would of course be welcome to join us." Though there was no welcome to her tone. Or her gaze. None whatsoever.

Yvonne spoke from her position of safety. "Mom has made *Scaccia Ragusana* and *Bolito Misto*."

"Arab-style lasagna bread and spicy stewed beef," Kelly explained. "My ex-husband's two favorite Sicilian dishes."

"How very interesting." Jerome's expression had shifted from apologetic to politely enraged. "How unfortunate the gentleman is not here. And never will be again."

"Unfortunate. Yes." Giulia Reid gave him frigid in return. "I was thinking the very same thing."

Kelly continued to view the drama from an emotional distance. There before her was the unending quarrel she had with her mother. The urging for Giulia's older daughter to forgive her ex and restart the family her mother so desired. The bitter disappointment over Kelly's refusal to do as Giulia ordered. The total lack of interest in Kelly's profession, her aims . . .

In who Kelly was.

Jerome showed no willingness to back down. "You must be so very proud of your daughter's many accomplishments, Mrs. Reid."

"Of course." She reached back and took her grandchild from Yvonne. All without releasing Jerome from her gaze. "Of course."

"I'll make sure you are the very first to receive a copy of the documentary now being filmed about your daughter's most recent find." He turned his back on the trio. "Kelly, I'm so very sorry to ask, but it appears our work will require . . ."

"Sure thing." She rose. "Mom, Yvonne, so sorry."

Yvonne asked, "You're not staying?"

"We really must register the *treasures* your *daughter* has unearthed." He continued talking as they headed for the front door. "Watch the papers. And the television newscasts." He opened the door, and turned back long enough to say, "Before you know it, Mrs. Reid, you will see your daughter's name in lights."

Chapter 29

Derek woke to a strong wind off the Pacific. The air through his bedroom window was tangy with the shore's fragrances. There was no dawn to speak of, just a gradual shifting of light through gray clouds, roiling and tossing like the waves he could not see. He lay and watched the light strengthen, thinking of past times. Weekend mornings like this, he would bring their first coffees back to bed and they would lie there together, languid with love and the prospect of a day that was truly theirs.

Thoughts of Erin stayed with him. Mug in hand, he padded through the house, taking in each room, remembering. Back in the early eighties a developer had bought a tract north of Miramar, where olive groves had climbed the slope. The homes were intended for families and retirees who wanted a refuge from the growing cities to the north and south. Miramar and the central coast were often referred to as the Middle Kingdom, and for good reason. It drifted between the two great behemoths of LA and San Francisco, suspended in salty animation. A joy for most of those who had the great good fortune to uncover these hidden gems.

The homes were small, the lots narrow. Their roofs climbed the slope like steps. While there was no view from inside the houses, all they needed to do was step outside, walk a few hundred paces, and the Pacific vista was theirs to claim. It was a wonderful place to call home.

Erin was not an easy person to live with. Not by any stretch of the imagination. A change of nature was unthinkable to her. She was sweet and happy, she filled their home with laughter and song, but only because Derek had adapted to her needs and desires. She loved art, but had no desire to possess, to own. This love of hers was generous to a fault, and shaped the art filling the walls of their home. Flowers drawn by a preteen had been hung next to the burning village of a Laotian refugee. Each told a story that was precious to her. Derek learned not to question, or object.

He returned to the kitchen, made himself a bowl of fruit and yogurt, topped it off with granola, and continued his walk through the corridors of memory. The day after her memorial, he had started taking down the artwork. Their continued presence had raked talons across his wounded heart. But in the four years since her passage, nothing had ever replaced the pictures filling seven boxes in his garage.

Erin had never understood his passion for fine art. The timeless quality of paintings, the way they marked transitions in society and culture and human civilization . . . Erin enjoyed listening to him. She loved his passion. But the works themselves meant little to her. She took busloads of students to the Getty and a half dozen other museums because she wanted to challenge and inspire. For Erin, it was all about nurturing the creative.

Derek finished his tour and stepped onto the rear deck. Watching the windswept clouds boil overhead. Studying the weights and workout equipment that littered his yard. For the first time in months, he felt no desire to run or cycle or lift, whatever.

He pulled the artist's portfolio from under his bed and carried it to the kitchen. He propped the Caravaggio on the cabinet, using a pair of clean mugs to keep it standing up. He poured himself another coffee and seated himself by the table, his chair turned to face the painting. The future.

All three faces dominating the central space held the key traits of Caravaggio's genius. Yet the mother and child looked at each other with an otherworldly calm, utterly disconnected from the shadows that approached on all sides. The play of chiaroscuro did not touch their faces. They were set apart. Already beyond the reach of earthly fears and agonies and loss.

The man who hovered above them, however, was something else entirely. The face was a masterpiece of emotional realism. His expression captured all the risk contained in earthbound love. The certainty of destruction, man's inability to protect his family from the grave, all there. Derek found himself gripped so powerfully he could reach across the centuries separating him from the widower and ask if the man had finally found the strength and the purpose to go on. To live again. To find joy in the next wounded day.

When it was time, Derek showered and dressed. He fit the painting back in the portfolio, packed the best of his own clothes, locked the front door, and loaded his belongings and Gwen's valise and the Caravaggio into his pickup's rear seat. As he backed from the drive and started down the hill, he had the feeling that he had finally, at long last, left his chrysalis behind.

When Derek pulled through Gwen's open front gates, he found her loading a small case into the trunk of her Bentley. The lady's ride was the four-door Mulsanne, a discreetly elegant alternative to her late husband's Continental GT. But still harboring a beast beneath the hood. Derek parked and transferred his cases. Gwen closed the trunk and asked, "You won't mind driving?"

"I would pay good money for the chance."

"Kind of you to offer, but not necessary."

Derek held her door. She accepted the gesture with a queen's regal grace. He handed her his phone and asked, "Can you set this up so we can hear it over the car's speakers?"

"Of course."

Derek walked around and settled behind the wheel. "If it's possible, we should patch both Trevor and Kelly in on this."

"This is a Bentley. If I could manage the controls, I imagine we could instruct your phone to dance a samba." Gwen set it on the console between them. "But first we need to discuss something important. You need to pay more attention to what you are due."

Derek took the freeway entrance and powered into the middle lane. The Bentley cut the traffic's rumble down to a soft murmur. "I'm listening."

"You know art," Gwen told him. "You know the world of treasure."

"A little," Derek said. "Not as much as I should."

"You know enough." Gwen waved her hand at the highway ahead. "But this world is something else entirely. And you need to *pay attention.* You're treating the mystery, finding any more missing treasure, as if that's all there is to this."

"There's more?"

"Of course there is. And you know it. Or you should, if you'd open your eyes."

"You're obviously heading somewhere with this."

"Derek, there is a very real opportunity here.

They are *filming* this. They are *using* you. You need to *use them back*."

"I don't disagree with you. In fact, I think you're absolutely right. But I don't know the first thing about what you're describing. This is a universe away from my comfort zone."

She swung around in her seat so as to face him, settling her back against the side door. "I could possibly teach you."

"Maybe. Probably. If we had time, which we don't. Things are about to go into overdrive. And truth be told, I really don't have the interest."

"You're not interested in money?"

"Of course I am. I'm frantically trying to hold on to my home. But what I'd really like . . ."

"Go on."

"Will you handle it?" When she remained silent, he pressed. "It's not the money. It's the maneuvering. The people. The deals."

"Try to put a little more disgust into that last word." But she was smiling now. "The *deals*. Make it something dirty."

"Is that a yes?"

She swung back around, facing the sunlit road ahead. "Trevor was right. You really are the most exasperating man alive."

"He never said that."

"Well, perhaps not in so many words. But that's what he meant." She gave that a beat. "You want me to act as your agent."

"Whatever you want to call it. Just get me what I need to keep my home."

"You're setting your sights far too low." She nodded. "All right, Derek. Yes. I accept the role."

"Thank you, Gwen."

"Don't you want to know what I'm going to charge you?"

"Not really, no. Can we please get down to business?"

"Can we . . . What do you think I'm trying to do here?"

"I have no idea." He pointed to his phone. "It would be best if Kelly and Trevor were both in on what comes next."

When the other two were connected, Derek asked, "Kelly, where are you now?"

"Leaving the Palisades. I just had breakfast with Brian. Now I'm late for a meeting with my boss back in Beverly Hills."

"I thought you were joining us at the Getty."

"I'll get there as soon as I can. Jerome called and said this was urgent."

Derek heard the firm tone, knew there was nothing to be gained from arguing. "How did the meeting go with Brian?"

"He showed up with two attorneys. Our lawyer was there as well. I think we've reached a basic agreement on terms. Want to hear?"

"No. Gwen is going to represent me on all business-related matters."

Kelly went silent. Then, "Are you sure?"

"It has to be this way. Gwen agrees."

"Reluctantly," Gwen added. "But yes."

Derek went on. "Have your lawyer write up whatever's necessary so Gwen can sign in my absence." Gwen shot him a look, but did not protest. "Trevor, the same goes for you. All right?"

"Well, somebody needs to be handling your end. And you certainly aren't."

"Moving on," Derek said. "The time has come to ask why Allen died."

Gwen's features tightened, but she remained silent. Kelly said, "Shouldn't we record this?"

"Trevor?"

"Wait a sec. All right. Go ahead."

Derek said, "First and foremost, it could have been an accident like the Sicilian police claim."

"Accidents do happen," Trevor said.

"Yes indeed," Gwen said.

Kelly said, "But you don't think that's it."

"No. I don't."

"A man who lived with a bad heart all his life does not simply get it in his head to go swimming in deep waters," Gwen said. "Allen was adventurous. But he was most certainly not an idiot."

Kelly asked, "Allen had a heart problem?"

"Yes, but that's for later," Derek said. "Moving

on to option two. Allen found the next item. Others found out what he was after, and killed him to take it for themselves."

Derek drove a number of sunlit miles. Giving them time and space. Waiting.

Kelly was the one to finally say, "If that's the case, I don't see what we can do about it."

"I agree," Trevor said.

Kelly went on, "If those people were to find out we were looking for the same item, we'd be toast."

"That can't happen," Gwen said. "I forbid you to even consider such a thing."

"Which is why we simply accept this might be what happened, and move on," Derek said. "If Allen was caught in the act of uncovering a new treasure, we will never know."

"And you won't try to find out," Gwen said. Stern now. "Say it."

"You have my word," Derek said. "Our trip is exclusively about the painting's provenance."

Another few miles, then Kelly said, "Which brings us to option three."

Trevor asked, "How many more are there? I positively loathe hearing you discuss various ways to have this end in two more drownings."

"Don't even think such a thing," Gwen snapped.

"Just one," Derek replied.

Kelly said, "And that is?"

"Back to the note he sent to Gwen," Derek said.

"Allen said it would restore my fortunes," Gwen said.

"And it was attached to . . ."

"The painting," Trevor said.

"By Caravaggio," Kelly said. "I'm sure it's his work."

"But why the painting and not one of the treasures in the bank vault?" Derek gave that another couple of miles. "I think this is the key."

Trevor's voice rose a full octave. "Key to what?"

Derek found it incredibly difficult to take that next step. Claim the unseen treasure. Open them to a hope that might have already killed Gwen's son. "At this point, what we need to focus on is staying alert to the possibility."

"I'm still waiting for an answer to the what," Trevor said.

"The possibility," Derek said, "that there is a second painting." He gave that a long pause, then continued, "Remember, we ask no questions. We make no suggestion that we even consider this a possibility. But all the while we're in Sicily, we listen. We listen and we watch. For the slightest hint, the first indication this is real. Staying as intent as we possibly can."

Soon as Kelly cut the connection with Derek and the others, her sense of crystal clarity faded.

It had been happening since she woke up that morning and went through the motions of starting another day. Her internal world had remained dominated by a complete and utter disconnect. During the breakfast meeting with Brian and the lawyers, the world had gone sharp and clear, her thinking precise. Just like when she had spoken with Derek. But now, as she passed Sunset and entered the Beverly Hills shopping district . . .

She drifted.

Thirty-six hours earlier, she had stared into the mirror and almost been swallowed by loneliness. Empty and bereft.

Then she had started just another day, taken just another trip to visit with just another client. And what happened? In the midst of just another busy day, she had stood in a bank vault with Professor Derek Gaines and seen . . .

What, exactly?

She could not put it into words. Not really. She could certainly say Derek was very easy on the eyes. She could even say she trusted him. She liked how his inner depths were reflected in everyone who knew him well. She really, really looked forward to working with him, traveling together, adventuring.

She liked him. A lot.

So . . . What?

She liked a lot of men. And they liked her. Normally, that was as far as it went. She gave what was comfortable, she maintained her distance, she kept herself and her world intact. This particular search for missing art changed nothing.

Or did it?

And then there was this latest development. The earth-shaker.

Jerome. Her boss. Declaring his affection.

And then, in her moment of exhaustion and weakness, he had defended her. The warmth and closeness of his actions, the implied intimacy, touched her still.

Jerome was there for her. Available. If she wanted.

But if she started a relationship with Jerome, what about Derek?

She stopped at a light, met her gaze in the rearview mirror, asked back, *What about him?* Was she suggesting that she was falling in love? With an almost-vagabond who loathed LA? No? Then why was she asking that question at all?

Her reflection remained silent.

But logic was not enough to still the burrowing doubts.

Kelly pulled into the upper deck of the parking garage fronting Rodeo, found a space, cut her motor, and sat there. Pondering the impossible question. What exactly did she want?

She had no idea.

Chapter 30

Nate 'n Al's was an old-style deli that had been home to Hollywood dealmaking and clogged arteries for over seventy years. The booths, lighting, linoleum floors, heavy china plates, massive portions, and snippy waiters were all throwbacks to a different era. The place still scoffed at cholesterol, and treated both grease and carbs as vital components of a good meal.

Kelly walked past the line of people waiting for tables and service at the deli counter. She spotted Jerome seated in a booth by the side wall with a heavyset woman who possessed a unique mélange of bloodlines. Southeast Asian, perhaps. "Sorry I'm late. Traffic was murder."

Jerome slid over and pulled his plate of cheese omelet and hash browns with him. "Kelly Reid, meet Aranya Lee."

"Hi." The waiter was typical for the deli, bored and alert in equal measure. "Just tea." To the others, "I've just come from a breakfast meeting."

"Aranya occasionally serves as our outside security consultant," Jerome said. "I've worked with her on several projects. I trust her, and you should too."

Kelly guessed the woman to be in her mid-forties, but she could be off by five years either way, perhaps even ten. Aranya was solid as a block of petrified mahogany, her skin pocked with old scars. Her gaze was hard, her voice calm. Toneless. A cop's voice. "I serve a number of clients, but Christie's is my number-one concern."

"Aranya was with Canadian federal security, then Interpol," Jerome said.

Kelly asked, "Why are we meeting?"

"The three items you found in Allen Freeth's safety deposit box," Jerome said. "I ran them by Interpol."

She nodded. Standard procedure for all items of questionable provenance. "And?"

Jerome gestured with his fork. "Tell her."

"And nothing," Aranya replied. "No red flags. No record of their ever having been stolen."

"So that's good, right?"

Jerome said, "Apparently there's been another person asking about these items."

"Very specific questions," Aranya said. "Very precise descriptions."

"Who?"

"A lawyer," Jerome said.

"A very powerful man in certain circles," Aranya said. "In Sicily."

Kelly looked from one to the other. "Mafia?"

"Anyone this powerful in Sicily has connections," Aranya said. "At least, that's the assumption my sources in Brussels are working under."

"Aranya could only go so far with her questions and make sure news of her interest didn't get out," Jerome said.

Aranya asked, "The man you're working with. The art specialist."

"Derek Gaines."

"Right. Him. He thinks your painting and the other treasures were taken from Sicily, correct?"

"It's where Allen Freeth died. That's basically all we have to go on."

She nodded. "So let's assume for the moment he's correct. A lot of art and treasure went missing from the island during that period."

"Six thousand items. I know."

"More than that," Jerome said. "A lot more."

"Six thousand pieces *officially* stolen," Aranya said. "Added to that are all the treasures never officially recorded."

"Not to mention treasures taken earlier in the island's history," Jerome said.

"A great deal of art went missing in the havoc following the Second World War," Aranya said. "Most of it was never recovered."

"Plus there are the items in private collections," Jerome said. "Items held for generations."

"As well as items taken from churches," Aranya said. "Many of these predated official record keeping."

"But they'd be insured . . ." Kelly stopped because both were shaking their heads. "What?"

"Remember where we're talking about," Jerome said. "Official records, insurance records, all these mean the federal authorities can tax them."

"And something else," Aranya said. "Records like those were often sold. Professionals on the look for treasure would pay good money for knowing who secretly holds what."

Kelly waited, then, "Same question. Why are we meeting?"

"Jerome tells me you're traveling with an official photographer."

"A documentary film crew," Kelly corrected.

"Working on provenance of a painting that might be by Caravaggio," Jerome said.

"Nothing more," Kelly said. "If someone who knows about the painting gets in touch, fine. But we ask no questions, we take no further steps to uncover anything else."

"That should keep you safe enough." Aranya passed over a card. "But at the first hint of danger or threat of any kind, contact me. I'll be standing by, in case you need anything. Day or night."

Jerome told Aranya, "I still think you should travel with them."

"A former Interpol agent, who's spent her entire career going after stolen treasure. You might as well paint a target on their backs." She slid a photograph across the table. "This is the attorney who put feelers out with Interpol. Antonio Orsini. I'm texting you a copy of this."

Kelly saw a man in his late fifties or early sixties, with leonine features and a flowing mane of silver-white hair. "Did he ask about the painting?"

"No."

"No one has ever registered a query, official or otherwise, about a missing unfinished painting from that era," Jerome said.

"Which means if he shows up, there's a connection we don't know about," Aranya said. "You see?"

Kelly nodded. "And if I spot him?"

Aranya leaned across the table. "My advice is, you get out while you still can."

Chapter 31

It seemed only natural to thank the security consultant, rise from the booth, leave the restaurant, and then hang about the entrance while Jerome settled the bill. He stepped outside and seemed genuinely pleased to find her standing beyond the queue waiting for tables. "Back to the office?"

"Can't. I'm due at the Getty." She pointed to the parking deck. "Walk with me?"

The sunlight was brilliant enough to defy the morning's crisp temperature and tasted like California champagne. Jerome waited until they climbed the stairs and she beeped open her ride to say, "About last night."

"I can't thank you enough, helping me out like you did."

"That's not what I meant and you bloody well know it."

His evident nerves seemed to calm her own. "I know."

"And?"

Kelly took her time responding, mostly because of how she viewed the man in a fresh new light. Tall, impeccably dressed, kept fit by a determined gym regime, every inch the successful city gentleman. At home in any number of lands. Intelligent, passionate about art, ambitious. They had so much in common. People would call them the perfect match. Several of her colleagues who had their eye on Jerome, married or not, would keel over dead with envy.

Kelly savored this beautiful, glorious moment. One where it was almost easy to say, "I am very fond of you, Jerome. I've liked you since the very first day you were appointed my boss. You're the finest person I've ever worked for. Truly."

He released a ragged breath. "That's it, then."

"Perhaps. Maybe even probably. I just don't know."

"Maybe even probably doesn't leave much room for hope."

"I want to be fully honest with you."

"That's one of the things I've treasured about you, Kelly. Your complete honesty. Even when it hurts."

She felt a faint tremor as the words resonated. How he *treasured* her. She was tempted to rush over, hold the man, let the moment's affection fill the sunlit hour. Instead she said, "I leave for Sicily tomorrow. It's all I really have room for. What if we just let it sit until I return?"

"No choice, really." Another breath, then, "I've moved into a furnished rental by the Penmar Golf Course. In case you change your mind."

She kissed him then. On the cheek, just the edge of his mouth. But still. "I'll call you as soon as we return."

Chapter 32

Evelyn Hardy, Getty's Senior Director, had alerted the guards of their arrival. Which meant Derek could once again glide past the long line of steaming cars and slip into the VIP section. A receptionist escorted them back to the restricted-access area. Judith Raimy, Getty's chief restorer, was there to greet them when the elevator opened. "Welcome to our secret lair."

"Judith, this is Gwen Freeth, owner of a truly remarkable private collection."

"At least for the moment," Gwen corrected.

"Much longer than that, if I have anything to say about it," Derek replied.

"A pleasure, Ms. Freeth. Truly." Judith wore a gray shirt and pantsuit, and over this a man's cashmere sweater that buttoned up the front, so large it fit her like an overcoat. The sweater had once been gray-green, but was now spackled with a rainbow of colors from her work. Reading glasses with magnifying overlays dangled from a gold necklace. "Derek, please tell me you've reconsidered. Please."

"I'm sorry," Gwen said. "Reconsidered what?"

"Evelyn's been looking for a number two."

"Ah. Yes." She shot Derek a look. "I heard about this."

Footsteps across the concrete floor announced the director's arrival. Judith's words accelerated to near light speed. "The other candidates are simply nightmarish. All brains, no heart. And pompous. And snippy. And they dared to criticize my work. A day in their company and I'm bound to be arrested for vile deeds I've already started planning."

Evelyn stepped up. "You must be Gwen Freeth. Evelyn Hardy. A pleasure."

From behind Evelyn's back, Judith clasped her hands together and mouthed, *Please.*

Evelyn said, "Perhaps you'd like to have a look at what we—"

"Sorry to interrupt. But we need to take just a moment for something that shouldn't wait." Gwen faced Derek. "You want me to handle your commercial commitments, correct?"

"Well, yes, but not—"

"There is no but. Either you do or you don't want me to help you negotiate your way through this morass of possible deals."

"I do. But Gwen—"

"Fine. It starts now." She turned back to Evelyn. "What are the details regarding this possible job?"

"I want to hire Derek. I don't know how I can make it any simpler than that."

Gwen looked positively affronted. "This man dared to tell you no?"

"Gwen—"

"You hush, now. I'm doing precisely what you asked me to."

Judith offered, "Derek doesn't like LA."

"What utter rubbish. You like the Getty, don't you? No, don't you dare interrupt." Back to Evelyn. "I assume he has some sense of attachment to a cottage or shack or somewhat up in, what's the name of your little town?"

"Miramar," Judith said. "Paradise on earth."

"It's not a shack," Derek said.

"Your job is to be silent." Gwen asked Evelyn, "Can this gentleman work from Miramar two days a week?"

"Absolutely." To Derek, "We also have a studio apartment that's gone vacant at the villa."

"The *Getty villa,* Derek," Judith offered. "In the *Palisades.*"

"Thank you very much. Derek accepts your offer."

Judith threw her arms in the air. "Break out the champagne!"

Evelyn said, "And here I thought it was going to be just another boring day at the office."

Derek asked, "Don't I have a say in the matter?"

The three women responded in unison. *"No."*

Kelly texted to say she was five minutes out. Evelyn responded to the news with, "It's not too late to send that Christie's person packing."

Judith said, "Oh, stop being such a pouty-puss. You like her."

"They're vultures, the lot of them."

"In this one single solitary case," Gwen replied, "I respectfully disagree."

"Kelly Reid is also lovely," Judith said. "You told me that yourself."

"I admit I had a weak moment after her last visit, nothing more." When Judith glared at her, Evelyn conceded, "She's certainly the best of a bad lot. Which is not saying much at all."

"Never mind Evelyn," Judith said. "When the mood is on her, which is all too often, dear Evelyn could pickle a shrunken head." Judith took Gwen by the arm. "Come have a look at the exhibition we're putting together."

Gwen gently freed her arm and turned to Derek. "Did I do wrong?"

"No. It's just . . ."

She gave him a moment. When he remained silent, she told him, "When we first met, I tested you."

Evelyn asked, "Tested him how?"

"I asked Derek if it was possible to heal. I've recently lost my husband."

"We heard. Our deepest condolences."

"Thank you." Gwen remained fastened upon Derek. "I've never seen anyone struggle with honesty as you did. The desire was in your eyes to lie. No, don't shake your head. You know it's true. You wanted to offer me the assurance I so desperately sought. Free of any contingencies."

Judith asked, "What did he say?"

"If I allowed, we can most certainly heal. If we want it badly enough to accept that it will never bring us what we really want. Which is how things were. Before. Instead . . ."

Evelyn said, "You may not stop there. I won't allow it."

"Instead we will find a different future. The question then is whether we wish to enter."

They remained locked in silence, the four of them, until the elevator pinged. Kelly stepped out, saw their faces, and demanded, "What did I miss?"

"Nothing," Judith replied. "We've been too busy mapping out your gentleman's future."

"He's not . . ." Kelly looked from one to the other. "Future?"

"Derek is to become my new boss." Judith smiled at Evelyn. "Thank the good Lord above."

Evelyn sniffed. "I resent that."

Judith happily motioned Gwen and Kelly forward. "Shall we?"

The cavernous central vault was used to both prepare and break down visiting collections. Judith led them through a partially completed exhibition of nineteenth-century American art. Tape was attached to the floor, marking the dimensions of the three rooms that would house the exhibit, with more showing the location of doors and connecting hallways. Most of the paintings hung from cables connected to ceiling rafters. A few more were attached to easels. This allowed the museum to shift the artwork around until they were satisfied with each placement.

Evelyn stopped before two landscapes by Winslow Homer, painted during his 1881 visit to London. Evelyn described how the mostly self-taught artist had employed techniques developed by the French Impressionists to paint a surreal illumination of the River Thames and the Houses of Parliament. Judith stepped forward and offered more detail on the brushstrokes.

Kelly took hold of Derek's hand, drew him back a few paces, and said, "You look worried."

"I am." He found an unlikely comfort in confessing. "And scared."

Kelly kept hold of his hand. "Of what?"

"Tomorrow."

She stepped in close enough for him to catch her fragrance, a distinct mélange of perfume and an already stressful day. "We're not talking about the trip to Sicily."

"No."

"Or taking this trip with me."

"Even stronger no."

She smiled with her eyes alone. "So this is tomorrow, as in . . ."

"Everything I don't know, haven't done, can't put into words. That tomorrow."

Her hand offered a comforting warmth that was one degree off molten. Just like her gaze. "How can I help?"

Chapter 33

As they approached Derek's old office, Judith made like an usher dressed in a paint-stained cashmere cardigan, welcoming each person in turn, bowing them into the room. She then used her cuff to polish the handwritten card taped to his door, and in the process smeared the letters with a rainbow of colors.

"You've only made it worse," Evelyn observed.

"Which is why he needs a new one. Copperplate would be nice, don't you think? Permanent."

Derek stood in the doorway, watching as the four ladies seated themselves around his center table. He studied the bare walls, where Erin's collection of amateurish art no longer hung.

Gwen asked, "Coming?"

"Yes."

Derek stepped inside.

At his request, Gwen had selected one of Allen's prizes and brought it along. She was a woman comfortable with treasure, and made a delicate process of spreading the black velvet display cloth, then laying out the emerald necklace. She took her time, turning over the gemstones one by one, revealing each of the faces, lining them up carefully. The connecting golden links shone with a ruddy light. There was nothing polished or contemporary about the necklace. It spoke of realms belonging to ancient worlds.

Evelyn was the first to recover. "What is it?"

"There is no provenance," Derek said. "And I haven't had time to do proper research."

"Tell me what you think, then."

"In 324, Constantine was crowned the first Christian emperor of the Roman Empire. Two years later, he sent his mother on a pilgrimage to Palestine. She also traveled as his royal representative. In the process, she effectively extended her son's rule to the eastern provinces. His *Christian* rule." Derek tapped the necklace. "My guess is, he had this made up as a symbol of her royal authority."

The news was greeted with the silence it deserved. Finally Judith cleared her throat and asked, "There's more?"

"I have two additional items in my possession," Gwen replied. "As lovely as this, in their own way."

"Plus the painting," Kelly added.

Evelyn drew the cloth closer and used her loupe to inspect the central emerald. "Exquisite. Quite simply astonishing."

Judith asked, "You will let us display them?"

"And the artwork from my husband's collection," Gwen confirmed.

"It's *your* collection now," Kelly said.

"Only if Derek succeeds in his quest."

"*Our* quest," Kelly said.

Gwen reached across the table and snagged her hand. "You really are a dear young lady."

Evelyn slipped the loupe back into her pocket and said to Derek, "I assume there's a price attached."

"There is," Derek replied. "But only if you want to help."

"We want," Judith said. "A lot."

"For once, I happen to agree," Evelyn said. "Tell us what you need."

Chapter 34

The planning and the phone calls and the further planning held them in the Getty vaults until after six. When they finally broke up, Kelly invited them all to dinner. Evelyn and Judith begged off, claiming they could not possibly leave, they still had the exhibition to complete. Gwen was clearly exhausted and declined, saying she would check Derek back into the Maybourne where she had booked them rooms.

Which left the two of them. It seemed only natural to invite Derek back. To her place.

As Kelly pulled into the garage to her building, she wondered at what on earth she was doing. The whole thing seemed surreal. Bringing this man into her home, her private space. Sure, she had men over. But there had always been very careful boundaries set in place beforehand. This far, and no further. They came, they stayed only so long as she allowed, they left. But this, a spur of the moment invitation to dinner, and then what?

She had no idea.

Instead, she heard herself say, "I don't cook."

"I do basics, myself. Salads, smoothies, like that. I do great boiled eggs."

"Actually, that's not completely true. I cook. But it takes a day of preparation. Sometimes two. I want everything just so. I choose a recipe and follow it like directions from on high. Which means shopping for just the right ingredients, and . . ." She saw he was smiling at her. "What?"

"Please tell me we're ordering in. Because I'm hungry *now*. Plus we have things to discuss."

She opened her door. Defeated by everything she had not put in place. Boundaries. What precisely were they anyway?

He followed her through the security door, into the elevator, watched her use the electric latch to code in her floor. Derek said, "A girl can't be too careful these days."

The doors pinged open and they stepped into her foyer. Derek gave the antique sideboard a careful inspection, the colorful splash of modernist painting on the wall, the double doors leading into her home.

Silently he followed her into the open-plan kitchen. Stood there between the dining table and the central island. Made a slow circle. Shook his head.

"What is it?"

"This is like Gwen's Bentley."

"What are you talking about?"

"All this time, I've made do by not wanting things. Looking no further than trying to keep my home." He continued circling. "Everywhere

I look are reasons to change my perspective."

She should not have been so touched by his words. "You like?"

" 'Like' isn't the right word." He walked over and inspected the antique crystal decanter and art deco palaver, the first two items she had purchased after the divorce. Her declaration of home and identity. "You have truly exquisite tastes, Kelly."

Something in the quiet sincerity of his words, the way he took time to ingest each item in turn, touched her deeply. "Let me order our meal and I'll show you around. Pacific Rim okay with you?"

He waved a hand in response and moved to the painting on the wall leading to the second bedroom, that was now serving as her office. "Whose work is this?"

"A young local artist. I think she has potential."

"This is tremendous." He stepped back, almost collided with the coffee table. "Sorry."

She called her favorite local restaurant and watched his slow progress around the living room while ordering. When she set down the phone, he had scarcely made it halfway. It was the most natural thing in the world to walk over, take his hand, and lead him down the main corridor. Stop so he could admire the Venetian glass in its tiny alcove, then guide him into the bedroom with the three black-and-white photographs autographed by Cecil Beaton. Back out and down to her office where he became frozen by the three paintings decorating her office walls.

"My nieces," she explained. "Two of them. The third is just a year and a half. There's space for her as well."

They were not presented as child's art, taped to the wall, there for the moment then consigned to a drawer of memories. Instead, the three watercolors were set in oversize silver frames. Each painting was surrounded by triple pastel mattes. They were silly things, a butterfly whose left wing was almost twice that of the right. A giraffe standing atop a pink elephant. And a woman with stick arms and legs who was supposed to be her. With a smile big as the sun overhead. She added, "They make me happy."

He turned to her. Derek's gaze had deepened to where it would have been the easiest thing in the world to dive in. And just keep falling. He said quietly, "You have a very good heart."

She had never, not in her entire life, wanted anything so much as to kiss that man.

Which was when the doorbell rang.

He was the first to move. A smile suggesting he felt the same way. "After that gallery opening, dinner is on me."

She lifted a hand as he departed, a half-hearted gesture to draw him back.

Crazy.

Kelly followed him back through the living room. She stood by the front doors as he touched the security button. "Yes?"

There was a pause, then she heard her mother say, "I'm sorry. I thought I had pressed the button for Kelly Reid."

She stepped forward and pressed the electronic door latch. "Come on up, Mom."

When they stepped into the foyer, Derek said, "Maybe I should go."

She had no idea how to respond. The number of times her mother had been here could be counted on the thumbs of one hand.

The elevator doors pinged open, her mother stepped into the foyer, studied Derek momentarily, then said to her daughter, "I am greeted by yet another strange man."

Derek responded by stepping into the elevator. "See you tomorrow."

And he was gone.

Chapter 35

The elevator doors clicked shut. Kelly remained frozen to the spot. Not so much angry or hurt as turned to ice.

Giulia looked over her daughter at the open entry. "Aren't you going to invite me in?"

Kelly studied her mother. Gave her the same careful scrutiny she would a suspect painting. Looking for all the hidden reasons to cast her out. Permanently.

Giulia must have seen something in her daughter's gaze, for her normal haughty demeanor slipped, at least a trifle. "I suppose I should apologize."

"Whatever for?"

"Clearly my words did not—"

"Why now? After so many wrong moves, what makes this any different?"

"What a way to speak to your mother." She started to slip around her daughter. "We should move—"

"Stay where you are."

Her mother had always favored russet shades. Tonight's outfit was the color of autumn leaves, sweater and skirt and a necklace of amber. She crossed her arms and clicked the beads with nervous fingernails. "Who was he?"

"Not my ex. And it never will be again. That's all you really care about. Isn't it." The words only seemed to feed the ice spreading through her middle. "And another thing. I'm not Yvonne. And I never will be."

"Not once have I suggested—"

"Here's your choice, Mom. You take the time and effort to actually, finally, learn who I am. And accept that. Or get out."

Giulia responded as she always did whenever anyone dared cross her. Only tonight the regal Sicilian fury was lacking. "How *dare* you—"

"You are *this close* to losing all contact with your elder daughter." Kelly tried to find a way to describe how she sounded. How she felt. The only word that came to mind was *funereal*. "If that actually matters."

"What a thing to say. Of course it matters."

"Good. You can start by apologizing."

"I already tried to, but you—"

"Not to me." Kelly slipped the phone from her pocket and forced her trembling fingers to scroll through her contacts. Found Derek. Touched the number. Stabbed the air between them with her phone. "To him."

"Kelly . . ."

"Call him or leave and never come back."

Reluctantly she accepted the phone. "His name is Derek?"

"Doctor Gaines to you."

Her mother raised the phone to her ear and spoke words Kelly could not bring herself to hear. The ice had almost consumed her now. She found herself recalling the last time she had felt this cut off from the world, from caring for anyone or anything. The night she finally confronted her ex. Forcing herself to accept it was over. That no matter how much she loved him or forgave him or remained blind to his deeds, he would continue to hurt her and crush her every chance he had. Because of who he was.

Giulia cut the connection and handed back the phone. "Now can we please move on?"

"Okay. Fine. I'd like a mother who doesn't measure me by her own personal yardstick. I'd like support in my hardest moments. I'd like her to take my side when it means the most. I'd like to be appreciated for who I am."

"That's not what I meant and you know it."

"But it's what I meant. Doesn't that count for anything in your book?"

"That's quite a lot of bile over a few misplaced words."

"You really don't get it." She could feel the ice severing the invisible threads binding her to what once had been her family. "First of all, you're right. Of course it's not just Derek. Or even how you greeted me yesterday with your perfect daughter, her perfect child, and dinner for the man who never, not in a billion years, will enter my life again. As if anything to do with that disaster was my fault."

Her mother started to protest, and was silenced by Kelly using one of Giulia's favorite gestures, the upraised hand ramming the space between them. Halting her in mid-breath. "All this is really about how you weren't there when I needed you most. Taking my ex's side when your *daughter* was hurting *so bad*. When she *needed* you most. And all you could think of, all you wanted . . ."

The words just stopped. The ice overwhelmed her then. All Kelly could manage was to turn away. "Just leave."

"You can't throw me out. I won't permit it."

"Fine. Stay. Whatever." She shuffled through the foyer, into her empty home. "I'm going to bed."

Somehow she managed to make it down the corridor and into her bedroom. She locked the doors and stripped as she crossed the room. Fell into bed. And cried herself to sleep.

Chapter 36

Three hours before their flight was scheduled to depart, the four of them met at British Airways check-in. Brian Beschel's travel department had set it all up, the packet with their documents was there waiting for them at the first-class counter. Derek and Kelly were traveling first, Noah and Shimmel in business. They went through security together, then Derek peeled off and led Kelly to the BA first-class lounge. Once there, he settled her into an alcove where they could have as close to privacy as the airport allowed.

Kelly . . . drifted.

She was there and not there. She presented the world a bright, professional attitude. But behind the calm facade, her normal vivacious energy was absent. After the strange call he'd received from Kelly's mother the previous evening, there was no need to guess what had transpired.

Kelly's mother had apologized with all the formality of reading the words off a script. Derek had stood in front of Kelly's building, waiting for his Uber to arrive. He breathed the strange mix of city-Pacific air and listened. Kelly's mother had spoken with a wooden precision, spacing each word, telling him how she had misspoken, how her comment could all too easily have been misinterpreted. She was truly sorry for any offense taken. She wished Dr. Gaines a good night and cut the connection. Derek had not spoken a word past hello.

When their flight was called and they boarded the plane, Kelly settled into her seat, pulled out several Christie's catalogues, and worked. She smiled brightly when the steward spoke to her, ditto for Derek's conversation. But the lady clearly wanted to be alone. Soon as dinner was finished, she stretched out her seat and slept.

Ten hours later, they landed in London. A three-hour wait in yet another lounge, then they boarded the BA flight for Palermo. Kelly continued to be there but not there. They landed in brilliant Mediterranean sunlight. A pair of drivers stood outside Passport Control, took their hand luggage, and welcomed them to Sicily. Derek saw Noah and Shimmel watching her settle into the first car, clearly concerned over her semi-absent state. He waited until they loaded their equipment into the second car, then said, "Kelly's had a family crisis."

Noah asked, "So you and her, all is good?"

He realized the two men had assumed they'd fought. "We're fine. And Kelly's a pro. She'll deliver when it counts."

The two men shared a look of evident relief.

"So tomorrow, we begin."

The Hotel Villa Igiea was located on the main coastal route at the heart of Palermo, situated in a park filled with flowers and palms and a rainbow assortment of birds. The hotel lobby was palatial and gaudy in equal measure, a sort of imperial spa meets designer chic. Derek hovered while Noah used a studio credit card to sign them all in. Then he drew Kelly over to a relatively isolated niche. She complained, "I need to shower and rest."

"This won't take long."

She faced him directly, but her gaze hovered two inches above his left shoulder. "What?"

"If there's anything I can do. Any way I can help. I'm your man. Just say the word. No explanation required." He released her arm and stepped back. "All done."

She remained standing there. Mute. He slipped the room key into her limp fingers. "You're in four-ten, I'm—"

"What are you going to do now?"

"I thought I'd go for a run. Not far. Not fast. Get some decent air in my system."

"A run sounds good." She started for the elevators. "Ten minutes. I'll meet you out front."

Derek swiftly changed into running gear and returned downstairs. By the time Kelly appeared, he had checked with the concierge and mapped out a route. He stretched longer than required for Kelly's sake, then led them down the hotel's sloping drive, across the main avenue, and along the broad sidewalk fronting the ancient seawall and the Mediterranean.

They passed Mondello Beach and covered the mile and a half to Palermo's ancient port. Derek held to the steady pace, making sure Kelly breathed easy. Which only gave the pretty-boy Italian Romeos more time to check out the American lady. Her in the shimmering Lycra shorts and near-perfect lines and bobbed dark hair, tall for an Italian, shaped like a model. With the blank gaze hidden behind dark Coach shades.

There was no threat or danger feel to guys and their inspection. This was, after all, Italy. Looking was part of the masculine DNA. After a kilometer or so, he was able to discount it. If the long looks and softly spoken comments didn't bother Kelly, so what? Let 'em look.

They rounded the port, set in place by the Greeks over three thousand years earlier. As they approached the central piazza filled with the early lunch crowd, Derek decided it was time to start back. He found it easier now to discount the locals and their smirking inspection, and take in the city. The light, the air, the architecture, the villas lining the seafront, the wooden fishing boats plying the blue-blue waters. There was only one word Derek could find to describe the scene.

Intoxicating.

When they arrived back at the hotel, Kelly declared she'd had enough. The porcelain mask was still in place, but she did manage a quiet thanks, and asked about timing the next day, and wished him a pleasant afternoon. All of which Derek took as hopeful signs.

He showered and ate a room-service meal on his balcony overlooking the Med. An hour's nap, then he checked in with Noah, planned the next day's activities, and slipped a detailed note under Kelly's door. Then he went exploring.

The city was bathed in an extraordinary luminescence. Derek had read any number of artists' descriptions of the Mediterranean sunlight, how it differed from any other place on earth. But nothing could have prepared him for the sunset aura that settled upon this scarred and primeval city. He wandered, became extremely lost, stopped for a meal, got directions from the waiter for his return, got lost a second time, then followed his nose to the seafront and eventually made it back to the hotel. He entered his room, was mildly disappointed to find nothing from Kelly, and went to bed.

They spent the next two days going through the motions. The city had been invaded and destroyed any number of times. The central districts, where the wealthy had their palaces and the city its museums, had been largely demolished by the

Allies' bombardment and invasion during the Second World War.

Caravaggio's time here had been difficult, to say the least. Wanted for murder, hounded by creditors and cuckolded husbands, not to mention having stolen funds from the Knights of Malta, Caravaggio arrived in Sicily a desperate man. Palermo had been his last stop on the island, a frantic period of deep depression and terrible uncertainty. But he was commissioned to paint a grand canvas, a nativity with Saint Francis and Saint Lawrence, and he needed the money. Scarcely had he completed work when the Maltese officials tracked him down. He slipped from his lodgings in the middle of the night, fled to the port, and bribed a fisherman to take him up the coast to Naples. Eighteen months later, he was dead.

All this made Palermo the perfect place to begin.

Thanks to Evelyn's preparations and the Getty's influence, their arrival made a lot of noise. Derek and Kelly spent the next two days at the center of a municipal whirlwind. Noah and Shimmel were kept frantically busy, trailing along in their rented van, setting up on the run, shooting footage of them in meetings and official luncheons and dinners and receptions. And of course in museums and churches.

Palermo's main Caravaggio, the *Nativity*, had

been stolen from the Oratory of San Lorenzo sixty years earlier. Which Noah assured them would make a great shot, staring up at the massive empty space, the frame still there, holding nothing but stones.

Kelly greeted Derek both mornings with a bright smile and perfect makeup and a stylish suit and glittering gaze. She held that fixed expression, tight and unwavering, for two days and nights of cars and people and events. Ever the pro.

Derek had made four oversize high-resolution prints of their unfinished Caravaggio, one of the center scene and three close-ups of the figures. Noah shot hours of him positioned in front of the photographs, discussing them with supposed experts who all agreed that the artwork could very well have been painted by Caravaggio. Then the locals all pointed out how over the following decades a number of other artists began copying his structure.

The municipal authorities were the best at showing a polished sympathy. Grimacing in almost comic regret, being forced by all the unknowns to disappoint the Americans and their film crew. But without a clear provenance, what were they to do? How possibly could they help?

Over their final reception in another palatial hall, Kelly used the loud chatter to say, "They're laughing at us."

Forty or fifty people held drinks and talked at something close to full shouts. Not to mention the high ceiling and the marble walls. Derek replied, "I see them."

"They think we're wasting everybody's time."

"Good."

"They think we don't know what we're doing."

"Even better."

"How much more of this do we have to endure?"

"We're all done. Let's say our farewells and get out of here."

The entire gathering seemed to have been waiting for this very moment when they could express their deepest sympathy over how they could not assist their American guests. How they wished them a nice holiday on Sicily. How Derek and the lovely Ms. Reid must take time to enjoy the island's unique flavor, the air and the food and the scenery, before they flew back to the United States. The unspoken was clear in their voices and eyes. How they should never have bothered them with such nonsense in the first place.

Chapter 37

The municipal authorities had supplied them with a dark Lancia sedan and a driver who spoke very poor English. Once they were headed back to the hotel, Derek asked, "What do you have on for tonight?"

"I need to check in with Brian." Kelly paused, then added, "Jerome's texted me half a dozen times. I better let him know we're okay. You?"

There was something about the way she spoke his friend's name. Jerome. A hesitation, maybe even fear. But Derek decided it wasn't his place to ask. "I need to check with Noah, make sure we're set up for tomorrow's trip. And I want to let Evelyn know how things are."

"Tell her thanks from me, okay? She did a bang-up job."

"Sure thing." He studied her in the passing headlights. To anyone who did not know her, Kelly would have appeared to be doing just fine. Bright and alert and fully there, despite the day of endless meetings. "Hungry?"

"Starving. You didn't eat anything at the reception?"

"Too busy being laughed at. Want to grab a bite?"

"As long as I don't have to walk more than fifty feet." Kelly opened her door the instant the car halted in front of their hotel. "Give me twenty minutes."

They dined in the hotel's terrace restaurant. They ate linguini and fresh-caught scampi big as his hand, salty-sweet and crisp and delicious. They had a candlelit view of dusk over Mondello Beach, while the moon rose ruddy and glowing in the calm Mediterranean. Kelly remained silent through the main course, but over coffee and a complimentary grappa she finally opened up. It was a quiet tirade, the words pouring out with weary sorrow. Derek listened to her describe the mother-daughter argument that had followed his departure from her apartment, and ached for his friend.

As she finished, the waiter returned, cleared away their cups, asked if they wished for anything more. Kelly gave no sign she noticed him at all. When they were alone once more, Derek wondered if she was hoping for a response from him. Then he decided what the lady most needed just then was a silent and attentive friend. He waited.

Kelly then took a step backward in time, and told him about Jerome confronting her mother.

In an odd way, the reverse order made sense. Derek listened and understood how Jerome's words had released emotions that had been simmering since her father's funeral and confronting her ex.

She went silent a second time, long enough to watch a fishing boat cut a swath through the sparkling waters. Nets dangling from the high boom seemed ready to capture the moonlight. Then a motorist passing along the coastal route broke the spell, blasting away with its horn. This had been happening all night, of course. Derek had only been in Italy for three days, and already he knew the locals applied their horns more readily than their brakes.

Only this time was different. Because as soon as the sound ended, she told him what Jerome had said in the car. The separation and coming divorce. The growing affection Jerome held for Kelly. How completely staggered she had been. How totally shaken she had felt, hearing him make his stilted declaration. Derek could almost hear his former best friend fighting against his natural reserve, confessing how he was falling in love.

Kelly then returned to the confrontation in her mother's front room. How she had been unable to do more than observe, because of the total disconnect caused by Jerome's confession. She had merely watched in silence as he had defended her. As if she was already his to protect.

This time, when she went silent, Derek knew she was done. The story had brought them both full circle, back to this terrace restaurant perfumed by night-blooming jasmine. He spoke the only words that came to mind. "Thank you for trusting me with this."

It seemed to him that the first words he'd spoken in over an hour served as Kelly's release. She rose from her chair and started away, only to lean over and kiss his temple.

She left, and the night closed in.

Derek was the one who drifted now. Across the terrace, through the lobby, into the elevator, along the upstairs corridor, into his room, and onto the stubby balcony with its wrought-iron railing. The same night awaited him here, the same rising moon and spicy-sweet jasmine.

Only now there was a difference.

Derek was increasingly drawn to Kelly. Her closeness was a spark to every day they spent here together. But that meant what, exactly? Derek watched the sweep of headlights on the road beyond the hotel park, and had no answer. The very thought of developing feelings for her seemed disloyal. Was he ready to fully step away from Erin? Was he done with grief and his lonely life? And why was he even asking himself such questions, after Kelly had described Jerome's emotional confession?

After an hour of wrangling with himself, he admitted defeat and went to bed.

Chapter 38

Kelly was downstairs at seven thirty the next morning, refreshed and fully there. Her sleep had been untroubled, her mind was clear. Her heart . . .

One thing at a time, she told herself.

When Noah and Shimmel arrived, she resisted the urge to rush over and apologize for the poor acting job over the past forty-eight hours.

Derek stepped from the elevator five minutes later. He was dressed in another of Gwen's borrowed outfits, the finest hand-me-downs she had ever seen. The threads fit him like a second skin, this one gray and navy, knit shirt and gabardines and tasseled loafers. She enjoyed how men and women alike were drawn to the sight of him. And how he showed no interest, perhaps did not even realize the impact he was having. She wanted to tell him what it had meant, sitting there on the terrace, spilling her heart out beneath the swollen Italian moon. But he was all business this morning, and she owed it to him and the others to follow his lead.

Derek had a word with Noah as they checked out, then walked over to where she waited. He wished her a good morning, asked how she slept, complimented her outfit. As pleasant as pleasant could be. Just the same, she detected a subtle difference. An interior wall that had not been in place the previous evening. She started to ask about it, but something held her back. Instead, she merely said, "Thank you for last night."

He smiled, but it only seemed to heighten the sense of a barrier now in place between them. "I was just being a friend."

"The friend I needed most. At such a crucial hour."

"I'm glad." Then he took a step away, making space for Noah and Shimmel to join them. Ending the moment completely. He told the three of them, "Today it all begins. You understand?"

"No more receptions," Noah said. "No more filming empty people saying empty words."

"Not to mention the empty frames of paintings that aren't there," Kelly said. Wishing she could understand what was different. Why he was not connected. She tried to tell herself it was just Derek being the professional. But there was something else, a new element that had created this wedge . . .

Derek said, "All that is behind us. Now we work."

Noah smiled. "Good."

They drove to Syracuse by way of Messina, a two-and-a-half-hour detour that took them around the elbow of Sicily, over to its closest point to the mainland. Their rental was a large Fiat people-mover with lumpy seats that smelled of cigarettes and bad cheese. All Kelly's carefully packed outfits now resided at the bottom of the rear hold, underneath the video and sound equipment, the metal stands, the lighting. Derek sat up front making notes, talking them through the coming shoot, all business.

Kelly stared out the side window at a glorious vista of hills and vineyards and villages beyond time's reach. She found herself thinking back over the previous night. She had lain in bed and watched the moon through her open balcony doors. Feeling satiated at heart level from the simple gift of a listening friend.

She remembered how Derek had spoken to her upon arrival at the Palermo hotel, reaching through her jet-lag fog and the regret, touching her with the simple words that he was there for her. How last night he had done precisely that. Been totally there. Doing what she needed most. Illuminating her heart and mind by the act of silent intent. Now as she followed the trio from the hotel, she felt as though the mental cobwebs had been cleared away. Revealing . . .

As they entered Messina, she decided she had no idea. The woman in the mirror was now a mystery.

And she was perfectly okay with that.

Messina was the port city from which the Allies had launched their invasion of Italy. Remnants of the town's historic past stood amidst the confused concrete chaos of modern Italy. The central museum was a dusty Baroque relic facing a noisy central thoroughfare. An entire floor, two great halls, were given over to the artists who had grabbed hold of Caravaggio's genius and created a new way of artistically viewing the world.

They were met by just one person, Dottora Valentina Russo. She greeted them with the brusque air of a busy professional woman, inspected Derek's photographs with minute care, and ignored how Noah filmed her every movement. She was a hefty woman aged in her sixties, with a deep sultry voice from the cigarettes that stained her fingers and scented her hair. She was stylishly dressed and possessed a calm, self-confident air.

She slipped the reading glasses from her nose, folded them into a finger-size case, and slipped them into her pocket. Dr. Russo handed Derek the photographs and said, "Yes. All right. I agree."

"You think this is an unfinished Caravaggio."

"I think. Yes. But what does this matter? Without provenance, you understand?" She waved at the grand marble staircase at the foyer's other end. "Three of our masterpieces in the main halls are unsigned. For over a century the experts, they come and they go and they argue. Is this a Caravaggio, is this a student, is this one person, is it another. You understand?"

"I'm not here to argue with anyone."

She mocked them with a smile and a bow. "Then you are most welcome."

Dr. Russo stayed with them. She showed no impatience as Noah and Shimmel prepped. She drew over a guard's chair and seated herself and observed in silence. Then Noah filmed Derek introducing Kelly to the museum's two prizes, a pair of paintings done by Caravaggio at his prime.

Kelly responded on cue, hit her marks, and gave it her all. Internally, though, she felt split in two. On the one hand, she reflected the fascination they all hoped would echo the audience's interest. On the other, she observed. At some deep level, Derek had become disconnected from her. Why, she had no idea. But she was certain it was so.

The longer he talked, the more electrified Derek became. These were the prizes of his world, and this was the first time he had seen either up close. Caravaggio's *Adoration of the Shepherds* and the *Resurrection of Lazarus*, both completed in 1609, were massive portrayals that had turned the art world on its head. Derek made the paintings and their long-dead creator come alive. His description of Caravaggio's disgust for the formal Baroque settings and stylishly dressed models became living testimony to what hung on the museum walls. He related how Caravaggio walked the streets and searched the taverns, looking for faces that contained the raw and ragged emotions he wanted to depict. He told how the artist had demanded they dig up a fresh corpse to be used as the model for Lazarus. The longer he spoke, the further removed Kelly felt from the draughty museum, the people, the lights, even the mystery of why he was no longer fully there for her. Here was the true Derek fully revealed, still quiet and respectful, but electrified by his passion.

She felt bonded to him.

Finally he stepped back, took a long moment to survey the two paintings, then declared, "There was the world of art before Caravaggio, and after him the world of art as we know it today. The turning point is here on the walls before us."

When Noah cut the lights, Kelly felt a keening regret. Which was silly. Ridiculous. But returning to the here and now, surveying the dusty halls and all the other art left her feeling, well, bereft.

Noah lowered the camera back into its case and declared, "Now we are making movies."

"It was okay?"

Noah and Shimmel began stripping the lights as Noah said, "Do not use that word. *Okay* is not good enough for this. *Okay* sounds almost profane."

Dr. Russo stepped forward and asked Derek, "You stay longer in Messina?"

"We leave now for Syracuse."

"A shame. I would like my students to hear you

lecture." She offered Derek her card. "When this is complete, you will send me the final video?"

Noah said, "That is a promise."

Her smile took in them all, and the two paintings as well. "I am certain the maestro himself would have been pleased."

Chapter 39

◇◇◇◇◇◇◇◇◇◇◇◇◇◇◇◇◇◇◇◇◇◇◇◇◇◇◇◇◇◇◇◇◇

They journeyed from Messina in silence. The day's filming, the trip, the heat, all of it weighed on Derek and he assumed the others felt likewise. The air through his open window carried a bouquet of arid fragrances, lemon and sage and sorrel and dust. Derek glanced over at Kelly; she met his gaze and offered a gentle smile. He turned back to his open window, and recalled the moment he had stepped through the Getty office doorway. How he had seen it as a portal into the unknown future. Had he somehow suspected this would be part of it? That he would come to Sicily and realize he had remained blind to his growing affection for Kelly until it was too late?

He was not going to compete against Jerome. That required no thought whatsoever. Another man might see it as a contest for her affection. The idea was repulsive, as far as he was concerned. Kelly was her own person. She had to decide. Plus there was his and Jerome's history. All the bad moves that had cost Derek his longest friendship. There was a bitter rightness to this situation, having a second chance to do the proper thing. And let her go.

Even though it hurt. Even though it rendered him hollow. And sad.

The highway followed a ridgeline bounded on one side by the sparkling Mediterranean. The other side was a wide valley carpeted by blooming fruit trees. The fragrance was strong enough to compete with the sunlight. Then the road turned inland, traversed a broad headland, and there it was.

The walled city of Syracuse stretched out before them, a timeless golden spell cast over the island's northwestern point. The Med surrounded the city on three sides, framing it in shimmering blue. The sun was ten degrees or so off the western horizon, strong as a torch.

Shimmel spoke for the first time since their departure from Messina. "The fairy tales of my childhood live again."

A lay-by appeared on their left. Noah swung in, parked, and opened the rear portal to pull out his camera. The videographer said, "You and Kelly, there by the railing. No, closer together. Good." He checked them in the viewfinder. "Now take two steps to your left. No, no, your other left. Look out over the city. Derek, stop squinting please. Kelly, off with the sunglasses."

She was close enough for him to catch hints of her perfume, tossed with her hair into his face.

"Kelly, look his way, good. Hold that."

She said softly, "Is everything okay?"

He breathed her flavor, the closeness of her. "Everything is fine."

"You seem, I don't know, distant."

"The key portion of our trip begins now. Syracuse marks the major step."

"That's all it is?" She searched his face. "Just work?"

He offered the smile she needed to see. "Of course."

"Have dinner with me tonight."

Which of course only made the internal turmoil worse. He heard himself say, "Thank you. I accept."

There were any number of cities that looked great from the air, or viewed through the lens of memories, or from a thousand miles away. Syracuse was something else entirely, at least for Kelly. The closer they came, the more brilliant the city shone, bathed both in the Mediterranean sunset and its incredible history.

Brian's team had booked them into the Ortea Palace, a Baroque jewel dating back to the time of Caravaggio. Kelly's room overlooked the strait separating Sicily from the tiny island that contained Syracuse's old town. Fishing vessels and tourist boats plied the still waters, making sunset rainbows in their passage. She showered and dressed in a somewhat wrinkled but otherwise fresh outfit, gold slacks of rough silk, a matching off-the-shoulder sweater. She took the stairs and arrived in the palatial lobby to find Derek seated by the front windows. He was dressed in another of Gwen's Rodeo Drive hand-me-downs, and drew glances from women of all ages. She started to approach, then stopped where a pillar partly hid her from view.

The man looked resigned. Or angry. Or . . . What? All she could say for certain was, he did not look happy to be where he was.

She recalled the very first moment they had shared in the Getty forecourt. How certain she had been of the right move, the words that needed saying. And now? Kelly had no idea.

Derek spotted her, rose to his feet, and offered, "You look lovely."

"I was just thinking the same about you." She searched for the right words, and could only come up with, "What were you thinking about just now?"

He nodded, as though she had indeed been right to ask. "Erin."

She gave that the moment it deserved, then offered her elbow. "Shall we?"

They left the hotel and walked through the heart of Ortigia Island and its pristine collection of churches, piazzas, and palaces. The architectural jewels on display had survived earthquakes and invasions and the Black Death, creating a honey-colored parade through nineteen centuries.

They stopped at one of the restaurants whose tables extended into the square's cobblestone heart. The waiter spoke no English, but offered

them two plastic-coated menus in multiple lan-
guages. He and the manager both greeted them
in a mangled combination of German and French
and Dutch, urging them to trust them and their
choices, flirting outrageously with Kelly in the
process. Even Derek smiled at their theatrics.

Their first course was palm-sized ravioli filled
with stewed veal, accompanied by a crisp Sicilian
white wine that Kelly thought tasted of the lemon
blossoms that had perfumed the day's journey.
Kelly told him about the meeting with Jerome
and the investigator. She drew up the attorney's
photo on her phone, passed it over. Derek studied
it intently, but showed no real concern. She
told him, "I should have mentioned this before,
I know. I had a dozen chances I didn't take.
Starting with the LA airport."

"You were otherwise occupied."

"You don't look worried."

He leaned back and allowed the waiter to
remove his empty plate. "Every time I've worked
on provenance for treasure dogs, there's been
issues like this. None of these finds are totally
clean. Divers are accused of working inside
territorial waters. A supposed former owner
shows up, declaring in court his or her rights
to the sale. A museum becomes involved. Or a
country. We're talking about art and treasures
that have been missing for centuries. It's a messy
business. Which is why they bring in somebody

like me. To keep a safe distance, clear away the detritus, and bring the item to market safely."

She liked how the spark was back in his gray gaze. How he was totally engaged with her. The two of them in the timeless square, enjoying each other's company. Totally together. "There's the matter of Gwen's dead son."

He shrugged. "We focus on our one job here. We're hoping to establish provenance. Nothing more. Which brings us to the matter at hand. You need to do the talk tomorrow."

"Derek—"

"No arguments, Kelly. You need to be front and center."

She was tempted to tell him just how handsome he looked, his features cast in the candle's golden glow. "Okay."

He was caught off-guard by her acquiescence. "I was expecting battle."

"I know."

"Hours of me insisting you'll do fine. Telling you how the world needs to see you as the expert you are."

"I did my undergraduate honors thesis on Syracuse."

"Why am I only hearing this now?"

"Because I knew if I told you, you'd insist on me doing tomorrow's talk."

"And you were right." He sipped his wine. "Why Syracuse?"

"My mother's father comes from a village about twenty miles from here. He died when I was six. I was brokenhearted." She looked across the square, watching the scene. A trio of strolling musicians sang Italian classics at the next restaurant, adding a musical backdrop to the theater. "He had this great snow-white moustache I loved to tug. And hands like concrete. He worked as a bricklayer when he first arrived in America. He was fourteen years old. When he retired, he was managing construction sites for one of Phoenix's biggest home builders."

"What is the village's name?"

"Sortino." She stopped talking when the waiter returned and deposited their main courses, fire-grilled Mediterranean snapper. Kelly did not speak again until their plates were empty. Then, "Where was I?"

"Your late grandfather."

"He almost never spoke about his beginnings. But I remember this one time, the adults were all sitting around the table late at night, a forest of empty wine bottles, a lot of laughter, I was curled up in the corner, they had all forgotten I was there. My grandfather called Sortino a village of tears. How he was lucky to have escaped. How he had tried to bring over his only brother and his parents. But they were infected by the Sicilian disease. That was how he described it. The island's affliction. They loved their land as much as they hated it. They were bound to the place, no matter how much it cost them, no matter how great the pain."

The manager returned then, offering Kelly a chance to step back from the memories. He accepted their compliments, then gestured the waiter forward, who carried a bottle of grappa and two slender glasses. The manager ignored their protests, poured double portions, and left them to the night.

When they were finished, Derek paid the bill and shook hands with both the waiter and manager while other patrons watched and smiled. Kelly could see how the customers thought they were a couple, enjoying a romantic getaway in the heart of a lovely Sicilian night. As he walked around to hold her chair, an old woman dressed all in black approached. She took a long-stem rose from the bundle she carried and offered it to Derek. His smile tightened, but he managed to hold on to it as he gave the woman a note, accepted the rose, and handed it to Kelly. His gesture was almost solemn. She thanked him with a voice she did not recognize.

As they started across the piazza, she discovered her vision was somewhat tilted. "Wow."

"What's the matter?"

"Your arm, good sir." Once she had a firm hold, she said, "Grappa on top of the wine has hit me like a hammer." She felt him try to draw away, but only drew closer still. Insisting on it. A very feminine demand.

They crossed the piazza like that, arm in arm, close enough to walk in tandem. As they entered the broad cobblestone avenue, Kelly found herself thinking about Jerome. Wondering what to do. Finding an odd sense of clarity in the heady mix of a strong man's support and the lovely Sicilian night. She heard herself say, "I just don't get it."

"What's that?"

"I'll have you know, I'm a very well-educated woman. And I'm smart."

"No argument there."

"I've read the poets and the philosophers. I know how they say, seize the day. I've heard the line, read the book, seen the play." Kelly sensed him gradually relax. Releasing himself into her closeness. "What if I don't know? The poets never talk about that. Nobody bothers to talk about that awful moment when the hardest thing in the world is just to know what to do."

They turned onto the grand avenue linking Ortigia to the mainland. "What's up with you tonight?"

"That is an *excellent* question." She heard herself slur the words and didn't care. "That is *exactly* the point I'm trying to make."

"Maybe the grappa wasn't such a good idea."

"What on earth am I supposed to do? How am

I supposed to handle this *ridiculous* situation, where *nothing* makes sense and *every* choice seems wrong?"

"I hope you're not looking at me for an answer. Watch out for the step there."

"I see the step. I see *exactly* where I'm supposed to be walking. And that's *not* what we're talking about."

"It's not?"

"No." She reared back a notch, but found it difficult to bring him into sharp focus. "Are you laughing at me?"

"Maybe just a little."

"I come to you with a perfectly good question and you laugh at me. Isn't that just perfect." She let him greet the hotel attendant for both of them. "Maybe we should go upstairs and call my mother. The two of you can laugh at me together."

He steered her toward the elevator. "Maybe we should get you to bed. You've got to be on tomorrow. And sober."

She loved how it felt, leaning on his strength more than she really needed. Him being rock solid for the two of them. The elevator pinged open, they stepped inside, then she said, "Tell me what to do, Derek."

"About what, exactly?"

"My head is full of conflicting thoughts." She pulled at her hair with the hand not wrapped around his arm. "It's like this *noise* only I can hear. And it just keeps getting louder."

He was watching her now in the mirrored doors. "Sometimes you just have to go with what seems right."

"If only it were that easy." Even so, it felt good, hearing him speak the words.

"You have to try. Take the risk."

"Even if it's a wrong move? Even if it ruins my life?"

The doors opened and he steered her down the corridor. When they stopped in front of her door, he said, "The first time we met, you talked about the terrible experience you'd had with your former husband."

She fumbled in her pocket and came out with her key. "You may refer to him as the louse."

He took the key from her and opened the door. "Did the louse ruin your life?"

"Sort of."

"No, Kelly. He didn't. Handling that crisis has made you who you are today."

"And who is that?" She refused to let go of his arm. "Scared, afraid to make a decision that can't wait, uncertain what's right, blind to my own future."

"Beautiful," he replied. "Smart. Totally engaged. Making it in a challenging world. Successful."

She desperately wanted to kiss him. The urge was so strong, she had no choice but release her hold and step inside. Putting distance between them was wrenching. A deep breath, then, "Thank you for a lovely evening."

He stood there, solemn and somber, his gaze a thousand miles deep. "I meant what I said, Kelly. I'm there for you."

Chapter 40

Half past five the next morning, Derek gave up on sleep and went for a dawn run. The grappa's sour aftertaste stayed with him for the first couple of miles, but eventually his legs found their strength and his lungs cleared and he moved easy. He made a tour of Ortigia Island, along the harbor walk and through the central piazza, then down the outer seawall's promenade with the sun's upper lip melting the Mediterranean.

He ordered a room-service breakfast, showered and dressed, and was downstairs twenty minutes before their departure time. Noah and Shimmel were already in the lobby's corner, packs of equipment by their feet. As Derek started over, he spotted the spotter.

At least, he was fairly certain the man seated close to the entry and supposedly reading the newspaper was the attorney Kelly had mentioned. Derek took a seat with his back to the side wall, which forced Noah and Shimmel to turn away from the lobby. He said, "We may have a problem."

When Kelly arrived seven minutes later, Noah and Shimmel both remained locked on Derek. Neither man had turned around or made any other move that might suggest to a watcher they knew who the man was, or were the least bit interested.

Kelly arrived wearing sunglasses and a tight expression. "He's here. The man I told you about."

Derek pointed to the seat opposite him. Lining her up so the man could not observe her face. "Sit there."

She lowered herself down. Took a breath. Said, "I think I've seen him before. When I spotted him just now it popped into my head, I'm pretty sure he was at that last Palermo reception."

Shimmel asked, "Do we quit?"

"Who said anything about quitting?" Noah pretended to fiddle with a camera lens. "We're here to do a job."

"My babies need a daddy."

"We do the job," Noah insisted. "No quitting allowed."

Derek waited until he was certain neither man had anything more to say. "If this is our guy—"

"It's him," Kelly said. "I'm sure."

"So in a couple of minutes he'll probably stroll our way, introduce himself, offer to be our best friend."

"The investigator said I should call."

"No calling," Derek said. "Noah's right. We do our job. We shoot everything we need from Syracuse . . ."

Kelly said, "What?"

Derek said, "Here he comes."

"Tell me what you were going to say."

"Follow my lead," Derek said. "We hide in plain sight."

The man who approached them wore a suit that probably cost upward of five thousand dollars and fit him like a beige glove. Cotton was the coolest natural material, but it wrinkled at the first hint of perspiration. To look this good all day, in Sicilian heat, the man had to be wearing wool. Woven so tight and fine it weighed next to nothing and breathed as well as cotton. White collared dress shirt, gold cufflinks with what appeared to be star sapphires at their heart, thin gold watch. Swept-back silver hair, tanned complexion, the features of a self-satisfied predator. He had just eaten, but given a reason, he would gladly feast upon them. "Dr. Gaines?"

Derek rose to his feet. "Can I help you?"

"Ah, good sir, it is I who shall hopefully have that honor." He beamed at Kelly. "And the lovely Ms. Reid. I see now why all of Palermo are still speaking of you."

"Sorry, you are . . ."

"Forgive me." He offered his hand. "Antonio Orsini at your service."

"You're with the museum?"

"Hardly. I am merely an attorney and member of the city council."

Derek pretended to study the man intently. "You're really here to help us?"

"Anything within my power to offer, Dr. Gaines, you need merely ask."

Derek turned to Noah. "This could be our lucky day."

Noah and Shimmel stood together. Noah's swallow was audible. "Okay."

Derek said, "Today and tomorrow we shoot our Syracuse segment. We leave for LA in three days. We really need to do a first-rate job here. Syracuse could well be the highlight of our visit."

Orsini beamed at one and all. "I most certainly hope so."

He indicated a wide-eyed Kelly. "Ms. Reid needs someone to talk to. The audience is going to be very tired of just seeing me as her counterpart. It would be so much more interesting . . ."

Kelly sprang to her feet. "Derek, no."

"She's never been in front of the camera before," Derek said.

Noah said, "This could be great."

Kelly said, "Derek . . ."

"What?"

"I thought, you know, it would be you and me."

"Look at this gentleman," Derek said. "He's perfect."

"I have been called many things in my day," Orsini said. "Perfect, well, that is a first."

Noah asked, "You'll do this?"

"What, precisely, is it you wish?"

"Walk with her," Derek said. "Listen."

"Be her sounding board," Noah said.

Derek could actually see the man's mind working. "You are asking me, a Sicilian male, to walk alongside a beautiful American lady and not speak?"

Shimmel offered, "I can still wire you up."

"Speak away," Noah said. "We can always cut you out."

Orsini shook his head. "No, no, this thing, I cannot do it."

Derek did his best to show disappointment. "It would add a new dimension—"

"An Italian *avoccato*, he survives by going unnoticed." The man's accent was stronger now. "This is especially true in Sicily."

"Our show is not going to be aired here. Just in the US."

"Who can say what may happen in the future? Regretfully I must decline."

Derek could not care one way or the other, but he liked how the man's refusal calmed Kelly's nerves. "Will you at least come with us? Hear what we have to say. Make sure we're representing your city in the proper light."

"I will not be on the camera?"

"Not unless you change your mind. Noah?"

"We won't include you in a shot. My word on it."

"This I most certainly can do." He made a formality of offering Kelly his arm. "Shall we proceed?"

Chapter 41

As they entered the lane leading from the hotel to the piazza, Orsini received a phone call and stepped away. Kelly took that as her chance to hiss, "Did you not hear a thing I said?"

"I heard everything."

"That man is dangerous!"

"Calm down and listen for a second. He wants to observe. Let him observe."

"Friends close, enemies behind the camera," Shimmel said. "Smart."

Kelly looked from one to the other. "Why do I have the feeling you're ganging up on me?"

"He is here for a reason," Derek said. "We're here for a *different* reason."

"The provenance," Noah said. "One painting."

"No treasure," Shimmel said. "Very smart indeed."

Kelly bit her lip. "I don't like it."

"Your job is to be beautiful and smart and passionate and shine for the camera," Derek said. He asked Noah, "Do you have a reflector he can hold?"

"No," Kelly said.

"Yes," Shimmel said. "Smarter still."

"He'll watch and he'll hear and he'll get bored and he'll leave," Derek said.

"A Sicilian getting bored watching this lady?" Noah grinned as he opened his backpack. The reflector snapped open like a blooming flower. "Doubtful."

"Now you are all laughing at me."

"Just a little," Shimmel said. "Sound check."

"I hate you and I'm scared."

"Sound is good."

Derek stepped directly in front of her. Loving the fire in those dark eyes. Loving her. "It's just you and me now."

Wishing it was so.

Derek could see Noah and Shimmel both shared his worries over how Kelly would perform. It was, after all, her first foray in front of the camera, at least with them. Plus they were starting the day's shoot in full public display. Noah wanted her to walk across the piazza, in the full view of literally hundreds of locals and tourists alike. Pretending it was just her and Derek.

Not to mention the man walking backward directly in front of her face. Holding a reflector.

Three paces in, even before Kelly spoke her first word, Noah stopped and declared, "This won't work."

Orsini was being hailed by passersby, and greeted others as he moved. Making a joke of his backward progress. Playing the well-dressed clown.

Each movement scattered ribbons of reflected light over Kelly's face.

Derek could see she was growing increasingly tense. Her smile had taken on a rictus quality. He approached the lawyer, waited until he had shaken yet another pedestrian's hand, and said, "Thanks, but we need to make different arrangements."

"Forgive me, it is hard for me to ignore my friends, you understand?"

"Sure thing. Even so, we can't work like this." To Noah, "Can you do without a reflector?"

"Kelly will need to angle her walk a little more, keep the sun from splitting her face into light and shadow."

"Chiaroscuro," Shimmel said. "Cute."

Derek told the lawyer, "We need a cone of silence around her while she talks. Shimmel, how far?"

"Twelve feet should do, fifteen is better."

"Of course you're still most welcome to attend us."

"Attend you." Orsini was clearly irritated, an important man used to being able to dictate all terms.

"We're here to do a job, and Kelly needs to be surrounded by silence." Derek pretended not to see the man's ire and pointed to a spot on the cobblestones. "Step back there, chat with all the people you like."

"You are telling a member of the council where he can and cannot stand? In his own city?"

Derek stepped in closer. Showing the man a blade of his own. "We're here to work. We are establishing a provenance for a painting and shooting a vital scene. You offered to help. Was that the truth?"

"The truth, the truth, what is the truth of your visit?"

"I don't understand your question."

"Where is this painting? What can you possibly find here that was not present in Palermo?"

Derek liked how the real man was revealed. The man of power who despised being challenged. "You really want to know?"

"Why do you think I am standing here?"

"I have no idea. You said it was to help."

"Tell *me* the truth. I will help. Or not."

"Again, I don't understand the question."

"There is no provenance. I suspect there is in fact no painting. You are here for another reason, no? A *secret* reason."

"You're the one with secrets. You're not here to help at all. You want to— What is it you want?"

"I want you gone. Out of Syracuse. Away from Sicily. You and your secrets."

"Provenance," Derek said. He pointed to the church. "We think the answer lies in there. All our work in Palermo? It was so we didn't have to deal with people who make promises and

270

don't deliver. You want to find out our secret? Stand over there, stay silent, listen carefully, and everything will be revealed the instant we enter your cathedral." He started away, then turned back and said, "Thank you for your help."

He walked back to where Kelly stood, eyes wide, staring at him. "Shimmel, come wire me up."

The soundman's hands trembled slightly. "Was that smart?"

"Probably not. But it felt great." Derek kept his back to Orsini. "What is he doing?"

"Taking aim, it seems to me."

"Long as I'm the target and not Kelly." He stepped away. "Let's do this thing."

Kelly was fully on.

Derek suspected it was the confrontation with Orsini, the adrenaline rush that came from proximity to danger. He felt it too. Orsini tracked them with a dark gun-barrel gaze. Now and then he spoke on his phone. The genial bonhomie he'd previously shown to everyone within reach was gone. Derek watched as passersby caught sight of Orsini's expression and veered away, as if living in Sicily taught them when to avoid this sort of man, this silent menace.

"Syracuse's Cathedral Square is one of the most beautiful in all Italy," Kelly said. Noah shot her over Derek's left shoulder, holding the camera with one hand and keeping the forefinger of his right hand held up—as in, look and talk here. Kelly went on, "The side to my right is flanked by the city's municipal buildings, a ruler-straight line following the route of a Greek thoroughfare. This road was laid down over three thousand years ago, and it still serves as the city's main artery."

Derek was not so much concerned as on full alert. He had heard his treasure dogs, the front-line hunters, describe this as the crystal moments. When life and the surrounding world became etched with a clarity that was beyond lucid. A completely different sense came into being. More than an adrenaline rush. A new and vivid means of parsing each second. Just like now. He had never experienced anything like this before. Even in the face of Orsini's silent threat, Derek knew he was hooked. In this one brief instant, he had become just another treasure dog.

"The square's left side follows the same gentle curve as the harbor wall, and is fashioned from one grand palace after another. Most of these structures were first erected over twenty centuries ago. But following a major earthquake in 1693, they were rebuilt in the style known as Italian Baroque." She continued walking as Noah panned away from her, taking in the sunlit splendor. "And up ahead is the square's crown jewel, the Church of Santa Lucia al Sepolcro. Our destination."

As she climbed the church's front steps, Noah said, "Now the both of you turn slowly, good, and smile for the camera. And cut."

They returned to the piazza's far corner and shot the approach once more. Orsini hovered on the perimeter, a walking shadow.

Derek was once again in the company of a calm, alert, intelligent woman. Only now there was an additional element, one so powerful not even Orsini's sullen presence could erase it.

She was also beautiful. Alluring. Magnetic.

Of course Derek had seen this before now. But now there was a difference.

And no matter how often he insisted he wasn't ready. No matter how much he missed what he and Erin had once enjoyed. No matter how conflicted all this left him. Honesty demanded he face the truth.

It would be all too easy to fall for this amazing lady.

Chapter 42

But as they started to enter the church, Kelly said, "Wait. I want to try something." She looked at Derek, uncertain. "Is that okay?"

"This is your day," he replied. "Your show. Try whatever you want. Right, Noah?"

They both did their best to ignore Orsini, who had climbed the stairs beside them and now stood with one hand on the church's door handle, glowering back at them. Noah said, "What we have so far, it is golden."

Orsini snorted.

Kelly glanced at the attorney, and Derek knew a momentary fear that Orsini had wrecked the mood. But Kelly turned back and said, "I'm going to start down at the bottom of the stairs."

Noah asked, "Where do you want us?"

"Derek, with me, please. Noah, you're fine up there."

This time, as they reclimbed the broad stone steps, Kelly said, "What we have is living evidence to the pair of events that have shaped modern Italy. The church's exterior is testimony to the Baroque era, the final chapter before Sicily entered a truly disastrous century."

She stopped as the church doors opened. A bizarre man stepped into the sunlight, a brutish figure in white priestly robes. He was massively built, at least as tall as Derek and a hundred pounds heavier. The face of a bruiser, heavy features and thick lips and a nose that seemed to have been broken and rebuilt several times.

All this framing the eyes of a child. Wide and dark and filled with secret delight.

The priest seemed to find great joy in everything he saw, including Orsini. He growled a hello and then swallowed the attorney's hand in a grip as large as the rest of him. The priest then stepped to Orsini's other side and said, "I am Father Lauro. Please to continue."

Derek noticed how the priest's appearance had unsettled Orsini even further. Kelly asked, "Where was I?"

"A terrible century," Derek said.

"Maybe you should start over," Noah said.

She returned to the cobblestones, waited for Derek to join her, received the signal from Noah, and began again. The repeat actually seemed to have helped. She moved more slowly, timing her steps to the points she was making. "Five hundred years ago, Sicily was one of the wealthiest provinces of all Europe. The problem then was the same as the problem now. Almost none of these riches touched the common people. They were governed by foreigners who treated locals as little more than slaves." Kelly climbed another step. "The Spanish viceroys and their inquisitors were replaced by the Holy Roman Emperor, who parceled out the island to nobility from northern Italy, France, even a pair of German counts. These rulers served as official parasites, and sucked the island dry."

Another step, then, "Added to this were invasions by the Barbary pirates, two terrible plagues that decimated the population, a crippling drought, and a series of taxations known as the *donavito*. All this regularly brought Sicily to the brink of starvation."

Another step. "The century of oppression has left a permanent stain. While northern Italy thrived as independent states, this island continued to suffer under the burden of horrible rulers. As a result, the cultures of Italy became permanently divided. Northern Italians came to see themselves as citizens, people who could determine their own destiny." Kelly reached the top step and turned to face the city.

Derek asked, "And Sicilians?"

"Still today, many locals see themselves as nothing more than neglected subjects. The majority of Sicilians look to the welfare state, or a sponsor, or a *padrone*, to meet their needs."

She reached for the door, and Noah said, "And cut."

Noah and Shimmel moved inside. After a moment's hesitation, Orsini and the priest followed. They were to give the team a couple of minutes to set up, then Kelly was to enter, continuing her talk as she did so. But once they were alone, the tight fear reentered that lovely dark gaze. "What do we do about the lawyer?"

Derek was ready because he had been expecting the question. "He's not here. You understand? This is just us now. You and me and Noah and Shimmel."

"He's not going away."

"He is also not the issue."

"Not right at this moment."

"Exactly."

"My job is to talk."

"And you're doing great, by the way."

"I like doing it."

"And it shows. Ready?"

She watched him reach for the door. "When I started up the steps did you feel a sort of, I don't know, electricity between us?"

Derek found himself frozen on the top step, the sunlight piercing and fresh, the air filled with the scent of lemon trees and the Mediterranean. "Here we go."

He opened the door, stepped inside, and watched her become silhouetted by the sunlight, as if her presence had become so powerful it could draw the light in with her. He heard her say, "Inside, the cathedral's Baroque exterior gives way to a very different chapter of Sicilian

277

history. This structure started life as a Greek temple, erected in the fifth century BC and dedicated to the goddess Athena. Archeologists believe it was one of the grandest structures of its time, testimony to the city's importance and wealth."

Noah pointed them down the left-hand aisle, between a line of massive pillars and the exterior wall carved with man-size niches for an array of sculptures. Orsini and the priest were seated a third of the way down, just far enough along the pew to keep them out of the camera's reach. Orsini continued to smolder, his gaze tight. By contrast, the priest showed genuine delight at what he was hearing, smiling and nodding with his entire upper body. Kelly matched her pace to Noah, heading toward the front, and continued, "In the sixth century AD, after this structure had seen a thousand years of use as a Greek temple, Christian conquerors rebuilt the nave and turned this into the city's cathedral. But our story does not end there. Three centuries later, Sicily was seized by Muslim warriors invading from North Africa. These new rulers turned it into a mosque."

Noah rounded the front pew and guided Kelly over to where she stood looking back down the cathedral's central aisle. "When the Muslims were defeated by Norman knights four hundred years later, it once again became a cathedral. The Normans ruled until the Spaniards were deeded the island, and that binds our two stories together." She stopped where Noah pointed and went on. "Three different religions have claimed this very building over three thousand years. That is the story of this island's heart."

The priest started clapping, startling them all. "*Brava! Magnifico!*"

Noah lowered his camera, grinned, and said, "I look forward to watching Brian do backflips."

Derek took over then, a segue so smooth Noah scarcely had time to reposition himself. Kelly slipped over to the side pillar, from which she observed as Orsini and the priest shifted to the front row. The attorney continued to scald everyone with his heat. Father Lauro, however, remained utterly unaffected. He stretched out his legs, crossed his hands over his ample belly, and smiled in benevolent approval as Derek introduced the painting that dominated the cathedral's nave.

"Caravaggio's *Burial of Saint Lucy* depicted the Syracuse mourners who raised her body from where she had been murdered—in the square outside the church. There were multiple variations on the basic story," Derek explained, "but on a few things all agreed—around the year 297 AD, a young woman dedicated her life to God. When she refused to recant her faith at the demand of her pagan suitor, he consigned her to a brothel. When she refused this as well, he knifed her in the throat and left her to bleed out on the temple steps.

"Added to this were eighteen centuries of legends. Such as, her prayers healed her mother and various others afflicted by blindness. Which was how she became the patron saint of the vision impaired, as well as electricians, candlemakers, eye doctors, and many others. The day of her martyrdom was still celebrated as far away as Finland."

Derek then described the painter's technique, comparing it to the Lazarus oil they had viewed in Messina. He spent a few moments describing what he called the "incredible emptiness" that dominated the painting's upper half.

Three and a half minutes, start to finish.

Noah lowered his camera a notch. "Are we done here?"

"Do you need another take?"

"Not from where I stand." Noah glanced at his soundman, who shook his head. "I think we're good."

"Okay, mark this as a new transition." He turned to the priest. "Father . . ."

"Lauro."

"Could you join us, please?"

"But of course." He lumbered to his feet. "I must say, the two of you make my heart soar. The history of my beloved land, the tragedy and the beauty, all is alive for me. And, I think, for many others." He smiled back at Orsini. *"Non e vero, avvocato?"*

When the lawyer did not move, Derek said, "You want to see this, Signor Orsini. You really do."

Still the lawyer remained stationary. Father Lauro smiled and motioned him forward, speaking in a rapid dialect Kelly could not follow. Nor did she need to.

Reluctantly Orsini rose and started forward. "You do not take my photo."

"Noah, shift around so he's out of the frame. Father, can we please put a mike on you?" He waited while Shimmel hooked him up. "Okay, are we ready?"

"Rolling."

Derek reached into Noah's larger pack and extracted a manila envelope. "Father, did the Getty tell you why we are here?"

"Something about a painting. You think by Caravaggio. But you are not sure."

"Right. We're after provenance."

Lauro watched him lay out the photographs. "I am sorry. But the technical aspects of art, I know nothing about this."

"That's not where we need your help. We can point to any number of aspects about these faces, their positioning, the lighting, the shadows, all say this is the work of Caravaggio."

Father Lauro ignored Orsini's snort of derision. "This the Getty director told me as well."

"Right. But there is one other element. The reason we came to Syracuse." Derek met Orsini's gaze. Heat for heat. "The only reason."

He set down the next photo.

Despite himself, Orsini leaned in close. "What is this?"

"This shows the entire painting. All the canvas you see surrounding the finished portion shows sketch marks done in charcoal. We're testing for date—"

Orsini almost shouted, "You did not show this in Palermo!"

"There was no need." Derek was watching the priest, who had leaned in so close his nose almost touched the photo.

Father Lauro murmured, "Can this be?"

"You see it, don't you."

"This window . . ."

"Exactly." Derek set down the final photo. "Here it is in close-up. Noah . . ."

"Step back just a moment, please. All right, that's enough."

Orsini's expression was thunderous. "You dare hide this evidence?"

"No. I show it when the time is right." Derek moved in tight. "I'm not the one hiding secrets, now, am I."

Orsini's face flamed. "You, sir, are a scandal!

We know how to deal with the scandalous!" He stormed down the central aisle. "You wait! I show you! I show you all!"

Father Lauro waited until the door thundered shut. "A man who spends all his days spinning lies can come to hate the truth."

"We don't have much time," Derek said.

"No. On that I agree."

"Can you help us?"

Father Lauro's smile transformed his brutish features into something almost saintly. "More than that, dear sir. I can solve the mystery that brought you here."

They left the church by way of a priest's door set in a narrow alcove beside the nave. The corridor was paved in ancient flagstones, cracked and rippled by centuries of sandals and shoes. Down a set of stairs, another, curving now as they descended farther and farther, finally entering a broad passage of hand-chiseled stone. Alcoves tight as library shelves were fit into both walls. Kelly realized she was walking through the cathedral's ossuary, but the only bones she saw were skulls carved into pillars flanking the shelves. Illumination came from bare bulbs strung from cables nailed into the domed ceiling.

The passage narrowed, then ended at a door peaked like the roof overhead. Father Lauro used an oversized key and led them up stone steps that swayed in the middle. Another door, another key, and they stepped through a narrow door hidden behind a boot rack.

They stood in the foyer of what was once probably a grand estate, perhaps even a palace. But there was little to show of its former grandeur. The marble floor and bare walls were seamed with cracks deep as old veins, filled with graying plaster meant to hold the place together. A cheap brass chandelier dangled from the high ceiling. Double doors leading to the main lobby were missing.

Father Lauro led them up a grand central staircase, along an open-sided gallery, and then paused by a closed door. "This is the private chapel for priests serving the cathedral. Wait here, please." He knocked and entered.

Only when Kelly turned around did she realize Noah had been filming the whole time.

He lowered the camera and said to Derek, "There are only two reasons I can think why he would bring us here by way of that tunnel."

Derek continued to watch the door.

"Either he was showing off, or he was hiding where he took us."

"Hiding means danger," Shimmel said. "I am not one who likes danger. When it comes to danger, I am the world's biggest coward."

"Maybe it wasn't such a great idea to bait the Sicilian bear," Noah said.

Father Lauro stepped back through the door as Derek replied, "The lawyer was our enemy from day one. Nothing's changed."

"After what you said, he has a reason to be angry, to take revenge," Noah said. "Everything is out in the open." When Derek did not reply, Noah pressed. "You *challenged* him."

Derek's only response was to hold the priest with his gaze. Kelly studied the two of them. They seemed locked in a silent dialogue. Then Father Lauro stepped farther into the hall. Closed the door. Crossed his arms. And waited.

Derek took that as his cue. "Treasure dogs operate by what they call a double-blind system."

Lauro said, "This word, 'dog.' I do not understand."

"Treasure hunters," Derek replied. "They sniff out clues. They stay close to the ground. They move fast."

Lauro nodded. "And double blind?"

"There are always people like Orsini. Maybe it's a government agency. Curator of a museum. Thieves waiting to see what the hunters dig up. Or other hunters after the same find. Or their agents."

"Or Mafiosi," Lauro said.

Noah muttered something. Shimmel might have moaned.

Lauro's gaze shifted over, then back. "Do you know, as recent as the late seventies, local authorities insisted there was no such thing as Mafia in Sicily. It was too dangerous to even speak the word. They were the shadow. The dark threat no one spoke of."

Shimmel said, "I am ready to go now."

"Soon," Derek replied.

"Truly, we leave?"

"We do this, we are done," Derek said. "We leave today."

Noah said, "We are booked to stay here for another two and a half days."

"That's right. We are."

Shimmel's accent had perceptibly thickened. "I am breathing again. Breath is good."

"You were speaking," Lauro said, "of double blinds."

"The enemy is there and they are watching. So you give them something to watch, make them think they have discovered what you're after."

"The unfinished painting." Lauro nodded. "Provenance."

Kelly said, "Why did this make Orsini so angry?"

"People like Orsini deal in secrets," Derek said. "They want to be the first to know. It gives them leverage, power, and sometimes profits. We refused to dance to his tune. We showed the father here, and let Orsini watch. We put him outside the circle. And even worse, we insisted we were after nothing else. On camera. In public.

Denying him the chance to use us and find a bigger prize. Of course he was angry."

Lauro asked, "You have been to Sicily before?"

"First time," Derek replied.

The priest nodded slowly. "And this secret hunt?" When Derek remained silent, watching, Lauro continued, "The unspoken, the second thing you hide behind this double blind? What is it, exactly?"

"If you have to ask," Derek replied, "it doesn't exist. There is no unspoken. No mystery."

"Of course," Lauro said. His voice had dropped to a near whisper. "Of course."

"We need someone to fly us to Rome," Derek said. "A private plane, a pilot we can trust. Total secrecy. You, us, the pilot. No one else should know. Can you help?"

"You can pay cash?"

"Noah?"

"I'm wearing a money belt. Just for this very moment."

Lauro said, "One phone call, it is done."

"Everyone have their passport?" When they confirmed, Derek turned back to Lauro. "We can leave now? Straight from here to the plane?"

"Most certainly." Father Lauro seemed to be enjoying himself immensely. "Where are you staying?"

"Ortea Palace," Noah replied.

"Perfect. It is best if I am not seen at the hotel.

They may be watching, you understand? A sister has a relative who works there. You can trust her to gather your belongings."

"Ask her not to check us out. We'll do that from Rome. Everybody, give the good father your room keys." As they did so, Derek went on. "We'll be making a major donation to the church building fund."

"Cash," Noah said.

"That is not necessary."

"Just the same, it's happening."

"I and the people of my congregation, we are indeed grateful." Lauro reached for the door. "Shall we proceed?"

"Noah?"

"One moment, let me stop my hands from shaking."

Chapter 43

The chapel was as spare as the public rooms. A few rows of mismatched chairs faced a scarred oak communion table and matching lectern. The chalice holding the sacraments was a simple stone goblet covered by a white linen napkin.

And on the wall behind the lectern was the window.

"We are speaking of a time beyond time," Lauro began. Shimmel was kneeling at the top of the central aisle, monitoring his portable sound board, while Noah shifted around, trying to fit the priest and Derek and Kelly into a shot that included the window. Kelly could see that neither technician was ready, and liked how they did their best and did not complain. Lauro went on, "Two, three, four centuries after our Lord's passage into heaven, less than one-tenth of parishioners could read and write. Symbols were used to illuminate the messages. One of these symbols was a wreath, or crown of light, used to designate a saint."

"Only this one for Lucy was different."

"*Esattamente*. Our Santa Lucia, patron saint of Syracuse, has a wreath of candles. No one knows why. After eighteen centuries, the legends are so many." He shrugged, happy with his talk, their company, the light, altogether a man who shared with the world a quietly contented glow. "And then there is this window's unique element."

"The dove," Derek said.

The window was a precise duplicate of the one in the painting. A woman's face silhouetted by a circle of candles. Above her, a white dove caught in flight, the illumination forming a cross with the bird at its center. "The dove," Father Lauro confirmed. "The two symbols together are unique to this room."

"Can you tell us anything about who lived here?"

"Legends again, and very little else. We know the family was a strong supporter of the church."

"The tunnel," Derek supplied, in sync with the priest.

"You see this in many Italian cities, where a powerful family will create a direct access to their church. They can come and go when it pleases them, in secret, even when the church is closed to others."

Derek lifted the photographs showing the portrait's figures. "We think the man has lost the woman and child shown here."

"Perhaps, yes, the painting does seem to suggest this." Lauro shrugged. "The *morte nera*, you understand?"

"Black Death."

"It struck here three times. The worst, more

than two-thirds of Syracuse perished in less than five years." Lauro gazed at the window. "We can only say two things for certain about this family. One is, they were great supporters of art. The painting you saw in the church, the Caravaggio, it was paid for by this family. We know because of records in the Vatican library."

Derek whispered the one word. *"Perfect."*

Kelly asked, "And the second thing you know?"

Father Lauro smiled. "Their name."

"And that was?"

The man's great humor surfaced once more. "Orsini."

Derek laughed out loud.

Noah said, "This is funny?"

Shimmel said, "Recording."

Noah reset the camera as Derek said, "So the man who's dogged our steps . . ."

"He has spent years seeking to regain what his family lost. This would make a lovely home for one of Sicily's most powerful attorneys, no?"

Derek returned the man's smile. "Are you sure you should be saying this on camera?"

Lauro shrugged. "Such matters are between Signor Orsini and the Vatican. Who am I, but a simple parish priest?"

"A lot more than that, is my guess."

"Ah, well. I entrust my safety to your good hands." Lauro gestured toward the door. "And now perhaps it is time that I see to *your* safety."

Chapter 44

Father Lauro settled them around a battered kitchen table. Soon after they arrived, a nun in a well-worn habit began preparing a meal. Only then did Kelly realize they had worked through lunch, it was past three in the afternoon, and she was famished. The nun set out cheese, fresh bread, olives, celery and cherry tomatoes, mozzarella with basil dressed in olive oil, salami sliced thin as paper, on and on the plates came. The only time she even glanced their way was when Kelly used her rudimentary Italian to ask if she could help. The nun responded with a smile that lit the room, at least momentarily. Otherwise Noah and Shimmel's mood darkened the chamber. Now that the shoot was complete, they were free to fret.

Shimmel said, "We're just leaving without our clothes?"

Noah replied, "The father said something about someone."

"This is very helpful, what you said. This some-one, they take our keys, they take our belongings, we get to LA and half our things are gone."

"This someone is a nun."

"A nun's sister," Shimmel corrected. "A Sicilian sister. Maybe the sister hasn't learned yet that stealing is not part of her job description."

"I am wondering the same." The two had retreated into an accented dialogue that fit their expressions. Noah fretted, "Maybe we should monitor the Italian eBay, look for our pants to show up."

"My laptop," Shimmel said. The man showed a remarkable ability to eat at full pace while talking. "The backup sound equipment."

"My second case of filters and lenses," Noah said.

"My travel stands and booms. Carbon fiber and titanium. Ten ounces, all three together. Eleven thousand dollars."

"Next week you can buy them cheaper on eBay Italy."

"Humor. Humor is good. Only not today. No more with the jokes about my lost equipment."

Derek pushed his plate to one side. "Do you have everything we've shot in Sicily?"

Noah replied, "We both carry hard drives with us everywhere."

"Standard procedure in all location shoots," Shimmel allowed.

"Plus we upload the raw data every night to the cloud," Noah said.

Derek thanked the nun as she filled his cup. "Then there's nothing to worry about."

The two men gave that a moment of sullen silence, then switched to what sounded to Kelly like Yiddish and kept moaning.

Kelly pushed her chair back, distancing herself from the three men, the nun, the scene. The moment felt trapped in Sicilian sunlight, and filled her with a heady thrill. The sensation was so intense she needed this moment to clearly define what was happening. It was far more than the growing affection she felt for Derek, the pleasure of working together on this project . . . Even the need to decide what to do about Jerome. How she genuinely felt, became a pleasant component to this amazing hour. And there was more besides. Because here in the completion of their time in Sicily, she recognized the joy found in this sort of work. Which begged the question, did she want to change jobs? For the first time, she was tempted to accept Brian's offer of an executive position.

The myriad of opportunities felt like champagne fizzing in her bloodstream. Not the choices themselves. The *freedom to choose.*

Five minutes later, Father Lauro appeared in the doorway leading into the main house. He took in the pair's worried expressions, Derek's calm, Kelly's steady gaze. He offered them all his trademark benevolent smile. The sister spoke to him in rapid-fire dialect, gesturing to the food at the table's center. Lauro responded with a few words, and the nun snorted her disdain. The priest switched to English. "Ten minutes. Perhaps fifteen. No more. Everything should be arranged." He then asked Kelly, "Can you help me a moment, please?"

She followed him into a downstairs bedroom as sparsely furnished and poorly maintained as everywhere else—single metal-frame bed, narrow mattress, cheap throw rug, desk, rickety chair. Crucifix on the wall. The bed was covered with four sets of used clothing. More clothes were piled on the desk. Lauro said, "Four men will soon be departing the *parrocchiale*."

"Not three men and a woman."

"Correct."

"The house is being watched?"

"Church, probably, house, who knows? It is best to be safe." He gestured back toward the kitchen. "You can help me size the clothes, yes?"

"Of course."

"The two technicians, where are they from?"

"Los Angeles. They're Jewish."

"They sound frightened."

"You got that right." She began the sorting process by dumping two of the outfits back on the desk. "These are too small by half."

"Americans. They grow them tall, no? I have two *accoliti*, both very tall. They don't know it yet, but they are volunteering to help."

"You're enjoying this."

Father Lauro started to reply, then he lifted his forefinger to his lips, offered a twinkling eye, and departed.

Three minutes later he returned bearing another double armload. Kelly began sorting. The clothes were simple, washed so often any hint of crease had vanished, but very clean. "These should do for Shimmel."

"The skinny one, yes?"

"Right." She selected a collarless white shirt, cloth shoes with a toe missing, dark gray slacks that would no doubt ride up his long shanks. "Derek will hate this."

Lauro plucked a pale gray vest with one button missing. "And this?"

She added it to Derek's pile. "He'll hate that even more."

Midway through choosing Noah's outfit, the day's energy just drained away. Kelly dumped the clothes from the chair to the floor, seated herself, sighed.

"Something is bothering you?"

With the morning's adrenaline rush no longer there to shield her, the problem loomed. "I have a wonderful situation."

"Those two words I seldom hear together," Lauro replied. "*Wonderful* and *situation*."

"I have to make some really important choices. Either way, I think I win. But it's not just about me and what I want. If I even knew what that is. Which I don't."

"Ah." Lauro lowered himself to the floor, settled with his back to the wall opposite the bed. "You speak of love."

"Partly. Yes. I do. One of the choices has to do with a man who is, well, interested doesn't go far enough. And . . ." She stopped. Because while she intended to speak about Brian's offer and her current work, what she actually found herself thinking about was Derek.

She realized Lauro was watching her. Smiling in a way that left her wondering if he actually knew what she was thinking. Which was impossible, of course. But still.

"Being a priest who remains true to his vows, at least until this day, I am not what you would call an expert."

"But you're a wonderful listener."

"I have heard this."

"And a good, kind man."

He rocked his head side to side. Enjoying himself. "Again, at least through this afternoon."

"I want to do the right thing. By both of these decisions." She felt an unseen weight lifting from her, just by speaking the words. "And I want to honor the people involved."

"Then you shall." This gentle man, a great brutish lump resting upon the bare-plank floor, spoke with utter certainty. "You will bring honor to yourself, your choice, your future. Simply by wishing, you help to make it so."

"But I don't know what to do."

Lauro rubbed his back against the wall, side to side, like a bear scratching an itch. "My uncle was also my godfather, two very important bonds here in my island land. He was a priest. But he was so troubled by what he saw happening in his city, his parish, his church, he fled. He broke his vows. He left his homeland. Some say he went to America. No one knows for certain. Or rather, if they know, no one has said."

The man might have been discussing the weather, his voice was so casual, so easy. Yet the dark gaze in that massive face, with the broken nose and mismatched cheekbones, was bright and tender as evening candles. "Such a disgrace this caused my family, you cannot understand this without being Sicilian."

"My grandfather was born here."

"Here, Syracuse?"

"Nearby. Sortino."

"Well, well. Perhaps after all you do understand." Something new appeared in his gaze, a piercing quality, a decision, something. "All through my childhood, I hear of this disgrace. The wound he caused my family. The shadow that lay over us all. And through this time, I myself had two great loves, two *passioni*. I boxed. And I was good. At sixteen I won the all-Europe heavyweight title for my age. There was talk of my representing Italy at the next Olympics."

His smile grew impish. "Unfortunately, there was also the other thing."

"The church."

"I could not have both, of course. And the more I fought, the harder I struggled in the ring, the clearer it became that I was actually . . ."

"Fighting yourself."

"There, you see? You are Sicilian."

"One-quarter."

"Enough to understand. You *honor* this man who seeks your hand, and the people who want to work with you, by wanting to honor them."

"But what do I do?"

"You ask me?" He showed mocked astonishment. "You bring this dilemma to a celibate priest? Who has never had another job but the church? Truly, you are this desperate?"

"Actually, yes."

He moved to his feet with a surprising grace. "Then get into the ring and box. I for one have nothing else to offer." He started from the room. "And now you must select your own *vestario*. I will see what is keeping your transport."

Twenty minutes later, they were dressed and standing in what once had served as the manor's stables. Two youths stood proudly beside a pair of

Vespas, small motorcycles that were ubiquitous in southern Italy.

Noah smiled for the first time that day. "This is a wonderful thing."

Shimmel was horrified. "You actually like this idea?"

"Like is not strong enough. We are just four more locals going about our business, our faces hidden beneath helmets. What is not to love?"

"I can't drive a bike. Can you?"

"I stopped riding dirt bikes when my wife offered me the ultimatum." Noah squatted down and inspected the first machine. "She doesn't have to know about this."

Shimmel asked Derek, "You or the lady, you can ride?"

"I've ridden motorcycles," Derek replied. "But I prefer using my own muscles for power."

"Not today," Lauro said. He gestured to four helmets lining the side wall. "Try those on."

Derek handed Kelly a helmet. "Unless of course you'd prefer to drive."

"I know how to be a passenger," Kelly said. "That's as far as I've gotten."

Shimmel took a helmet from Noah and complained, "I want to dance at my daughter's wedding."

"I know for a fact," Noah said, straddling the bike, "that you have two sons."

"There is always hope."

Lauro and one of the youths strapped a valise holding Noah's camera and two sets of clothing to the back of Derek's bike, then lashed a bulky canvas sack containing Shimmel's sound equipment to the other Vespa. "Now you travel like true Sicilians."

Shimmel asked, "How fast do these machines go?"

Noah replied, "Fast enough. Right, Father?"

Shimmel moaned.

Lauro said, "Your destination is the Fontana-rossa Airport beyond Catania. Your plane arrives in exactly four hours and ten minutes. There are two ways to travel from here." He motioned to one of the youths who pulled a map from his rear pocket. Lauro opened the map on the Vespa's handlebars. "You can travel the coast highway, the E45." He looked at Shimmel. "Very crowded road. Very fast traffic."

Shimmel asked, "Is there perhaps a taxi? A fruit truck? Donkey cart?"

"Slow road it is," Noah said.

"Then you must travel by way of the Roman road here, inland." Lauro traced the route. "Eighty kilometers. Even a donkey cart can make this journey in time." The priest smiled at Kelly. "Plus there is the one special spice to this slower road."

It was Derek who first realized, "It takes us through Sortino."

• • •

As they readied for departure, four figures in shapeless dark clothes and rope-soled sandals, Kelly handed her helmet to Derek and drew Lauro over to one side. "I can't tell you what it's meant. Knowing you. Talking with you. Hearing your heart in your words."

"Boxing," he replied. "Boxing is the key to a good relationship. Ask any Sicilian lady."

She kissed his cheek. "You made the right choice."

He touched where her lips had been. "You will give your friend Derek a message from me?"

"Of course."

"Once you have left Italy. He should know this. My uncle, he was priest at the Oratory of San Lorenzo."

Chapter 45

The Roman highway ran north by west, carving its way through the island's heart. Steep-sided ravines were traversed by ancient fairy-tale bridges. They passed olive groves whose trees were gnarled and weathered like the people walking alongside the road. Open valleys were clouds of orange and lemon blossoms, their fragrance as heady as champagne.

Derek followed Noah and let him set the pace—or rather Shimmel did, by shouting and gesticulating every time Noah goosed the engine. Kelly was a warm and fragrant bundle, her body tight to his, her movements in sync as they leaned into curves and flew through descents. He touched her arms from time to time, and was rewarded with a brief tightening of her grip. Almost a hug. But not quite.

Never in his wildest dreams did he ever imagine he would find himself in such a situation. Riding the high ridges of central Sicily, the arms of a beautiful woman tight around his middle, her hair brushing his neck below the helmet. The joy found in caring for a woman who was not Erin. The glorious and heart-wrenching conflict that came from knowing she belonged to his former best friend. Every Italian love song now made perfect sense, even the lyrics he could not understand. Even the songs he had never heard.

The town of Sortino crowned one of the highland's many peaks, a jewel sculpted by time and made to shimmer with each fading day. They entered the town's central square just as every other person in Sortino did the same, or so it seemed to Kelly. A great swath of people dressed in evening finery, three and four generations walking together, strolling to the sound of street musicians and their own rapid chatter. Children scampered and played in happy clusters. Every seat at every café table was filled. The talk was a constant wash of sound, like an orchestra with five thousand players all preparing for the great crescendo of sunset.

Ten minutes later, she had seen enough.

Too many faces were clenched tight at the shuttered windows. Too many women her age dressed in black, head to toe, their eyes hard as agate. Too much like her mother in a rage.

No one looked directly at them, four strangers dressed in local garb, two more Vespas puttering down the central lane. But Kelly had the sense that everyone saw, and they all knew. These four did not belong.

They halted by the piazza's main church. Derek and the two technicians were watching her, waiting for a signal. Kelly told them, "We can go now."

"I'm sure we can find a place away from the main square and grab a bite," Derek offered.

"Or the church," Noah said. "We can park the scooters—"

"No. Thank you, but I've seen enough." She settled back into position. As they puttered down the cobblestone avenue, Kelly found both sadness and pleasure in leaving the town behind.

This was not her world.

Chapter 46

Their ride was a twin-engine Beechcraft, positioned fifty feet from the private air terminal when they arrived. The pilot was lean, sunburnt, and Italian enough to give Kelly's form a careful inspection. They had stopped in an empty cul-de-sac about ten miles from the airport and changed back into their former garb. Which meant the pilot surveyed her dressed in the clothes she had selected for the morning's shoot. About ten thousand years ago.

Derek stepped between them and said, "What is the range on this plane?"

The pilot started to lean over so as to keep Kelly in view, but something in Derek's gaze halted the motion. He straightened and replied, "Thirteen hundred kilometers."

"How far is Marseille?"

"Just under eleven hundred." His attention was fully on Derek now. "I was told to fly you to Rome."

"Will you take us to Marseille?"

"It will cost you double. Cash."

Noah opened his shirt, unzipped the money belt, and said, "We will pay you double. Cash."

Kelly settled into the back row and motioned

for Derek to join her. They waited while Noah and Shimmel checked the plane's cargo bay. She asked, "You don't want to see if your things are all there?"

"Everything of value is Gwen's. You?"

"I'm too tired to care."

Noah clambered on board and announced, "All our gear is intact. And packed better than Shimmel does. Miracles do happen. Even in Sicily."

Shimmel slid into the seat beside him and said, "Don't speak too soon. We haven't made it out yet."

The takeoff was smooth. As they circled the airport, Kelly spotted two men wheeling away their Vespas. "Derek . . ."

"I saw." He smiled. "Priests have friends everywhere."

"Speaking of which, I have a message from Father Lauro." She leaned in close and told him.

Derek released his seat belt and turned to face her full on. "Start from the beginning of that conversation," he said. "Don't leave anything out."

Just the same, she edited. Giving him instead a roundabout sort of conversation as to how she came to be discussing the priest's background. The boxing. The church . . .

Derek said, "His uncle and godfather fled the church and Sicily both?"

"Right. And moved to America. At least, Lauro

thinks he did." She watched as Derek shut his eyes, leaned back, and smiled. "What is it?"

But he shook his head in response. "I need to think."

Derek did not speak again until they landed in France.

Chapter 47

In the end they only stopped in Marseille to refuel. While on approach, Derek asked if the pilot would take them farther still. Another glance at the contents of Noah's money belt, and the pilot was only too happy to fly them straight to Paris.

By the time they landed at Le Bourget, Noah and Shimmel had worked their phone magic, arranging for four business class seats on the next Air France nonstop flight back to LAX. A limo was waiting for them when they landed, and Derek and Shimmel transferred all their luggage while Noah settled with their very happy pilot. The twenty-minute ride to Charles de Gaulle Airport was cramped, but no one saw any need to complain. When they passed through Customs, Shimmel did not actually sing with joy. But he might have hummed a few bars.

By the time they landed in California, the heady relief of being home was overwhelmed by jet lag fatigue. They hugged one another at curbside, gentle embraces and soft smiles, four people bound together by experiences they would probably never fully share with anyone else. Kelly waited until the two technicians had settled in a cab before asking Derek, "Can we meet tomorrow?"

"Whenever you like. I'm not going back to Miramar. Not yet. I need to be here in case . . ."

"In case something breaks. I understand."

"It's hard to even put it into words, what this might mean."

Which was exactly how she felt about him. And Jerome. She shivered at the prospect of what she would soon be facing. "Where are you staying?"

He pointed beyond the airport's confines. "Noah's booked me a room at the Crowne Plaza."

"Quite a step down from the Maybourne."

"I'm so tired, I probably won't notice."

She hugged him then, felt the strength and the goodness. Wanted to tell him everything. The conflict, the need to decide, the questions, the doubt . . .

He was still standing there, watchful and motionless, as her taxi pulled away.

Kelly slept well and took the next day in soft stages. She went for more of a fast walk than a run. She spent over an hour doing stretches. She waited until almost noon to turn on her phone. Her mother had called fourteen times and texted six. Almost double those of Brian Beschel. Only Jerome had contacted her more often.

She called the studio executive first and started

to apologize for being out of touch, but Brian would not let her finish. "I've gotten the short version from Noah. Sounds like you've come back with the prize."

"Two prizes, if you count the film he and Shimmel shot. They were great to work with, by the way."

"Sounds like Shimmel lost his nerve there at the end."

"We all did. Except Derek."

"Yeah, Noah tells me your guy is a natural." There was the sound of muffled voices in the background. "I'm tied up all day. Tomorrow breakfast?"

"Done. Brian, one thing more."

"Give it to me fast."

"It might be a good idea to keep Noah and Shimmel available for another round."

The man's voice took on a tight, electric quality. "There's more?"

"Nothing definite. But I think maybe. Actually, it's a little stronger than that."

He breathed, then, "Those two will be ready and waiting. You call, they come. And Kelly."

"Yes?"

"Have you thought any more about my offer?"

"Brian, I've been too busy just trying to make this work."

"Well, my guys say you've succeeded. If it's money—"

"No, Brian. It's not."

"Just saying. The offer is there, and the terms would be excellent."

She thanked him, hung up, and called Derek. When his voicemail responded, she left a brief message saying they should talk the next day.

Kelly then scrolled through her mother's messages. She had not been sure what she would say, how she would handle it. But by the time she cleared her phone, she was ready.

What she had to say needed to be in person. Kally texted that she would meet her mother at the Caffe Luxxe on Montana at four. When she finished, she saw her hands were shaking.

She did not call Jerome.

Kelly's mother was already seated at an outside table when she arrived. Kelly slowed her approach, studying this woman, her mother, the stranger. Giulia Reid was striking and attractive and Sicilian in ways that Kelly had not fully realized until now. The strength, the ability to dismiss with a casual flick of her hand or even her gaze, the closed walls she had seen in so many island women. All there.

"Hello, Mother."

Giulia waited until Kelly was seated before saying, "How formal she is. Did you not receive my messages?"

"This morning." Kelly ordered a green tea.

Caffeine, yes. But no more coffee, not on her stomach.

"Do you not wish to know how I am?"

Kelly started to go through the standard routine. Then decided, *not today.* "Do you not wish to know where I've been? What I've seen? What I've accomplished?"

"Such a tone she uses." Giulia lifted her face a notch, the sign Kelly had witnessed since childhood. The woman readying herself for battle. "You should be ashamed."

Kelly waited while the waitress deposited her tea. Poured a cup. Took a sip. Found comfort in her hands' steadiness. She carefully replaced the cup. Watched the passersby. Wondering if she should just stand and leave.

"I am speaking to you." When Kelly remained silent, her voice tightened. "Answer me!"

She asked a cluster of teens bouncing down the sidewalk, "What's the point?"

"I am your mother!" Only the presence of others kept Giulia relatively quiet.

"And I will never be the daughter you want me to be." Kelly faced her mother. "So why cause you more disappointment, and me more hurt?"

What Kelly was actually suggesting struck Giulia with the force of a slap to her face. "You actually . . . You don't want to see me?"

"Maybe it's better. For us both." She turned away. Feeling so fragile she could just evaporate, join with the sunlight. "We can love each other from a safe distance."

There followed a silence long enough for Kelly to finish her tea and pour a fresh cup. Then her mother surprised her. "I wish you could have known your grandfather."

"I did know him. He was my favorite person in the whole world."

"I mean, as an adult. He would have so loved your fire. Your spirit. Your . . ."

Kelly faced her. "What?"

"You knew your grandfather as a man of kindness and gentle strength. And he most certainly was that. But he could be so fierce, so hard, so . . ."

Kelly recalled the people she had just come to know. "So Sicilian."

"Cross the man, cause him offense, and he would turn away." Giulia brushed her hands against each other, back and forth. "Finish. Not for a day or a week. The feud was total. For the rest of his life, it was over."

"I never knew that."

"How could you possibly? You were four when he died."

"Six."

"Four, six, you were a child and his favorite. And now I see why." Her fingers trembled as she reached under her sunglasses and cleared her eyes. "Your grandfather had that very same fire. He was a man of great passions. And yet you had to be careful. Even those closest to him could never be certain he would still love them tomorrow."

Kelly leaned back, studying this stranger seated across from her. Seeing how the constant lifelong fear of being cut off, abandoned by her own father, could result in a woman who valued family above all else. "I went to Sortino."

"When?"

"Three days ago. No, four."

"How was it?"

Kelly started to say, *I saw you everywhere.* But there was nothing to be gained from such words. Nor did she feel the need. She settled on, "Beautiful. And tragic." Then she decided it was time. Kelly rose and signaled for the bill. "Thank you for coming."

Giulia rounded the table and gave Kelly a fierce embrace. "Of course I came. How could I not."

Her mother was still standing there on the sunlit pavement when Kelly rounded the corner and disappeared from view.

Chapter 48

Kelly was just finishing dinner when her phone buzzed. She turned it over, saw it was Jerome, and stared at it through five rings. "Hello?"

"You're back. I know you're back because I've spoken with Derek twice."

"You're angry."

"Kelly, of course I'm upset. Why didn't you call?" When she remained silent, he pressed, "Doesn't your boss deserve a safe arrival call?"

"We both know that's not what this is about. Not to mention the multiple messages and texts. It has nothing to do with work and everything to do with us." She carried her phone out onto the balcony. Stood staring at the night. Amazed at her own calm. "And that is why I didn't call."

The irritation was still there in his voice. "Unpack that for me, please."

"You already know why. I don't have an answer for you, Jerome. Either way. If I knew, I would have contacted you."

"You said, when you got back—"

"That was what I hoped. But it hasn't happened."

"Kelly . . . I don't know if I can wait much longer."

"Should I quit?"

"Should . . . What?"

"It's a simple enough question. Will this personal situation get in the way of our working relationship? Because if so, now is the time for me to leave. I've received another offer."

"Kelly, no, don't leave."

"Are you sure, Jerome? This is a real offer, and I need to respond."

"I don't know what to say. I was calling you about, you know."

"Yes. And you have my answer. I don't have any idea how I feel. I'm exhausted, I'm over-whelmed by all that's happened. And I don't know if or when things might change. On the personal level. Between us. Which is why—"

"Don't take the other job. Please."

"You need to be perfectly certain, Jerome. This personal situation cannot in any way impact our working together. If it does, if I get the slightest hint, I will have no choice but to leave."

"You sound, I don't know, so cold."

She nodded. She could hear it herself. Almost as if the hard edge had surfaced of its own accord. She sounded almost, well, Sicilian. "I'm sorry. But that's how it is."

"It breaks my heart to say it, but it sounds to me like you've already made up your mind."

She stared down at the flow of passing head-lights. A gentle sea breeze brought her a tangy hint of the Pacific.

"Kelly?"

"I don't know what to tell you. You could be right."

He sighed, then, "Who wants to hire you?"

"Brian Beschel. He's looking for a number two."

Another hard breath. "Word is out. The board wants me to transition into a London director-ship."

"That's wonderful, Jerome. A dream come true."

"It would make things easier for you, wouldn't it."

Kelly saw no need to respond.

"If you stay, if I go, I'm putting you in as my successor."

She mouthed a silent *wow*. "Thank you, Jerome. So much."

"I had hoped it might be the two of us making that transition." When she did not respond, he pressed, "Don't go, Kelly. This is work you're great at. Christie's needs you."

"Thank you, Jerome. Very much. I will think on everything you've said. Good night."

She cut the connection, walked back inside, and prepared for bed.

Chapter 49

The night before everything came together, Derek dreamed of an emerald tide.

He was there on the shore where they had scattered Erin's ashes. In the dream, his wife was there with him, watching the sun dissolve into the Pacific waters. The tidal pools glowed a gemstone green, meant for them alone.

Erin did not speak. She did not touch him. She did not need to. Her presence was a salve upon his weary spirit, an elixir he drew with every breath, deep into his bones. He did not weep, though he wanted to. He refused to let the tears mar this almost perfect hour. Almost, because he knew it would end. And he would return to the life he was making. One without her.

They stayed like that, not touching, silent, until the light was almost gone. The last he saw of her was the smile, the gentle light in her gaze, the feel of her breath upon his heart.

He awoke to the sound of a ringing phone. The caller identified himself as Raol, night security at the Getty. "This woman, she's called like nine times. She says it's urgent you talk with her."

"Did she give a name?"

"Yeah. San Lorenzo. You want me to spell that?"

Derek felt his heart rate spike. "No need."

"Probably a crazy person. She uses a saint's name. She says you got to reach her before the world wakes up. Her words, man. Not mine."

"Give me her number. Hang on." Derek scrambled for his desk, got pen and paper. "All right. Go."

He repeated back the number, thanked Raol, hung up. Went into the bathroom and washed his face. Breathed deep. When he was ready, he called. The woman answered instantly. "This is Derek Gaines."

"How do I know it's you?"

"I imagine because Father Lauro said you should trust me."

"You know who this is?"

"The relative of a former priest—"

She had a raspy cigarette-laden voice. "I'm his daughter."

"And he left something in your care."

"I'm fed up holding on to this stuff, waiting for the shadows to form into a killer and a gun and a bullet. You understand what I'm saying?"

"All too well."

"You want this, it's gonna cost you."

"I understand."

"We're not talking some token cash. I want

enough for me and my husband to vanish. Permanently."

"I can make that happen."

"We need to meet somewhere totally safe. I mean, not a shred of risk. Else I won't come, and you will never hear from me again."

Derek nodded. "I know just the place."

Chapter 50

Derek made a pot of coffee and drank two cups while he placed the calls. Gwen first. Then Trevor. Evelyn and Judith. He phoned them both because they deserved to hear it from him. Then Kelly. And because she asked, he phoned Brian Beschel. Then he went for a run.

The Crowne Plaza was located one block off the main road leading to LAX. Derek traced his way through rental car lots, low-slung industrial buildings, and bars that once had served wild-man test pilots escaping the desert heat. Back in his room, he stretched and showered and dressed in the last clean set of Gwen's secondhand finery. He ate a leisurely breakfast downstairs, then drove to the Getty and pulled into the parking garage forty minutes before the lady was scheduled to appear. He had texted her his photo and said he'd meet her at the entrance to the monorail station. He settled on one of the concrete benches and watched the arriving crowds. The sun reminded him of Sicily.

"Dr. Gaines?"

He rose to his feet. "Derek will do."

She was much like he expected, a stout heavyset woman whose features held a feminine hint of Lauro's bulk and strength. "I'm Fabiana."

"Very nice to meet you." He gestured to her tattered case and a cardboard tube longer than she was tall. "Can I help you with those?"

"I got the tube. The satchel, sure." As they started toward the monorail station, she said, "I decided to bring it all."

"Thank you for trusting me."

"Lauro said I should. And to tell the truth, I'm tired of worrying over who else might turn up looking for it."

The pack was weathered canvas and had to weigh sixty pounds. It clinked softly as Derek set it on the monorail's metal floor. "Dare I ask what's inside?"

"I think you know."

He nodded. The woman's directness was refreshing. "Do you have any idea what happened to Allen Freeth?"

"That man was a fool on a mission." She had a Sicilian's ability to shower every word with a frigid, hard-edged scorn. "We told him not to go. Not directly, mind. Through our middleman. We warned him there was nothing anybody could do if the Freeth kid got himself into trouble. Which he did."

"How did you make contact with Allen?"

It all came out then. How her husband had contracted cancer. And they didn't have insurance. And she had started digging for a way to sell some of her treasures.

She had come into contact with a middleman working with treasure hounds, and that had brought Allen Freeth into the picture. And she had sold him the four items. The painting. The treasures. "Six hundred thousand was our cut. I got no idea how much Allen paid the middleman. Our share was enough to cover the bills. And pay off our mortgage. We were set. Ready to get on with life. But that Freeth, he was like a dog with a bone. He kept pressing and pressing the middleman. Wanting to know our name. Certain we had more, or had a handle on where he could uncover more treasure. Scared us to death, worrying the middleman might give us up. Finally Freeth took off for Sicily. And you know what happened next."

"He asked the wrong person. He was forced to have an accident."

"I've held on to my old man's secrets long as I'm able. Now my husband and I just want to live the rest of our days in peace." She softly nudged the canvas sack with her toe. "I can't tell you how much I want to have this over and done."

"Allen's mother will be joining us today."

Fabiana showed very real fear. "I had nothing to do with that man's death."

"She knows that. She's part of this big picture. Nothing more."

Chapter 51

They were all present.

They formed a silent semicircle when Derek led Fabiana into the vault. He introduced them, drew over a chair on rollers where Fabiana could sit, but for the moment their guest insisted on standing. Now that she was here, Fabiana looked terrified. "These are all people I trust with my life," Derek began. "I think you should too."

Fabiana's words trembled like the rest of her. "Let's get this over with."

Derek felt like there should have been trumpets. An angelic choir. Something more than him pulling the stopper from the long cardboard tube, drawing out the contents, unfurling it slowly, and using seven padded pins to hang it from the metal wires. He stepped back and forced himself to breathe.

He said, "On the night of October seventeenth, 1969, the heaviest rain in history poured down on Palermo."

"My father had nightmares of that storm all his life long," Fabiana said.

"Thieves picked the ancient lock on the Oratory of San Lorenzo—"

"They didn't pick anything. My father had

the key. And it was just the one thief. One was enough."

"The church had no alarm system," Derek went on. "The thief removed the frame from its place above the nave, and cut out the painting you see here."

"My father left Sicily, left the church, left his own name." Fabiana settled into the chair. "All his life, he told me the tale of why he did it. Became a thief." She pointed to the painting, then touched the carry-all with her shoe. "How the Mafia hitmen and their bosses would come in and kneel before the painting there. Touch the crown and the Cross and the diadem in the sack. Take the Sacraments from the cup and bowl. They're inside as well. All gold, all centuries old. Plus the other treasures my father took from the church's cellar.

"These men, they'd cross themselves. Then go out and do murder. Extortion. Kidnapping. Drugs. And come back and go through the motions all over again. Not to mention talking about it in the confessional. All their deeds. All their poison heaped on my father, his homeland, and his church. Finally, he'd had enough. He stole, and he stayed there for another two long years until the investigators were gone and public attention turned elsewhere. Then he left. He never regretted it. Not for a minute was he sorry what he'd done."

"Of the six thousand works of art looted in that horrible decade," Derek said, "Interpol still has this painting at the top of their list of missing treasures."

Derek had spent the past three and a half days and nights studying the painting. Even so, nothing had quite prepared for seeing it in reality. "Caravaggio painted the *Nativity with Saint Francis and Saint Lawrence* in 1600, at the very height of his powers. The use of chiaroscuro, the features of these common folk he used as subjects, the visual and psychological intensity, it all results in an energy that seems ready to explode from the canvas."

Brian cleared his throat. "You're going to have to say all that again for the camera."

"Not while I'm around." Fabiana forced herself to her feet. "Like I told Derek here, I want two million dollars. Cash."

Brian asked, "If I front the money, can I assume the Getty will be assisting with this?"

"You have my word," Evelyn replied.

"Works for me." Brian reached for a pair of wheeled cases at his feet. "Madam, your money."

"Let me give you a hand," Derek offered.

"No, I got this." She extended the handles, tilted the cases, then paused. "My name, my father . . ."

"No one outside of this tight-lipped crew need ever know how these items came to be in our possession," Evelyn replied. "My word on it."

Derek escorted the woman up through security and onto the monorail. She did not speak another word, just stood at the window and watched him until the train rounded the corner and disappeared.

When Derek returned to the vault, they were all there, still waiting. The canvas satchel remained unopened. Derek resisted the urge to kneel on the floor and start unveiling the treasures. There was something he had to clear up first.

"These articles belong to Gwen until the court says otherwise," Derek said. When Brian looked ready to argue, he continued, "This was not a request. It's a take it or leave it situation. Whatever reward the authorities end up paying for this painting's retrieval, it goes to her. Everything coming from the Vatican or the Italian government, it's hers. Call it payment for Allen's death. Or bringing us all together and trusting us with his legacy."

"On behalf of Christie's," Kelly said, "I agree."

Derek went on, "Trevor is to serve as Gwen's agent. Christie's will partner with him and share the proceeds."

Kelly nodded. "Agreed."

Trevor would have collapsed had Judith not settled him into the chair Fabiana had vacated. Once he was seated, he asked her, "I am awake, yes?"

Judith pinched him.

"Ow."

"You'll be fine." She smiled at Derek. "Don't stop now. You're on a roll."

He turned to Gwen. "The rewards to be negotiated will be large enough to cover your debts."

She looked almost as unsteady as Trevor. "Are you certain?"

"I concur with my newest employee," Evelyn said. "And the Getty will back Christie's play." She smiled at Kelly. "Words I never in my wildest dreams ever thought I would utter."

"If that's the case," Gwen said, "the Getty would be welcome to put all these treasures on display until everything is settled."

"Then my day is complete," Evelyn said.

Brian complained, "Don't I have any say in the matter?"

"Absolutely," Kelly said. "You have right of first refusal on every item we're not required to return to Sicily and Gwen does not care to keep."

"I want none of it," Gwen said.

"Don't be too hasty," Derek warned.

"Keeping these things would only remind me of the loss. Of both my good men."

Derek found himself recalling the boxes in his garage of Erin's prize art. "That I can definitely understand."

Kelly said to Brian, "You also have the documentary."

"The early church treasures," Derek added. "There's no record of these anywhere. Which means Trevor and Christie's will be only too happy to put them up for sale."

Trevor covered his face with both hands.

"And the painting," Kelly said.

"The unfinished Caravaggio," Derek said. "Now with unimpeachable provenance."

"Thanks to you," Kelly said.

"To us all," Derek said. "This was a team effort."

"It still is," Gwen said, and pointed to the canvas satchel. "Now open this before I burst."

Chapter 52

Derek was seated on the retaining wall by the Getty's front steps when Kelly stepped through the entrance. The sunlight seemed to gather around her, or perhaps it was simply how the entire day was encased in something so new he could not yet give it a name.

"Fancy meeting you here. Shift over and give a girl room." When she settled, she asked, "Why didn't you stay downstairs for the celebration?"

"No idea, really. I guess I was too busy trying to fit all this inside my head. You?"

"I followed you out. We've got a lot to discuss."

"You don't need to say a thing, Kelly."

"Are you sure about that? Absolutely certain? You know exactly what I'm wanting to tell you? Right down to the very last word?"

He liked the sharpness that crept into her voice. A strong woman, smart and certain and steady on her own two feet. "That came out wrong."

"It sure did."

"I apologize. I take it back."

"Tell me what you thought I was going to say and I'll consider accepting your apology."

"Kelly . . ."

"Tell me, Derek."

He resisted the urge to take her in his arms. The flame in his heart was that strong. And for once he felt no need to maintain the careful distance. The conflict, the sense of abandoning his former marriage . . .

Gone.

"Derek, I'm waiting."

He cleared his throat. "When you were going through that rough patch with your mom—"

"One of many. But go on."

"I told you I was there for you. I meant it."

She had such an amazing gaze. Such power. Such emotional heat. It threatened to melt him. "You're my friend."

"I am. Now and forever."

"I like the sound of that. So much." She reached out then, and traced one finger along the line where his hair met his temple. Down, slowly, gently, until she touched his lips. "But what if I want more?"

In that moment, Derek found the answer to a question he had not even shaped. He took her hand, squeezed once, then rose to his feet. "Have dinner with me tomorrow."

"Wait . . . That's your answer?"

"No . . ." He was already moving, drawn forward by a need strong as the afternoon light. "But there's something I need to do."

Kelly rose and closed the distance between

them. Her eyes showed a bottomless depth, an invitation to dive in and just fall.

"I'll see you tomorrow . . ." She kissed him. "Hurry back."

The northbound traffic was heavy but moving at a steady pace. Derek made good time. Half an hour beyond Santa Barbara, he took the exit for Vandenberg and stopped in the town that serviced the air base. He bought a sandwich from what had once been their favorite shop. Then he headed out, retracing his steps from the previous week. Only now it felt like a different lifetime.

He pulled into the same graveled parking area, opened the cargo bay's cover, traded his city clothes for hiking shorts and boots, shouldered his ready-pack, and headed off.

There were a dozen or so trails leading off from the parking area, each designated by a weather-beaten sign naming just another solitary cove. Derek took his time, selecting one where the sandy path showed no recent footprints. Just as he used to do with Erin. Many years ago.

The central coast held any number of such regions, where the cliffs fell straight down to rock-strewn tidal pools. There was no room for coastal roads, no sandy beachfront to develop. So long as the weather held, hiking in from where the road ended took a couple of hours max.

Late afternoon shadows painted the dry hills

in a hundred different hues, all of them copper and russet and brown. Erin used to call these the shades of Indian summer, an in-between state she cherished in her own special way. Erin treated each wind-carved crevice as a sculpture that had waited eons for her to appreciate. Ribbons of light creasing the sky overhead left her breathless.

Derek emerged from the final vale just as the tide turned. He knew this place so well, he could name the moment when the outermost pools began to empty. The sea was almost calm, with just enough wave action to send foam cascading gently over the rocks. He settled on a ledge where he thought Erin had once perched and brought out his sandwich, then replaced it in his pack untouched. He watched the vista go emerald green, and remembered.

When the sun vanished beyond the Pacific's golden rim, he headed back. The night was so clear he left the flashlight in his pack. The trail was illuminated a brilliant pewter by the light of an almost-full moon.

Soft, bright, gentle as Erin's smile.

Center Point Large Print
600 Brooks Road / PO Box 1
Thorndike, ME 04986-0001 USA

(207) 568-3717

US & Canada:
1 800 929-9108
www.centerpointlargeprint.com